RICHARD C. MEREDITH is the author
of several novels and widely acclaimed
short fiction. He is perhaps best known for
his highly successful novel WE ALL DIED
AT BREAKAWAY STATION.

In AT THE NARROW PASSAGE, this
brilliant new star in the science fiction fir-
mament has created a far-future adventure
that paradoxically seems to occur in the
present—or something like it.

AT THE NARROW PASSAGE

RICHARD C. MEREDITH

A BERKLEY MEDALLION BOOK
PUBLISHED BY
BERKLEY PUBLISHING CORPORATION

This book is dedicated to the memory of H.
Beam Piper and to the Paratime Police, to
Verkan Vall, to Tortha Karf, to Hadron Dalla,
and to all those who guard the multiple worlds

Library of Congress Catalog Card Number: 72-94264
SBN 425-02730-9

BERKLEY MEDALLION BOOKS are published by
Berkley Publishing Corporation
200 Madison Avenue
New York, N.Y. 10016

BERKLEY MEDALLION BOOKS ® TM 757,375

Printed in the United States of America

Berkley Medallion Edition, JANUARY, 1975

CONTENTS

AT THE NARROW PASSAGE

At the narrow passage there is no brother, no friend.

—ARABIAN PROVERB

Some billion years ago, an anonymous speck of protoplasm protruded the first primitive pseudopodium into the primeval slime, and perhaps the first state of uncertainty occurred.

—I. J. GOOD, *Science*, February 20, 1959

1

FRANCE, LINE RTGB-307,
SPRING, 1971

It was spring in France when I contracted to kidnap Imperial Count Albert von Heinen and his wife.

It was a spring that had been too long in coming, and the bitter winter that had come before it had frozen all of western Europe and brought the war to a virtual standstill until the weather, in its own fickle way, finally began to warm and allowed us to return to the bloody games we were being paid to play.

The trenches in which we lived were very old and deep and muddy and cold when those first spring days came suddenly, almost unexpectedly, and though warm breezes blew across France, the trenches still remained cold, down deep in them, and it seemed that they would never dry out.

Trenchfoot was rampant. It seemed that most of us who hadn't come down with frostbite or pneumonia or one of the other diseases of the trenches that winter, finally gave in to that disgusting flesh rotting that I guess has been feared by foot soldiers as long as men have fought wars.

At least I had been lucky so far. We had a small stove in our dugout—the one I shared with Tracy and two subalterns—and I had kept my boots and socks more or less dry most of the time, and even though my feet stank a good deal more than my nose liked, they hadn't begun to rot. I was grateful for that, though that was just about all I was grateful for. Maybe I was getting a little bitter even then.

Above the intricate mazes of trenches, beyond our most remote lookout post, on the broken, muddy surface of the ravaged earth, the barbed wire still hung just as it had all winter, now rusty and looking even more forbidding than it had when we had first strung it the autumn before. Fragments of clothing—Imperial gray, they had once been—here and there a high-crested Prussian helmet, a rusting rifle with a broken bayonet, the barren, whitened bones of Imperial horses enduring the rain and snow and frigid winds that had blown across France during the winter. These were the silent, solemn reminders of the few foredoomed Imperial attacks that had taken place since the first winter snows came down and locked us into our positions.

At first the Germans had not seemed willing to admit that a British colonial division had set up housekeeping just a few miles from Beaugency. That was too damned close to their staff headquarters!

And during the first winter storms, and during the lulls between them, the Sixty-fourth Imperial Hussars, mostly on foot because of the terrain, had thrown a few feeble, bloody attacks at our lines. They had failed, as their commanders must have known they'd fail, but the attacks had been in the grand Prussian style, if for no other reason than to appease and glorify His Imperial Majesty, Franz VI, by the Grace of God, Emperor of the Romans.

Ha!

Well, during that bitter winter, suffering more from the weather than from the activities of the Imperials, the Second, Fourth and Ninth New England Infantry had sat on its collective ass a few miles southwest of Beaugency in our old, much-used trenches, a few hundred yards south of the Loire River and a mile or two from a battered little village whose name I don't know to this day.

But, as I said, spring had finally gotten around to coming, spring of the year 1971, by the Christian calendar used locally, the thirty-second year of the Great War, the War to End All Wars, they said. And with spring had come a renewal of the fighting and the end of my current contract with the Kriths.

Cannon had begun firing from the vicinity of Beaugency, the

German equivalent of our two-and-a-half-, three-and four-inch howitzers, from the Imperial artillery battalion that sat there. And big guns fired back from the south, British four-inchers answering the Germans.

Rifle and machine-gun fire crackled intermittently along the lines. Now and again there was the muffled roar of a hand grenade or a mortar shell lobbed into either our trenches or theirs. And occasionally a German or a British head would be foolish enough to show itself above the trenches and would promptly get itself blown apart, steel helmet or no steel helmet.

Off to the east, just about every morning an hour or so after dawn, a flight of British airships moved north, bombers for the most part, bound for the Imperial encampments in the area of Fontainebleau, the railyards that led to Paris and what industry still functioned in the French city. They would unload their crude bombs on Fontainebleau and then return home, those of them that hadn't been blasted apart by Imperial antiairship guns.

At times we hoped that some of the airships might even get as far as Paris itself, to begin bombing the Imperial household that we had heard was setting up spring quarters in what had once, long years before, been the capital of France, the City of Lights. But we knew, when we stopped to think about it, that our—the British—airships stood a snowball's chance in hell of getting much beyond Fontainebleau. Between that city and Paris the Germans had ring after ring of antiaircraft guns that could knock down the fastest airship that the British Empire could put into the sky.

German-occupied Paris would hold out, and would keep on holding out until the British infantry marched right up to the gates of the city and took it from the Holy Roman Emperor, and that was a thing that in the spring of 1971 seemed very unlikely, no matter what the Kriths did to help. Well, short of nuclear weapons, that is, but I damned well knew that the Kriths weren't going to put nuclear weapons into the hands of the British. Hell, the British didn't even know there was any such thing—at least that's what I believed then.

As I said, it was spring of 1971 and I was a captain of the British Infantry, American Colonial Forces of His Britannic Majesty, King George X. More exactly, I was the commanding

3

officer of Company B, Fourth Virginia Infantry.

My name then was Eric Mathers and I was supposed to have been from the city of Victoria, Province of Virginia, in the British North American Colonies, sometimes known collectively as New England. The men under me, colonials themselves, believed it, but that wasn't surprising since the Kriths had given me a damned good schooling in what Virginia was like in this Timeline, or at least the area of North America that they call Virginia here, which isn't exactly the same geographical area as *your* Virginia. I spoke and acted like any other good Virginian, a loyal subject of George X and the British Empire.

The true facts were somewhat different. I had never been in *their* Virginia in my life. I was simply a mercenary soldier in the pay of the Kriths, but that made me no less a good soldier for King George. The interests of King George and the Kriths happened to coincide, which was damned fortunate for George and his empire. So it seemed at the time, at least.

But then I was pretty ignorant in those days.

CHANGE OF COMMAND

On the morning when all this began to change I was late rising. I didn't do that very often, sleep late, but a group of us had consumed a great quantity of gin the night before and my head ached like hell and I was halfway sick to my stomach and, as they say, RHIP—Rank Hath Its Priviliges. I was exercising those priviliges, what there were of them, when Tracy came stumbling into the dugout, urging me to get the hell out of bed and into my uniform.

I waved him away sleepily, but threw back the cover and gingerly put my feet on the burlap-covered earthen floor, carefully testing the ability of my legs to support me.

"Blast it all, Eric," said Lieutenant Hillary Tracy—whose real name was Darc HonGlazz, but that was in another world. "Get your arse out of that bloody bed. The muckin' colonel's coming round."

Yes, Tracy really talked that way. Well, of course, it was customary, almost necessary for us to mimic the speech of the British we served under, but I thought Tracy was carrying it a little too far.

"Cheerio, old son," I mumbled, mimicking Tracy more than the British, and discovered to my surprise that I could stand up.

I glanced once around the dugout, saw nothing that was new, wished vainly for a hot bath, and then reached for my pants, which hung on a peg driven into the earthen wall beside my bunk.

The dugout that had been the home of Tracy, myself, and two other officers for the past four and a half months was small and dark and damp, a cave hacked out of the French soil a year or two earlier by another band of British soldiers when they had held this area before. When the Imperial Germans had taken the trenches from us the previous spring, I supposed some of their officers had lived here, though it didn't look as if they had done much to improve it. They had just existed here until fall, when we had come in and driven them back out again. I wondered whether Germans or British would be living here after the next big offensive or counteroffensive or countercounteroffensive or whatever the hell the next battle would be called at headquarters. That's the iind of war it was.

There were four bunks, little more than field cots, a table, three folding chairs, a box that served as the fourth chair, a rickety wooden table that the Germans had built the spring before, an old, battered, cracked potbelly stove of prehistoric British origin, three carbide lanterns, innumerable sandbags, and four footlockers. The dugout's single entrance was covered by a moldy, moth-eaten old blanket that still, somehow, carried the Imperial German insignia. The ceiling was supported by rotten boards, beer-barrel staves, a hodgepodge of bits and pieces of wood placed there to support the soggy earth above. Below, the cold, damp, half-muddy floor was covered with burlap sacking, some British, some Imperial, and even some that might have been of native French origin. Come to think of it, that might have been the only thing in the dugout, save for the earth itself, that was French. But then, there was very little of France left anywhere after thirty-two years of war.

But the dugout was home. All the home that Tracy and I had anywhere. We were both Timeliners.

"Hurry it up, Eric," Tracy said. "The colonel's aide just rang up to say that the colonel is coming round with our replacements."

"Replacements?" I asked, coming awake at last, activating certain artificial circuits of my body that would bring me to a level of awareness known to few men.

"Bloody well right," Tracy said in all seriousness.

"Oh, cut it out," I said. My head was still aching.

"Cut out what, old boy?"

"That bloody damned accent."

"We've got to stay in character."

"You're overdoing it."

Tracy snorted through his broad nose but didn't reply.

"Now, what's this about replacements?" I asked, finally pulling on my trousers, British issue, heavy woolen winter uniform, a dull, sick olive that was as unpleasant a color as I could think of that morning.

"That's all I know, old boy," Tracy said. "The aide just said that the colonel was coming round with our replacements first thing."

"Then where are we going?"

"Haven't the foggiest."

I found a poplin shirt that was relatively clean, though perhaps not neat enough to suit the colonel, but since it was the best I had, it would have to do. I pulled it on, stuffed it into my pants and said to Tracy, "I can't say that I'm too surprised."

"No, I'm not either," Tracy answered, finally sitting down on his bunk and fumbling for a cigarette. "Our contracts are about up anyway, y'know."

"Well, this assignment's been a waste of time," I said, more to myself than to Tracy.

Tracy nodded a vague reply, struck a match, lit his cigarette, said, "Aren't you going to shave, old boy? You look absolutely ghastly."

I peered at my face in the fragment of mirror that hung on the earthen wall between our bunks, frowned, nodded. "You're right. I guess I'd better."

I wished desperately for an antihangover shot, but they hadn't invented it yet. I'd just have to suffer, though I cut back on my awareness circuits so that I didn't feel quite so uncomfortable.

"There's hot water on the stove," Tracy said. "Tea too. Want some?"

"Yes, if you don't mind."

"Righto."

I would have preferred something stronger than tea, but then tea doesn't smell on your breath as strongly as gin, and I rather doubted that there was very much gin left after the night before anyway, considering the way we'd put it away.

I fumbled in my footlocker, found my razor and soap while Tracy poured me a cup of tea and brought it and a basin of steaming water over to me. He sat them on my bunk.

"Thanks," I said.

"I do wonder where we'll be going now," Tracy said as I worked up some lather in my shaving mug.

"Your guess is as good as mine."

I smeared my face liberally with lather, stropped my razor a few times across the belt, and then began scraping the stubble off my chin. Being fair and blond doesn't prevent me from having a very heavy, very tough beard that's hideously difficult to remove after a bad night.

Outside the dugout, through the yard of earth that separated us from the surface and through the tunnel that connected us to it, I heard the roar and whine of the big howitzers firing from our rear. A shell or two passed over us, headed for the Imperial trenches a few hundred yards away. It wasn't much, just a few rounds to let the Imperials know that the British Army was awake and still as nasty as ever.

"Anything else going on this morning?" I asked Tracy.

"Nothing much, so far as I know. Heard that there was a bit of action along the river about dawn. A German patrol coming down, I suppose. Lost their way and stumbled into the Ninth's trenches."

"Any prisoners?"

"Not so far as I know. Didn't ask."

I scraped away at my chin and speculated about the news that Tracy had awakened me with. So we were being replaced. Well, it was about bloody time that the Kriths realized that we were wasting our time in these filthy trenches. We had muddled along for four and a half months now, Tracy and I, waiting for the weapons to arrive that we were supposed to show our men how to use. Some new rifle, I understood. Something that would give the British a little more firepower, a little more accuracy. Nothing very startling, mind you. Nothing too much in advance of the current local technology, just enough for everyone to believe that it was a British development, a weapons breakthrough that would help, maybe, to change things, to turn the tide of history against the Holy Roman Empire, as Ferguson's breechloader had turned the tide of history against the American insurrectionists nearly two hundred years before—a pivotal point in this Timeline's history.

But the rifles had never arrived for some reason that was never explained to me. The Krithian weapons supervisor Karhinter seldom took the time to explain anything that wasn't absolutely necessary. And we who were supposed to test the rifles in combat, we two Timeliner officers leading a company of American colonials, had sat in our dugout and waited and killed time and told dirty stories and played cards and drank gin when we could get it and shivered through the winter.

Now it seemed that the Kriths had given up playing this particular game with us and were going to pull us out of here and give us another assignment. I wondered whether it would be in this Timeline.

In a way I hoped it would be in another Line. I'd lost the little finger and part of the ring finger of my left hand during a fracas the autumn before, and I would have liked to have an opportunity to get new ones grafted on. But you can't do things like that in a Timeline as backward as this one was.

At last I finished with my face and splashed away the remaining soap, inspected myself for cuts, found that I had been luckier than usual and hadn't cut myself—I never had got used to shaving with a razor. I dried my face on a more or less clean towel Tracy had thrown on my bunk and drank about half the steaming cup of tea, scalding my tongue.

"How soon's the colonel supposed to be here?" I asked.

"Don't know. Anytime, I suppose."

"No time for breakfast?"

"I doubt it."

I shrugged and then found my jacket, a tight-fitting woolen garment of the same sickening green as the pants, distinguished only by the captain's bars on its collar.

"Hand me my pistol, will you, Tracy?" I asked as I buttoned my jacket.

Taking the pistol belt from the peg where it hung, Tracy handed it to me.

It was an awkward belt to wear and the pistol in the holster was big and ugly and efficient. The seven-shot, .62 caliber Harling revolver was the standard sidearm for British officers There and Then, and it was a damned big pistol. I had rather grown to like the feel of it on my hip and hoped that whatever our next assignment was, I would be allowed to carry it. A .62 caliber slug is big and messy, especially when propelled by the 200 grains of powder in the standard issue cartridge. It certainly wasn't a sporting weapon. It had been designed to do just one thing—kill men, and that it did very well.

"How do I look?" I asked Tracy.

"Halfway human."

"That's an improvement, I take it?"

Tracy nodded.

"Any more tea?" I asked.

"Yes, I think so. Want me to look?"

"No, I'll. . . ."

" 'Tention!"

The voice was Tracy's. He was sitting so that he could see the dugout's "door" and could see the figure who was shoving the blanket aside and stepping into the man-made cave.

As I snapped to my feet and turned, I saw him too. Colonel Woods.

"As you were," Woods said gruffly.

I relaxed, said, "Good morning, sir."

"Morning, Mathers, Tracy," the colonel replied in the clipped fashion that I suppose was natural to him.

Woods held the flap open until the other two men accompanying him came into the dugout. As I expected, one of them wore captain's bars and the other was a lieutenant. Our replacements.

Colonel Woods quickly made the introductions. The captain was a tall, slender Floridian named David Walters. The lieutenant was a shorter, stockier man named Carl Boland. He was a Virginian, the same as I was supposed to be.

"Spot of tea, Colonel?" Tracy asked once the three newcomers had seated themselves at the table—in the three chairs. I guessed that left the box for me and Tracy would just have to stand.

"No. Just had a cup," Woods answered. "No time, anyway. Must get back to headquarters."

Walters and Boland accepted Tracy's offer, and he began to rummage around for two fairly clean cups.

"Sorry to come in on you so abruptly, Mathers," Colonel Woods went on to say. "Orders, y'know."

"Yes, sir. Of course."

"You and Tracy will have till noon to get your gear together and introduce Walters and Boland to your men. A signaler will come then to accompany you to brigade headquarters."

"Brigade, sir?" I asked.

Woods nodded, shrugged, then pulled a mimeographed sheet of paper from his pocket and handed it to me. "Orders just came round this morning."

The orders were quite explicit. We were relieved of our commands as of 0900 and were to report to brigade at 1300.

"Brigade is sending a man round for you," Woods said. "Understand that HQ's been moved or some such. You'll have to wait for him."

"Yes, sir." Odd, I thought. Were we going to brigade at all? Probably not, but Woods wouldn't know that. He would never really know what became of us.

I knew for a fact that Woods wasn't a Timeliner; he was exactly what he was supposed to be. He knew nothing, suspected nothing of the existence of the Kriths or of the fact that men from other universes were here helping him and his British Empire wage war against the Holy Romans.

Nor did either Walters or Boland seem to be other than what they claimed. They gave no indications and we Timeliners have a thousand secret ways of letting other Timeliners know of our presence.

No, it appeared that the Kriths had given up on this one rather minor aspect of their master plan for this Line. They had something else in mind for Tracy and me. We'd learn what that was soon enough, I suspected.

"Well, must be shoving off," Woods said abruptly, rising.

He offered his hand to me. "Been nice knowing you, Mathers, Tracy. You'll both get good reports from me."

"Thank you, sir," I said, shaking his hand.

After briefly clasping Tracy's hand, Woods turned, ducked out under the flap that covered the dugout's door and vanished.

I turned back to my replacement.

"Well, Walters," I asked, "ready for me to show you around a bit?"

3

KEARNS

Long before noon I had completed all the introductions, said all my good-byes, and packed what gear I had.

After a trip to the latrine, Tracy and I sat down on the bunks that had, a few hours before, been ours, and waited for the man to come who was to lead us to "brigade headquarters," whatever that might be this time.

Walters and Boland, after saying their good-byes to us, had gone to mess, so Tracy and I were alone when the sergeant came into the dugout, snapped to attention and saluted.

"Captain Mathers, sir?" he asked.

I nodded. "This is Lieutenant Tracy."

"I'm Sergeant Kearns, sir." Then he paused, his face relaxing. "Are we alone?"

"Yes, we are."

As I answered, Kearns deliberately placed the tip of his right thumb against the tip of his right ring finger. It was one of *our* signals. I replied by performing the same gesture with my left hand, though since most of my left ring finger was missing, I used the middle one. Tracy signaled with a similar gesture.

"*Ca kasser a Shangalis?*" Kearns asked, which loosely translated means: "With your permission I shall speak in Shangalis." It was actually an abbreviated form of the complete sentence "*Retam ca kasser a rir nir paredispo Shangalis?*"

"*Swen ro,*" I replied.

The man who had called himself Kearns smiled, sat down on

one of the vacant bunks and dug into his pocket for a cigarette.

"You don't mind if I smoke, do you?" he asked, still speaking Shangalis.

"No, not at all," I replied in the same language, the language that some believe to be the native tongue of the Kriths; I doubt it, though. There are too many Indo-European roots in the language, too many *human* words. It's probably something the Kriths picked up far to the Temporal East and carried with them as they moved West. At least it looks that way to me, but I'm certainly no language expert. I'm just a hired gun, but men who know more about such things than I do have come up with that theory, and since the Kriths have never denied it, I assume that it might well be true.

"Care for a smoke?" Kearns asked, offering the pack to me.

"Might as well," I answered, accepting the offered pack and knocking one of the brown-paper cylinders out into my hand.

Then I looked up abruptly, peering into Kearns' eyes. It wasn't a *local* brand, and by local I mean from this universe. It was a Toltec-Line weed, from a long way East.

"I assure you that it's okay, Mathers," Kearns said suddenly when he realized that I was staring at him. "I just got in this morning, and I'm supposed to be leaving as soon as I take you to the meeting place. Only you two will see them."

I suppose that it was none of my business, Kearns' having brought in Outtime cigarettes. That wasn't my responsibility. The Kriths were running the show, and if they wanted to let Kearns do it, then it was their business. I told myself to forget it.

While I passed the pack on to Tracy and then lit my own cigarette, I took the time to study unobtrusively this man who had come to take us to our meeting with the Kriths. He was tall and slender, what they called wiry in build, though quite strong-looking. He was rather dark, but there seemed to be enough north European blood in his veins to prevent anyone from wondering whether he really belonged in the British Army. And then there were some far more exotic types fighting in the trenches of France under the Union Jack: Amerinds from the Indian Nations of middle North America; dark-skinned Punjabis from East India; South Sea Islanders from the Polynesian Colonies and the Aussie Commonwealth; and a host

14

of others. No, Kearns, whatever he was other than European, would go unnoticed among the motley crew that fought for the British Empire.

His face was made of sharp angles, craggy planes like a half-finished piece of sculpture and bore what appeared to be the scars of battles fought a long, long When from Here and Now. Still, there was something more to that face than just its simple ugliness, something strange and remote, something that seemed even more remote than just the cultural differences between him and me, though I could not guess from what line he had originally come. I can't say that I instantly disliked the man, but there was something about him that put me on edge, and it was not until a very long time afterward that I even began to have an inkling of what it was.

"What's this all about, Kearns?" I asked, still speaking Shangalis.

"Damned if I know," he answered. "They just told me to come in and get you two."

"Where are we going?" I asked. "I mean, where are you supposed to take us?"

"The village a ways back," he said. "If you're both ready, we can go now."

"I suppose I am. Tracy?"

"Righto."

"Sorry," Kearns said as he rose to his feet, "but you'll have to carry your own gear. I wasn't allowed to bring anyone else to help."

"Okay," I said, hefting the haversack that carried all my wordly possessions, fifty pounds of nothing very much. A Timeliner learns to get along with very little more than himself and the clothes on his back. "Let's go."

4

KAR-HINTER

Around the village the land was flat, without trees, except near the river where the ground was too marshy for plowing and the poplars and willows, those that had survived the shelling of the bloody summer before, still grew as they pleased, now beginning to bud in anticipation of summer. I wondered how many of those few trees would still be standing when the next spring came. It was not a pleasant thought.

The village itself stood not far from the Loire, a quiet, slowly winding river that must once have given a sensation of peace and gentleness to the now-ravaged countryside. I had been told that last spring the Loire had turned red with the mingling of British and Imperial German blood, and from the looks of the river's far bank, craters that the winter rains and snows had not yet obliterated, I rather suspected that it was true.

There were only two streets in the village, unpaved, crossing at right angles, one running from the ford of the river where a bridge must have stood at one time, though there were few traces left of it now, the other road parallelling the river, running a few hundred yards from its bank, back far enough to remain on solid, dry ground, curving away from the river at times and then back closer at others. The two roads met in the village, crossed, and then ran on their ways, leaving what had once been a sleepy little human habitation. But the spring and the summer of the year before had done their damage to the village, as well as to the country.

The crossroads had been the center of life of the village, when it had had a life. A few buildings still stood, and there was enough left of some of them to tell what they had once been: the church, Roman Catholic, of course—years of British protection and then occupation had never been able to make any fundamental changes in the religious views of the French, though they had accepted the British with good enough grace, considering; a blacksmith shop, half-burned to the ground, though the forge and anvil were still visible through the wreckage, and a few rusting tools; what had once been an inn, its sign still hanging on one hook, weather-worn and fading—though the image of a wild boar was still fairly recognizable, the French words that had once been written below it were now nearly obliterated; a store of some sort, probably a general merchandise store, I guessed; a few other buildings that had lost their identity; and empty, broken-windowed houses.

I suppose I must have paused for longer than I should have, looking at the ruins and speculating about their past—a weakness of mine; I had once, very long ago, intended to be a historian—and it was Kearns' harsh voice that finally made me realize that we had more urgent business to attend to.

"Let's go," he said curtly. "Kar-hinter is waiting for us."

It was the first time that Kearns had said the name of the Krith that we were to meet. I hadn't thought of asking before, assuming that he wouldn't know, and also knowing that it wouldn't make a hell of a lot of difference anyway.

Kar-hinter, I repeated the name in my mind. He was the Krithian weapons supervisor for this Line, an old Krith who had been my chief on several assignments before, including the one I was just completing. He wasn't so bad to work for, even if he was a bit taciturn. I rather liked the old beast; well, better than I liked most Kriths, at least.

Now I don't want you to get the idea that I disliked the Kriths then. I didn't. Not at all. Nor did I particularly like them, as individuals. I admired them as a race and appreciated what they were doing, but they were, by and large, a rather repulsive-looking bunch that I had never really learned to like in all the years that I had been working for them. But Kar-hinter, well, he was okay. For a Krith.

And please don't accuse me of racial prejudice or xenophobia, not until you've heard all my story, at least.

I obeyed Kearns' urgings and followed him through the village, my feet squelching in the mud that even by the middle of the day had not dried very much. It would take several warm, clear, sunny days for the mud that lay over the whole of the Touraine to become solid earth again.

We passed through the center of the village and went on down the muddy road that led out of the town and toward the now-barren landscape beyond. Off in the distance, sheltered by two or three naked-limbed trees, stood a house that was virtually intact, its damages nearly repaired, the windows boarded over, smoke rising from the remains of a chimney.

"That's it. Over there," Kearns said, apparently realizing that I had noticed the house.

"Kar-hinter's there?" I asked.

"Kar-hinter and a British general named Asbury," Kearns answered.

It was then that I saw the British staff car parked beside the house, half-hidden by naked bushes that grew beside the house, by bare vines that in the summer must have covered the house with leaves and clusters of grapes. This was the wine country of France, or it was in other places and had been here once, when France had had the time to make wine, when foreign armies weren't ripping it apart.

By this time you may have gathered that I wasn't altogether happy with the way I made my living. I had outgrown a lot of the misplaced idealism that had led me into it in the first place, but then it was a living, and the only one I knew. It was often a dirty, nasty job, but, like they said, somebody had to do it.

Two men in British uniforms flanked the house's front door, tommy guns held across their chests, standing ramrod-stiff and staring off into space like automatons. Each wore the double chevrons of a corporal, which meant something in the British Army. Men like them had built the Empire, I said to myself, almost admiring their stance, though I myself was not that kind of soldier. I sometimes wonder if I was ever any kind of soldier at all. But I got by. Most of the time. At least I'm still alive as of this writing, and that's saying something.

The two guards came to attention as we approached, saluted me and Tracy across the receivers of their weapons, and one of them said, "May I help you, sir?" He was addressing me since I was the ranking officer.

Kearns answered for me: "Captain Mathers and Lieutenant Tracy to see General Asbury." He produced a sheet of paper from a breast pocket and handed it to the corporal who had spoken.

The corporal relaxed his grip on his tommy gun, took the paper, glanced at it, then back to me. "Certainly, sir. The general is expecting you. Go right in." He handed the paper back to Kearns, gave me another salute across his weapon.

The other corporal turned, opened the door, and I entered the house, Tracy and Kearns behind me.

The first room we entered was empty, though the floor was littered with paper and debris left behind when the former occupants had fled.

"In here," a voice called from another room.

In the next room there were three beings, two of them human, and enough furniture to make the place look as if it were habitable.

A large oak table occupied the center of the room, and a gas lantern sat in its middle. Below the lantern lay a map, but from the distance I could not tell what the map was of. Six chairs of assorted sizes and shapes sat around the table. There was a bed, a sofa, a cabinet on which sat a bottle of wine and some glasses, and three overstuffed easy chairs completing the furniture. A picture of Jesus hung on the wall, holding open His robes to expose a radiant heart. I suspected that the picture belonged to the former occupants of the house, not to any of the present ones.

One of the men was Sir Gerald Asbury, Brigadier General in His Britannic Majesty's Army. I had seen his picture often enough—he had been something of a hero the previous spring when the Touraine, or part of it, was recaptured from the Imperial Germans—though I had never before met him in person. He was a short, stocky, redheaded man, with a huge cavalry mustache, the stereotype of a British officer, but despite that, a bold and imaginative man, so I had been told. I rather liked his looks.

The other man I had met before. His name was Pall, and his nearly seven-foot frame was all muscle. His swarthy face was expressionless, as always, as he stood behind Kar-hinter, his hands hanging at his sides. He was dressed in a harshly-cut black uniform, without decoration save for the ugly energy pistol that hung on his left hip. He was Kar-hinter's bodyguard and one of the deadliest beings I had ever met. I don't know what Timeline he came from, but I don't think I'd care to visit it, not if it's inhabited by very many like him.

The third occupant of the room I knew also. That was Kar-hinter himself. A Krith.

I suppose that this is as good a time as any to describe the appearance of the Kriths, and since Kar-hinter was a fair representative of his race, at least the males of the race, I'll describe him.

Kar-hinter stood six foot four or so in his bare feet, which were always bare, as was the rest of him. Always. His coloring was brown tinged with green, a color that might have been olive had it been a little greener, but wasn't quite. I have seen Kriths who were a sable-brown and some who were a true olive. Their skin coloring varies within these ranges, though there seem to be no racial distinctions as there are supposed to be with human beings.

His head was big and almost.egg-shaped and somewhat lumpy-looking. He had no hair on his head, or on any part of his body, and his skin was a not-quite-shiny satin surface. His eyes were enormous, brown, liquid, equipped with two sets of eyelids, but without distinct pupils, irises, or anything else. They were like big brown marbles. I'm quite sure that they don't work anything at all like our eyes, and of course, it was impossible to tell just where he was looking. A reflection of light on the moist balls gave the impression of pupils, but it was not so.

Below his eyes was a row of tiny openings that dilated with heartbeat regularity. These were the nostrils of a Krith and all they had of a nose. The mouth below the nostril row was, like the eyes, enormous. Kar-hinter's lips were thick, heavy, moist, and hungry-looking. When his mouth opened, you could see rows of sharp, fanglike teeth. Kriths are primarily carnivorous and live mostly on a diet of uncooked meat, I understand.

Along the sides of Kar-hinter's face, running from about where his temples were to the middle point of his jaws were two rows of feathery membranes that twitched in the air like a fish's gills. These functioned as ears and as something more, though I'm not quite sure what.

He had virtually no neck, his head seeming to sit right on top of his broad, muscular shoulders. The arms that dropped from the shoulders were remarkably human, as were the five-fingered hands that grew from the slender wrists.

His chest was broad with prominent, almost feminine nipples. His stomach was flat, well-muscled, and flowed smoothly into his pelvic region. And it was there that you could see that Kar-hinter was very obviously a male.

His legs, in proportion to his long torso, were short and thick and terminated in wide, webbed feet. A short, prehensile tail grew from his buttocks and twitched aimlessly in the air as he rose to greet us.

Kar-hinter, as I said, was absolutely naked. He wore no decorations, no instruments, not even a watch, nor did he carry a pouch to hold personal belongings. I had never seen a Krith wearing anything at all. Whatever they carried with them was locked inside their huge heads, and that was enough. More about that later.

One more point about the Kriths: I assume that there are two sexes to their race—else why would Kar-hinter have the masculine equipment he had?—but in all the years that I had been working for them I had never seen a female Krith, nor had I ever heard of anyone who had. They refused to discuss the matter with humans. Krithian sex life was a complete mystery to the people who worked for and with them.

I gave both Sir Gerald and Kar-hinter a British salute, which they both returned, though Kar-hinter seemed to have a mocking expression on his alien face.

"Please be at ease, gentlemen," Sir Gerald said. "Sit down, won't you?"

"Thank you, sir," I said in English.

"I am sir Gerald Asbury," the British general said, "and, I say, you might as well drop the formalities. I am quite aware of who and what you fellows are. And the men outside"—he gestured toward the front of the house—"are yours as well. I am the only *local* here."

I nodded, took off my cap and dropped it onto the couch near me. After unbuttoning my coat, I took one of the chairs that the general indicated.

"Greetings, Kar-hinter," I said awkwardly, since I never did know quite what to say to a Krith.

"Hello, Eric," Kar-hinter said, clasping his hands behind his back. "And you, Hillary, and you, Ronald." The last was directed at Kearns. "Please, do all of you sit down and make yourselves comfortable. You, as well, Sir Gerald."

When we were all seated, Kar-hinter gestured to Pall, who got the bottle of wine and five glasses from the cabinet behind the Krith. He poured wine into each of the glasses and passed them around without speaking. I noticed that he poured none for himself. Then he returned to his statuelike position behind his master.

"Again, gentlemen, please make yourselves comfortable," Kar-hinter said. The Krith spoke local English without trace of an accent, a policy which the Kriths prided themselves on, though at times it must have been quite difficult. Their speaking mechanisms aren't made much like ours, but they do a damned good job with them anyway.

"I am sure that you are wondering why you are here," he said when we had each taken a sip from our glasses—the wine was excellent.

Tracy and I nodded, though Kearns didn't seem concerned at all. He had said before that he was going Outtime later on in the day, but for some reason I felt some doubts about that, though I didn't know why.

"Good wine, is it not?" Kar-hinter asked. "French, though not local. Pall acquired it from a few Lines East of here where they are not plagued by war. Not just yet, at least. Please, drink up. I brought this bottle especially for this meeting, and I would hate to see it go to waste."

Obediently we drank our wine and waited for Kar-hinter to

get around to telling us why we were here. Kriths don't hurry very often, though they certainly expect it of humans when it's necessary. Well, that's what they paid us for. And I rather liked the pay. I could never have made that kind of money back in my Homeline.

"Now," Kar-hinter finally said after he had Pall refill our glasses, "let me tell you about it. Or, rather, I shall let Sir Gerald begin. Sir Gerald, please."

"Yes, certainly," the British general said awkwardly, reaching for the map that lay on the table and then pushing it back, apparently deciding that it wasn't time for it yet. "To get straight to the point, gentlemen, Royal Intelligence has reason to believe that the Imperial Germans are working on something called an atom bomb. Kar-hinter assures me that you fellows know of such weapons, Outtime, that is."

"Yes, we do," I replied.

"Our scientists seem to have suspected that such a weapon is possible, but they are a very long way from developing it. Kar-hinter tells me that it is basically quite a simple thing."

Right then I was hardly listening to Sir Gerald's words. I was too stunned by what he had said. The Imperials building atomic weapons! It was fantastic. They were still three or four or even five decades from *that*. Hell, the locals hadn't even developed a really decent radio yet.

"Nevertheless," Sir Gerald was saying, "the Germans seem to have gotten somewhere with the idea. Seems they have a rather bright group of young scientists working for them, developing the theories of some fellow named Eisenstein or something. He has been dead for years, I'm told, but he left some rather impressive theories that weren't published until a few years ago, and then only in the Holy Roman Empire. The book fell into our hands only a few months ago. And then we began getting reports that the Imperials were actually trying to build such a bomb."

Kar-hinter waved Sir Gerald to silence with a careless, unconscious gesture of one accustomed to command.

"It is not necessary to tell you," Kar-hinter said, facing the three of us, "what atomic weapons in the hands of the Holy Roman Empire would do to our efforts here. They could, of

23

course, if produced in sufficient quantities, put the Imperial Germans in command of this entire Line, even with their primitive delivery systems—and we certainly cannot afford that." He paused. "Please go on, Sir Gerald."

"Yes, of course," the British general said. "Well, as soon as we learned of the German efforts, we sent intelligence teams in to gather more detailed information." Sir Gerald paused reflectively for a moment, then continued. "The first two teams failed to report back. The third team did come back, rather badly mauled, I must say, but with *some* information." Sir Gerald paused again.

"Yes?" I asked.

"The Imperial Germans have a plant on the Baltic, near Königsberg, actually on the Gulf of Danzig," Sir Gerald went on slowly. "It's very well hidden and extremely well guarded. We are not exactly sure what they're doing there, but it is in some way connected with the atom bomb project. That is all we know." The British general looked at Kar-hinter.

"Thank you, Sir Gerald," Kar-hinter said. "As you might suspect, His Majesty, King George, ordered that this information be turned over to us. When we learned of the Imperial efforts to build nuclear weapons, we gave His Majesty a simplified explanation of just what they are. His own physicists were able to confirm this to his satisfaction.

"Sir Gerald was then put in charge of the British operation to prevent the construction of the bomb, with our technical advice. We *do not* wish nuclear weapons in this Timeline at this stage." The Krith looked at Sir Gerald. "As much as we admire and respect the British Empire, we are in no position to give them nuclear weapons, nor will we assist in their local production. Considering the world conditions on this Line, we cannot tolerate nuclear weapons. I hope you understand, Sir Gerald."

"Of course," Sir Gerald said without conviction. "It has been explained to me several times."

"Very good," Kar-hinter said, imitating a human smile without much success. "Will you proceed, please, Sir Gerald?"

"There is very little more to tell," the British general said. "We have made three attempts to gain entry into the Baltic

24

plant. All have failed miserably. Considering its location within the Empire, it is, of course, impossible for us to get a large force near it, even by sea. Nor, I doubt, would it do us much good. As I said, the plant is well guarded: there are several regiments of infantry stationed within a few miles of the plant, and the Third Imperial Fleet is presently situated at Gdansk. The emperor is taking no chances of our getting anywhere near it. And, of course, we have now put him on guard."

"Then I assume you're planning a cross-Line attack?" I asked Kar-hinter.

"Ah!" Kar-hinter exclaimed, then made another of those expressions that were supposed to be smiles. He motioned to Pall to refill our wineglasses, scratched himself thoughtfully in an intimate place, and finally spoke. "It has been considered." He looked at Sir Gerald. "What Eric is asking, Sir Gerald, is whether we will establish a force in an alternate Timeline where the area is uninhabited and then skud the force into the plant and destroy it."

"Well, I was thinking of simply skudding a bomb across," I said.

"As I said, such things have been considered," Kar-hinter said, "though if we were to do so we would probably skud a spy in first to see exactly what they are doing there. But, ah, no. To answer your question, we will not do that. We are already interfering with this Line a bit more than is wise, or so the *Tromas* in the Homeline tell us. They will allow a cross-Line venture only after we have tried all other avenues. If all else fails, then we will be allowed to cross-Line at the Baltic plant. As I said before, this Line is not to be allowed nuclear weapons under *any* circumstances." He glanced at Sir Gerald.

"I'm sure you know best, Kar-hinter," Sir Gerald said, though he didn't seem to really mean it.

"Then what?" I asked.

"Now it seems," Kar-hinter said, belching politely and raising his wineglass, "a very fortunate set of circumstances has arisen that may allow us to gain all the information we need without ever approaching the Baltic plant." Kar-hinter, like a second-rate actor, paused dramatically.

"And what's that?" I asked on cue.

"The Imperial Germans have placed Count Albert von Heinen in charge of the atomic project. As well as being a distant cousin of the emperor, he is a highly trained engineer —for this Line—and has made himself an impressive record as a military field commander. Quite a young man, as well, I understand.

"Now it seems that Count von Heinen is presently visiting Beaugency. I am not sure why, but as I said, he is a man of many talents. Just why he is in Beaugency is of no great moment. The fact that he is here is of great importance to us. We shall kidnap him."

Kar-hinter paused again, finished his glass of wine, placed the empty glass on the table with a flourish. As he continued to speak, he paced back and forth at the head of the table, his short tail whipping in the air.

"Von Heinen will be spending the night in a villa just north of Beaugency. His American wife is with him, I understand, so we shall take her when we kidnap him. It may be that she can give us some additional information."

"I don't follow you," I said.

"The wife?" Kar-hinter asked. "An American, I said. Doesn't that mean anything to you, Eric? Ah, well, let me tell you. The Countess von Heinen, née Sally Beall, is the daughter of the late Archer Beall. What does that mean to you?"

"The ARA leader?" Tracy asked, speaking for the first time since the conversation began.

"Exactly, my dear Hillary," Kar-hinter said. "The late Mr. Beall, killed recently in the New York riots, was one of the major leaders of the American Republican Army, as well as president of the Mad Anthony Wayne Society. A very, very important man in American revolutionary circles."

Sir Gerald's red face showed obvious anger at the mention of the Bealls. As a loyal British officer—though he was, I believe, born in the American colonies—he was properly outraged at the rebels in America who were causing so much trouble during the war, siding with the Imperial Germans by their very presence, draining desperately needed troops from the European war.

"Beall's daughter married Von Heinen for purely political

reasons, I am told," Kar-hinter said. "To cement German and American rebel relations, so to speak. But her capture will be merely a by-product of the main effort—an in-depth interrogation of Count von Heinen."

In-depth interrogation, Kar-hinter had just said. Mind probe! Now just how in hell were they going to pull that off, I wondered.

"Let me outline the plan, gentlemen," Kar-hinter said, scratching his more intimate parts again. "We will go into greater detail later. But for now, the high points. You, Eric"—Kar-hinter pointed a finger at me—"assuming that you wish to take out a new contract, will lead the kidnapping party. At approximately midnight you will take four boats into the Loire, row upstream across the German lines and into Beaugency."

"How do we get across the German lines?" I asked. "You make it sound awfully simple."

"For you, it shall be," the Krith said. "Just after dark the British right flank will launch an attack against the German positions east of Beaugency and sweep toward the city. By midnight the whole British right will be entangled with the Germans. Then, just before you start up the river, a squadron of airships, laden with fire bombs, will proceed across the British right toward Beaugency. It is a suicide mission, I will admit"—Sir Gerald bit his lower lip but did not comment—"but it should do well in putting the city, or a good portion of it, to flames." Kar-hinter paused, smiled, belched. "Then, Eric, with all this going on to your right, with the Imperials so preoccupied with the battle, you should be able to pass up the river in the darkness and confusion with little difficulty."

Finally Sir Gerald could contain himself no longer.

"I must protest, sir!" he exclaimed.

"You have protested before, Sir Gerald," Kar-hinter said calmly. "You have protested straight to Buckingham Palace."

"I bloody well have!" Sir Gerald almost yelled. "And mucking little good it's done. But, sir"—he addressed the naked, alien Krith as a superior officer—"I just cannot condone sacrificing hundreds or thousands of British lives, not to mention a whole squadron of airships, just to allow a handful of men to—to . . .''

''Sir Gerald,'' Kar-hinter said firmly, his tail lashing sharply behind him, ''please restrain yourself. You have registered your complaints.''

Sir Gerald muttered something else under his breath and then was silent.

''When you reach the villa,'' Kar-hinter went on as if Sir Gerald had never spoken, ''you will kidnap the count and his wife.''

''And then what do we do with them?'' I asked.

''There will be a skudder waiting for you,'' Kar-hinter said slowly.

''Now wait a minute,'' I said. ''You told us that cross-Line movement had been forbidden.''

''Yes,'' the Krith said, ''for the Baltic plant. But this action will not be *direct* interference, so to speak. You will take Von Heinen and his wife cross-Lines to a designated place where there will be an interrogation squad waiting for them. They will probe the count and his wife, and then you will return them to this Line and release them. They will be conditioned to believe that they escaped from you—and no one will be the wiser for it.''

''I don't understand it,'' Tracy said. ''Cross-Lining in the Baltic is forbidden, but it isn't here. Why?''

Tracy should have known better than to even ask.

''Because it *is*,'' Kar-hinter said firmly. ''You will do as you are told within your contracted terms.''

''Why the bloody hell can't you just skud them or whatever it is you do right into the villa?'' Sir Gerald asked angrily.

''It *must* be done as I have outlined it, Sir Gerald. This is the only way it may be allowed. There are reasons that I would find impossible to explain to you.''

I could well understand Sir Gerald's mystification. Countless times in the past I had run up against the same sort of thing from the Kriths. I don't suppose we can ever understand their reasons for doing things the way they do them. They just don't think the same way we do.

Kar-hinter looked at Tracy and then at me, scratching himself thoughtfully. "There is one final matter to settle, gentlemen," he said. "Your present contracts are about to expire, and they certainly do not cover an operation of this nature. I have new contracts which I beg you to consider. You are the best men available for this job, and I would consider it a personal honor should you accept."

With this he pulled two sheets of paper from a folder lying on the table and handed one to Tracy and the other to me.

I read over my copy quickly and smiled to myself when I came to the part about the pay and the benefits offered for this job. All things considered, it was one of the best contracts the Kriths had ever offered me.

When I looked up, I saw that Tracy was smiling too.

"I take it that you accept?" Kar-hinter asked.

Without replying I signed my name on the bottom of the contract, thumbprinted it, and handed it back to Kar-hinter. Tracy did the same.

"Thank you," Kar-hinter said with a nonhuman smile-thing on his face. "That will be all for the time being. Food will be brought to you shortly. I suggest that you rest now. There are bunks ready for you in the back room. At nightfall the remainder of your party will arrive, and we will go into the plans in more detail. Do you have any further questions now?"

"I have one," Kearns said, speaking for the first time.

"Yes, Ronald?" Kar-hinter asked.

"When do I leave?"

"When Eric, Hillary, and Sir Gerald leave," Kar-hinter answered slowly. "You shall accompany them to Beaugency. You are to be their skudder pilot."

Kearns just smiled, nothing more, as if he had known all along that he would be going with us.

Kar-hinter then nodded politely to Sir Gerald, to the rest of us.

"You will excuse me, gentlemen," he said. "I have work to do. I shall be back by dark." He left the room with the black uniformed Pall at his heels.

Then we waited for our meal.

5

THE LINES OF TIME

I suppose that Kar-hinter's intention in giving us so much wine was to make us sleepy, to force us to rest some before the activities of the coming night. Though, of course, that might not have been his intention at all. You can only guess at what a Krith's purposes really are.

Still, if that was his idea, it worked. Three glasses of strong wine on an empty stomach—for I hadn't eaten all day—had almost put me to sleep when a mess steward came in with three tins of beef hash, bread, and tea. It wasn't a particularly tasty meal, but it was nourishing and filling, and I felt much better after eating, and even sleepier.

As Kar-hinter had said, there were beds in the back room of the house, old metal-framed beds, worn and rusty, but supporting thick down mattresses. It had gotten quite warm by afternoon, and the golden French sunlight streamed in between the boards that covered the windows, illuminating the motes of dust that swam in the air like galaxies of stars.

Tracy and Kearns fell asleep almost at once, and I lay back, half-dozing as the afternoon came and slowly passed, moving toward night, not at all concerned about what Kar-hinter had planned for us. I had been through worse often enough not to be concerned. What would happen would happen. You can call it Greek fatalism, if you like.

I don't know where Sir Gerald went. Shortly after Kar-hinter and Pall left, the general got into his staff car, saying that he would be back before dark, and drove off. I sort of suspected that he was going somewhere to make another complaint about the Krithian plans, but I doubted that it would do any good. Apparently the plans for the British attack against the fortified German positions had come straight from the top, the General Staff or maybe from the king himself. I was sorry that it had to be that way—so many lives expended just to get us into the villa where Von Heinen was staying, but it had to be that way. There wasn't a damned thing *I* could do about it, and I didn't think that Sir Gerald could do any more.

So I rested and half slept and did something that was midway between remember and dream. Fragments of images, half-forgotten events, a girl's name, a glimpse of a childhood a long way and a long When from Here and Now. A blond Greek boy who was big for his age and had a way of getting into more trouble than he should have. At least I considered myself Greek, even if my blood was half-Saxon and I had been born on an island that is called Britain in a lot of Lines.

And I remember how my father had been hanged for treason by the governor of North Ionnia and a girl named Kristin had been raped by a gang of the governor's bullies and how I joined an underground student group in college and nearly got myself hanged before the general revolution broke out—backed by the Kriths, though I didn't know that until later—and how the Kriths, when it was all over and we had won, asked me if I wanted to join the Timeliners. My family was dead. Kristin had committed suicide. Why the hell not?

And I remembered another girl named Marissa in one of the Carolingian Lines and how she had died terribly slowly and terribly painfully and how I had made the man who killed her die even more slowly and more painfully because I had loved her and would have quit the 'Liners and married her and settled down if it hadn't been for that goddamned war.

And I thought about the month I had once spent in one of the Rajaian Timelines—trying to forget about it all. That was a hedonistic Line where machines did the work of men and left people with nothing to do but spend their lifetimes in pursuit of pleasures of one sort or another. And while I was there, I had tried just about all of them, except for some that were even a little too perverted for me. Like the three girls and the trained monkey and the goat who all got together. . . . Well, never mind that.

But what I thought about mostly, for some reason, was the Kriths, who and what they were, and why. My thoughts weren't in any kind of order, but I'll try to present them as if they were. Maybe you can understand a little bit of it.

Who exactly are the Kriths? Friend, I don't know. I'm not even sure that they know themselves. They come from some Line a long, long way to the T-East, so far across the Whens that men hadn't even evolved on Earth. Whether the Kriths were even natives of Earth I don't know, but I sort of doubt it. Or if they are they came from a Line that branched off from ours millions of years ago, back when the first mammals were developing, for there was some fundamental differences between them and the mammals of our Lines that would take millions of years to produce. More likely, I thought, they came from another planet, a lot of Whens closer than a sixty-or-seventy-million-year-old split.

Kriths are totally unable to do anything with machines. This is a fact—or at least I thought it was then—and I'd seen it proved countless times. They could never have developed spaceships, but with their built-in Line-skudding ability they could easily have come across someone who *had* developed spaceships, men or some other beings, and in those come to Earth. Hell, I know that doesn't sound much more likely than their having evolved here. So let's drop the subject. I don't know When and Where they came from, but they *are*. And the fact that they are is very important. Maybe one of the most important things in all the universes.

Let me tell you about *that*. Given a nearly infinite number of universes—at least I'm told that the number is nearly infinite, if that means anything, all beginning back when the first universe was created, if it ever was *created*. But the Lines are there, stretching East and West farther than any Krith has ever gone, extending almost forever. I've seen a few hundred of them myself, but that's nothing, absolutely nothing. But to get back to the point I was trying to make: Given an almost infinite number of Timelines, just about anything is possible. Even Kriths.

The Kriths have a nervous system that isn't very much like ours. Oh, they have a brain, of course, three of them in fact. One is for, well, *thinking,* conscious thoughts like those you and I think. The second is for involuntary actions, the general running of the body, and it's located somewhere in the chest area so that a Krith can go on living for a hell of a long time with its head blown off, and I've seen it happen. Of course without his head a Krith isn't good for very much, but that's the way things are.

The third brain isn't really a brain at all; it's more a series of nervous ganglions extending the length of the spine, but well inside the body cavity, pretty well protected. What this setup was first evolved for, I don't know. I can't even guess, but then I have no idea what kind of environment the Kriths evolved in. Maybe it was originally a protection against, well, magnetic fields or something, or maybe it was a means of radio communications—for they do have that or something like it. As I said, I don't know why it ever started evolving. I just know where it led.

It led to cross-Lines.

The Kriths have their own built-in skudder. They can, at will, cross the Timelines from one universe to another.

Impossible? Damned near, maybe, but not quite. They exist and they do it.

I don't know whether they evolved intelligence before or after they developed their skudding ability. Maybe they both developed together. I suspect that maybe you can't have the ability to skud without a rational faculty to guide it, but that's only a guess. And sometimes I wonder just how rational the Kriths are. I mean, they can talk and think and act rationally, but they have no mechanical ability at all. They can't even build their own shelters. In other ways they're bright enough, so I don't know. I suppose they had to sacrifice a great deal to develop skudding to the level that they have.

Anyhow, they did learn to skud, and they began jumping across the Lines, into the parallel universes. I don't know what they found to the East of wherever they started, but to the West they found men.

At first the Kriths didn't interfere with humans. They just dropped in, so to speak, saw things they liked, and finally found a means of communicating. Shangalis was developed, either by them or by men, and a cross-Line language was born.

At some point men began to investigate the Kriths' means of skudding, but whether the Kriths prompted them to do it or whether men did it on their own, I don't know. Probably both in different Lines. And eventually men built skudders and the Kriths began to use them with human pilots. When the Kriths used their own built-in mechanisms to cross the Lines, all they could take with them was their own physical bodies. If they wanted to take anything else—men, machines, weapons, books, tapes—they had to have mechanical help. They got it when men built skudders and the Kriths took advantage of them.

So, a long, long way East of here, cross-Line trading began to take place, cultures of parallel worlds began to mingle, merge, change, and a whole new kind of civilization was built.

Still, all this doesn't explain much, doesn't explain, for example, why a mercenary soldier from a Europo-Macedonian Line was fighting a war in a Romano-British Line. Let me try to explain that to you.

Time travel is impossible.

I mean, travel into the future or the past. A lot of places have tried it, and they have always failed. It simply can't be done. Don't ask me why. I'm no mathematician. It just can't be done.

However, they tell me there is a way that communications from the future to the past can take place. It's pretty complicated and awfully costly, but it can be done. At least the Kriths have said it can and has been done. But you can judge for yourself.

A long way East, so the story goes, there's an Indus Line where technology developed early and reached a high level some hundreds of years ago. They had even got so far as building spaceships and exploring the nearer stars. It was there that the first future-to-past communication was attempted. The Kriths were in on it, so I'm told; they helped finance it by bringing in a great deal of Outtime wealth and materials to try the experiment.

A huge transmitting station was built on the moon. From what I've been told it was the biggest transmitter ever constructed in any Line, more watts of energy than would be needed to run a dozen high-level technology worlds. They tell me that the energy of the sun was somehow drained to power the station —and I don't means by solar cells or something like that. They tapped the sun and poured its energy directly into the station.

This transmitter, though, was never connected to a real antenna. All its power was fed into dummy loads, huge chunks of the lunar surface converted into resistors just to drain off the transmitter's power. They set up this monstrous station and burned up half the moon just to get rid of the power it produced.

All this was done just to get a standing wave on a huge bank of solid-state devices. A gigantic quasi-modulator was fed by power, and it just sat there and waited . . . but not for long.

The idea goes something like this, as well as I can explain it: The signal is generated, and it exists and will continue to be generated and continue to exist for centuries. The quasi-modulator will be—is—was waiting for a signal to be fed back to it from the future.

They tell me that there are certain activities of subatomic particles that get cause-and-effect backward. A thing, they say, can happen *before* the cause of it takes place. They go on to say that if a radio signal is existing in a certain type of solid-state quasi-modulator it can be affected by this backward effect and cause, that a whole chain of these backward effects and causes can happen in this quasi-modulator.

Now, it's like this. Somewhere way in the future they decide it's time to send a message back to the past. They feed this message into the quasi-modulator—and somewhere down in the subatomic particles, down even below where the radio energy is bouncing around, this effect-before-the-cause chain will begin. The cause had happened, but a nanosecond before that the effect had already taken place; this effect had, even prior to that, been the cause for another effect even another nanosecond before, and so on. Backward through time the effect and then the cause, the effect and the cause, until it finally gets back down the chain of time to the beginning.

Okay, now you can forget all that. The Kriths say it works,

and you can take their word for it if you like. I once did.

So, the Indus Line people built this station on the moon, drove all this power into it and sat back and let it operate for the next half million years, if that's what it would take to get a message coming the wrong way in time.

Well, even before the station had gotten up to full power, a message came in. From the future!

Translated into local English the message read something like this:

FROM THE YEAR 7093 [WHICH IS ABOUT TWO THOU-SAND YEARS FROM NOW BY THE RECKONING OF TIME IN THAT INDUS LINE]. GREETINGS. WE HAVE WAIT-ED UNTIL THE LAST POSSIBLE MOMENT TO SEND THIS BACK TO YOU. BUT WE KNOW THAT WE CAN WAIT NO LONGER. WE ARE ALL DOOMED. WHILE THERE IS STILL TIME LET US TELL YOU WHAT HAS HAPPENED TO US ALL.

THERE IS A CIVILIZATION OF BEINGS ON THE FAR SIDE OF THE GALAXY. THEY ARE TOTALLY ALIEN, INIMI-CAL TO ALL THAT IS HUMAN AND KRITH. THEY HAVE BEEN BIDING THEIR TIME, AWARE OF US, BUILDING A GREAT ARMADA OF INTERSTELLAR WARSHIPS TO COME AND DESTROY US ALL.

WHY THEY HATE US WE DO NOT KNOW. NOR DO WE KNOW HOW TO FIGHT THEM.

HUMANITY AND KRITH STAND ALONE AGAINST THE ALIEN HORDES THAT ARE COMING TO DESTROY US. AND WE ARE ALL BUT DEFENSELESS AGAINST THEIR WEAPONS.

ALL THE WORKS OF OUR GREAT MUTUAL CIVILI-ZATIONS SHALL PERISH UNLESS. . . .

And there the message ended. That was all there was of it. And it was the only message ever received.

The station is still in operation to this day—assuming it's all true—beaming its power into the moon, and I suppose that it will continue to operate until the day two thousand years from now when it is destroyed—if the future is not changed.

But that one message came through. The aliens are coming to destroy us, mankind and Kriths together.

Across the Lines six more stations were built, beaming their power into the future. And each one received substantially the same message, asking for help from the past.

Crazy, isn't it?

The first time I was told the story I went out and got myself senseless drunk and got laid by the ugliest old whore in North New Ardhea.

But, to go on—the final analysis was this: All across the Lines there exists this same menace two thousand years away. A menace that will totally destroy everything human and Krithian unless something is done to stop it. That's when the Kriths really got started. They decided to do something about it. They decided to change the future, to change the message being beamed backward in time.

Using the sociodynamics of the Haldian Lines, they began to move across the Timelines, mostly to the West where men could, perhaps, someday be strong enough to fight the invaders, and began to build worlds that could meet and withstand the aliens.

They would move into a Line, the Kriths and the Haldian sociodynamicists, and analyze where the current trends would lead in two thousand years, what kind of world would be there to meet the invaders. Then they set about making the necessary changes to meet the countless invasions of the future.

Guided by their own strange logic and the sociodynamics of the Haldian Timelines, the Kriths would bring in what forces were necessary to make the changes, aiming the Lines in the direction of maximum strength in the distant future. They used sociologists, anthropologists, scientists of a hundred kinds to add, to subtract, to build, and to change, and they used mercenary soldiers where necessary.

Mercenary soldiers like me.

Now the world in which the British and the Holy Roman Empires battled was a fair example of how they worked. Haldian sociodynamicists said that without outside help the Holy Roman Empire would defeat the British within a decade. Before the century was out, it would consolidate its hold on the Western Hemisphere and then turn to face the growing Nipponese Empire. The twenty-first century, by local reckoning, would be devoted to another war between the Holy Romans and the Nippons, which would ultimately lead to nuclear warfare that would destroy both empires and most of the rest of civilization.

It would take a thousand years for even a primitive agricultural society to redevelop and at the end of the two-thousand-year span allotted to us the inhabitants of this Line would probably have barely reached the level of ancient Rome, local history. Hardly a match for the invaders.

On the other hand Haldian sociodynamics indicated that a victory by the British would ultimately lead to a mutual coexistence with the Nipponese, the eventual rise of republican forms of government within the next three hundred years, a falling apart of the old empires, and the gradual rise of a peaceful, united world with a high degree of technology.

By the end of the two thousand years *this* culture would have colonized a good chunk of the galaxy and be in a position to more than take care of itself against the invaders.

So there Tracy and I and a few hundred other Timeliners were, with a handful of Kriths, helping the British defeat the Holy Romans and create this better world.

That's the sort of thing I believed then, and that's what I thought about as I waited for the sun to set and for Kar-hinter to return and prepare us for our mission—the kidnapping of Count Albert von Heinen and his wife.

I had no idea what else was going to happen before that mission was over.

6

UP THE LOIRE

The moon had set early that night, and had it not been for the flashing of cannon along the British right and the answering flashes of Imperial German artillery and the red glow in the east where the city had already begun to burn, it would have been a night of pitch blackness, unbroken even by stars, for a low cloud covering had moved in shortly before nightfall, forewarning us of the rainstorms that the meteorologists had predicted for tomorrow's dawn.

At times we could see airships moving in and out of the clouds to the east, their bellies lighted by the glow of the city burning under them, by the flames of their own bombs exploding, and by the fainter flashes of Imperial cannon and antiairship weapons. And once or twice as we watched we saw an airship burst into flames, its catalyzed hydrogen, impervious to flame most of the time, but still unstable and liable to explode when the proper degree of heat was reached, bursting out, lighting the undersides of the clouds with a brilliant glow. Then the fireball would begin to fall apart as the hydrogen was consumed. And I wondered how soon the Kriths were going to help the British "invent" heavier-than-air craft.

But we had little time to watch what was happening or to wonder about things. We were in the boats, in the dark river, in the shadows of the willows and the poplars, and we were quietly paddling toward the cables and chains that the Imperials had laid across the river to prevent just such a venture as ours.

The lead boat held three British soldiers: a sergeant and two privates, dressed in rubber swimming garments, equipped with cutters and saws to hack a path for us through the cables and chains. Those three were really what they appeared to be —simple British soldiers given an assignment that they didn't fully understand, but about which they asked no questions. Not of us, at least, we officers.

I was in the second boat, sitting in the front position, a paddle in my hands dipping softly, quietly into the dark water, moving us forward, while we listened. My own senses, augmented by artificial electrobiological systems, were at their peak and more acute than those of other human beings who did not have the Timeliner modifications.

Behind me sat General Sir Gerald Asbury, dressed now in the uniform of a common soldier, with only a glint of metal on his collar to betray his rank. He too held a paddle and alternately dipped it right and then left and then back to the right again. Behind him sat Ronald Kearns, our skudder pilot, showing no emotion at all. Though he was a Timeliner like myself, I could not fathom what was going on in his head, though that is not strange in itself, for Kearns or whatever his real name was was probably from a world as different from mine as mine was from the one in which we both now found ourselves.

The third boat held Tracy and the two corporals who had been guarding the house in which we had met with Kar-hinter.

In the final boat there was another corporal and two privates, at least that is what their British uniforms said they were, though like the rest of us, save for the three in the leading boat and Sir Gerald, they were men from worlds other than this, men who moved across the parallel branches of time fighting a war for the Kriths that would not end for two thousand years.

We Timeliners have a lot of history in front of us.

"How much farther do you think it is?" I heard Kearns ask.

"A good distance," Sir Gerald answered. "We are still a mile or two short of the German lines, as best I can estimate, and the villa is a good five miles beyond that."

"Several hours then?" Kearns asked.

"At the rate we're going, yes," Sir Gerald whispered back.

40

"We will be doing very well for ourselves to have the count in our hands by dawn."

"We'll have him before dawn," I said over my shoulder.

"I hope so, Mathers," said Sir Gerald.

"I know damned well, sir," I replied. "We don't have any other choice."

"It's your show," Sir Gerald whispered bitterly. "I'm just an observer."

I said nothing, for it was true. This wasn't a British patrol. It was strictly Krithian and Timeliner. The poor British were only causing a distraction for us, a bloody, nasty, costly distraction that Sir Gerald hated with all his guts. I can't say that I blamed him.

It seemed like hours, though it could have been no more than a few minutes later, when the sergeant in the lead boat held up his arm and signaled for us to stop. Not that I could really see his arm even with my augmented retinas; it was only a shade of blackness somehow slightly distinguishable from the other shades of blackness along the river.

We slowed in midstream and carefully turned our boats toward the shore, up to the marshy ground, in close to the trees that grew on the water's edge. And there we stopped and waited, silent, hardly breathing, listening to the distant sounds of war and the closer sounds of German sentries marching along the edge of the river.

Then there were two soft, watery sounds, not quite splashes, more like the sound of two heavy bodies slowly lowering themselves into the river, down under the water. There was silence as the sergeant and one of the privates swam underwater up to where the first set of cables lay across the river.

There was nothing to do but wait and wish for a cigarette and know that I couldn't smoke one and then chew on my lip and recite an old Greek poem my father had taught me and think about women and wonder what was going to happen when we finally did get to the villa—though that sort of thing, long experience had taught me, was a complete waste of time. I'd do whatever I had to do when the time came, and that's all there was to it.

We were still a mile or two from Beaugency and the two bridges that spanned the Loire there, if they were still intact, and aerial photographs hadn't been too clear about one of them; it might be half lying in the water for all we knew.

Beaugency was an old town, I understood, or rather the name was old. The present town was relatively new, for this part of France, having been built from the ground up around the turn of the nineteenth century. The earlier city by that name had been a few miles farther up the river but had been burned during the Peasants' Rebellion in the late 1799's that tried to overthrow the French monarchy and had very nearly succeeded before the British stepped in on the side of the royalist defenders of the crown and helped put down the rebellion with the same deadly Ferguson breechloaders that had stopped the American rebels two decades before.

The old Beaugency had been a stronghold of the rebels during the last stages of the rebellion. When their main forces had been crushed by the royalists and their British allies, the shattered armies had somehow converged on the Touraine and finally retreated into Beaugency. It was the last major rebel fortress to fall and the angry, victorious king had ordered that the city, like Carthage nearly two thousand years before, be leveled and salt sown upon the earth where it had stood.

The survivors of Beaugency, those who weren't beheaded or hanged under the king's eyes, were allowed to settle along the river a few miles from the spot where the old city had been. The new Beaugency had gradually grown up there—and that is the city toward which we moved or had been moving before we had stopped to wait for the cutting of the cables.

All this is of absolutely no importance, of course. It was just one of the bits of information I had picked up while we sat in the trenches during the long, cold winter.

At last we heard the movement of water again, the soft splashing of careful, highly trained swimmers returning to their boat. Again I saw the sergeant, once he had got his dripping body back into the boat, give me a hand signal; this one for us to follow.

Back out into the river we rowed, though not as far from the shore as we had been before. From here on we would have to do our best to avoid being seen, though I doubted that very many Germans were peering down into the river that night. There was too much going on to the east for them to worry much about the river.

After a while we passed the trenches and the last of the cables that had lain across the river. Soon the Germans would discover that they had been cut, but it would not be soon enough for them to do very much about it. We hoped.

Then we came to the parts of the city that lay along the river. The main sections of the city had grown up to the east, away from the river and that is where Beaugency's industry had been and that is where the Imperial forces were camped most thickly and that is where the bombs fell.

I had halfway expected to see refugees streaming toward the river, trying to cross the bridges or perhaps swimming the river itself, but there were none. Maybe there were no civilians left in Beaugency and the Germans who retreated from the battle—that would only be the wounded now—would be going north, not west. Kar-hinter had known pretty well what he was doing when he sent us up the river.

The first bridge showed no sign of damage, though about all I could really see were the two guardhouses on either end of the bridge and the two sentries who paced back and forth between them and threw occasional, disinterested glances down into the water. I doubt that they could see a thing in the blackness that surrounded us.

We passed the bridge without incident and came to the second about half a mile up the river, the one that the aerial photographs had indicated might be damaged. It was.

At one time a blast had struck the bridge on its extreme right, blowing it completely apart. The spans of twisted, rusted metal drooped down to the water and rested on the river bottom. Half the river was blocked to navigation. We were forced to cross over to the left bank and proceed there along the side.

There were no guards visible there. The Germans must have been fairly confident that no one would get this far up the river without being detected, I thought.

Soon the center of the city was behind us and even the glare in the sky was falling off to our right rear. We were well behind the

Imperial lines—and without detection.

Funny, I should have known by then that the time to be most careful in war is when you feel sure that you've accomplished something. That's when you get careless and when the enemy is most likely to do something deadly.

It came suddenly, without warning.

A light flashed above us from the riverbank. An instant later a second light came from the other bank. The two beams met on our lead boat. And a German machine gun opened up on it.

For an instant I was tempted to switch my body to full combat augmentation, to speed up my actions and reflexes to five times their normal speed—for that had been built into me too—but I did not. Full combat augmentation, though it makes a man the most deadly fighting machine in all the known universes, also drains a man's metabolism at an astonishing rate. And I knew that I would need all my strength when we reached the villa. I did not will those electrobiological circuits into operation.

One of the men in the lead boat came to his feet, a tommy gun in his hands, aimed toward the nearest of the spotlights. The tommy began to chatter within a second of the barking of the German gun, and its first slug must have hit the spotlight's lens. But even as the light was going out, the British soldier's body was cut in half by the machine gun's rain of bullets.

Then the boat seemed to come apart, two more bodies tumbling out as rifles from both sides of the river began to fire.

I grabbed up the rifle that lay in the boat beside me, swung it up, and pulled off a shot at the second spotlight. I heard another Enfield crack in unison with mine, off to my rear. Tracy had been just as quick as I.

The other German spotlight went out.

We dropped our rifles, all of us in the three remaining boats, grabbed our paddles and began paddling like mad up the river. We had only a few minutes of darkness, at best, before the Imperials brought up another light. We all knew that we'd better make the most of it.

It was still totally dark in the river and I'm sure that the Germans on the bank couldn't see us, but they could hear us, and they could fire in our direction. I just hoped that their hearing wasn't good enough to pinpoint us all, and I thought that echoes from the buildings along the river would aid us. My main fear was that one of our own men would be foolish enough to fire back, revealing our positions with the flashing of his weapon. I should have known better. All these men were experienced mercenaries—not heroes.

The river curved slightly, carrying us away from the spot where the machine gun was set up, though it continued to fire into the water around us until we finally got out of its range. The rifles, however, moved along as easily as we did and continued to pelt the river around us. More than once I heard the whistle of a bullet that missed my head only by inches.

"Ach!" came a sudden expletive from directly behind me. "Bloody hell!" It was Sir Gerald's voice.

"What is it?" I asked, hoarsely whispering.

"I'm hit," Sir Gerald said weakly.

"Where? How badly?"

"Right thigh," he gasped. "Don't know how bad. Really doesn't hurt much yet."

"Give it time," I said. "Is the bone broken?"

"Don't know."

"Kearns," I whispered, "see about it."

I heard movement behind me, Kearns slipping into position to investigate the general's wound with the tips of his fingers. Now I had to paddle the boat alone.

"Not too bad," Kearns' voice said a few moments later. "It's going to hurt him, but I don't think it got the bone."

"Can he walk on it?" I asked.

"If he has to."

"My God, man," Sir Gerald gasped, "I don't even know. . . ."

"If you have to, you'll walk on it, *sir*," Kearns said slowly, bitterly. "Or I'll blow your bloody head off."

"What are you saying?" Sir Gerald asked in a pained voice.

"I'm saying you're not going to slow us down when we hit the ground," Kearns said as if speaking to a child. "Mathers?"

"Yes?"

Kearns was silent.

"Oh!" I said, realizing what he meant. "I'm sorry, Sir Gerald, but you'll have to walk on that leg or surrender yourself to the Imperials."

That was enough for Sir Gerald; he said nothing more.

"Kearns, help me. I can't handle this boat alone."

But already I heard the splash of Kearns' paddle in the water.

By now the city was thinning, gaps appearing between the lower, smaller buildings and the light of the burning portions of the city was beginning to play on the water. In a few more moments the riflemen on the shore would be able to see us.

"Right," I whispered to Kearns. "Head for the right bank."

We began to cut toward the center of the river, out to where we stood a better chance of being seen, but I figured that it was a chance we had to take.

The men in the boats following us must have been able to see us well enough to realize what I had in mind, for they began cutting out toward the middle of the river and then toward the right bank.

My boat had passed the midpoint of the river and was nearing the darkness of the right bank, Tracy's boat was now no more than a yard or two behind mine, and the final boat was very close to his, though I could barely see it. The Imperials on the left bank had momentarily lost us in the confusion, and we dipped our paddles silently, carefully, to try to avoid detection.

Then a brilliant explosion from the burning portion of the city lighted the river, revealing us.

"Balls!" Kearns muttered.

Then a voice screamed something in German from the bank.

Rifles and submachine guns began chattering, lacing the river with shot, here and there a tracer showing the paths of their bullets and many of them were very close to their targets.

"Let 'em have it!" I yelled back, grabbing up my rifle and hoping that inertia would carry the boat the rest of the way to the bank.

Kearns' tommy gun began to fire only seconds after my rifle. To my surprise Sir Gerald, who had been silent, fumbled with his Enfield for a moment, then placed it to his shoulder and began to snap off shots with a marksman's ease. He seemed to have forgotten about his wound, for the moment at least.

From a quick estimate of the number of rifle and submachine-gun flashes from the now-distant left bank I guessed that there were about fifteen Germans there. There seemed to be none on the right bank now, and I wondered why, though I thought that now and then I could hear small-arms fire from the vicinity of the broken bridge and I wondered if the British had overrun the German trenches and driven the Imperials that far back into the city.

But I didn't take much time to think about that sort of thing. I was far more worried about the fifteen or so firing from the left bank.

In a few seconds the brilliant light of the explosion passed, and the river was again plunged into darkness, save for the flickering red glow that reached it through broken buildings and naked trees. Then the Germans could see us no better than we could see them, and that was only by the flashes of our weapons.

Suddenly, unexpectedly, the boat's prow bumped against something solid. I spun around, felt forward, and my hands met slimy stone, the bank of the river and the stonework that had been built there.

"We're there," I gasped, grabbing the stone as best I could and pulling the boat in closer. The river's current turned us around so that the boat's side bumped against the old, slimy stones.

"Kearns," I said, "out! Help Sir Gerald."

"But I. . . ." Sir Gerald began to protest.

"Out!" I said and then turned my attention back to the far shore, slipping a fresh clip into my Enfield.

I heard Kearns' harsh breathing as he clambered around me and out of the boat onto the uncertain footing of the stones.

"Take my hand," he said.

"Be careful, you fool," Sir Gerald gasped.

"Shut up and get out," Kearns snapped, hauling upward on the general's arm.

Sir Gerald came to his feet awkwardly, gasping under his breath, but British enough not to cry out from the pain.

He came out of the boat, half falling onto the stones, struggling and then with Kearns' help stumbling up the sides of the slippery steps to drier ground.

The boat began to slip away from the shore. I slung my rifle across my shoulder, grabbed the stones with both hands, pulled the boat back against the bank. Then, barely able to keep my footing as the boat tried to pull out from under me, I half stepped, half jumped onto the slimy stonework. For a moment I almost fell back into the water, dropped to a crouch, grabbed for a handhold, and then pulled myself up to where Kearns and Sir Gerald stood. Even as I reached his side, Kearns had begun to fire again toward the distant bank.

The second and third boats came up against the stones, and the men tumbled out. One man did not get out of the final boat, and his body was still in it when it began to pull away from the bank, bumping against the stones and then moving out into the current.

"Come on," I said. "We've got to get a couple of miles up the river and then cross back over. The villa's on the other side."

"Oh, shit!" someone muttered under his breath. A few of us fired parting shots at the Germans on the far bank and then we moved away from the river into the dark ruins of the city.

7

THE VILLA

The villa had been built in the early part of the century, back in the days before the war. Then France had been, in theory at least, a free and sovereign nation, though in reality it had been little more than a British satellite.

When the bloody Peasants' Rebellion of 1789-93 had been put down by the remnants of the French nobility and the British Army and the king restored to his throne mainly by British aid, France had been unable to sever all ties with its British allies. Normandy and Brittany had been ceded outright to the English throne by a grateful French king, but the king had not bargained on the redcoats who remained stationed near Paris and half a dozen other French cities to, as the British claimed, "guard the person of the rightful King of France."

When Louis XVI died in 1803, at the age of forty-nine, and was succeeded by Louis XVII, the British found a faithful servant in that weak-willed monarch. For the remainder of his reign Louis XVII was more than happy to allow British troops to protect him from his own people.

A string of other Louis' followed, none with the will or power to try to throw off the British occupation. A brief attempt was made, however, by the Duke of Gascony in 1868, but since no Joan of Arc stood at his side, the duke found the only reward for attempting to free his nation was a cell in the Tower of London and the hangman's noose.

By the beginning of the twentieth century local France accepted its vassalage to England and perhaps not unwillingly, realizing now the growing power of the reborn Holy Roman Empire and the inability of France alone to maintain its independence from the German Empire, even more hungry for continental land than Britain.

The villa itself had been built by the Earl of Kent as a summer retreat on a parcel of land deeded to an ancestor of his by the grateful Louis XVI after the putting down of the Peasants' Rebellion.

Sitting on the bank of the Loire, five miles or so north of the center of the new Beaugency, the villa's ground covered perhaps fifty or sixty acres, half of it devoted to vineyards, for the Earl of Kent had had a great weakness for French wines, and half to stables, for he had also had a weakness for racing horses, mainly those of British Arabia.

The main house was an enormous, rambling, gingerbread structure, all frills and lace and useless ornamentation, three stories of rococo ugliness that the late Earl of Kent must somehow have found attractive.

Half a dozen outbuildings, servants' quarters and such, ringed the main house, half protecting it from attack, half hiding it from the beautiful countryside in which it had been built. The stables and their related buildings were located some distance from the main house and as far as we knew they were now used as garages for German motorcars. A company of elite, handpicked grenadiers inhabited the servants' quarters, and Intelligence had told us that there were six black-booted bodyguards living on the villa's main floor. Just where Count von Heinen and his wife were dwelling in the house, we did not know, though we believed that they and the guards were at present the villa's only inhabitants. Von Heinen, according to reports, had a passion for privacy. He had been warned against it—this morning he would learn why.

There were eight of us who came shivering out of the Loire into that cold predawn drizzle in the spring of 1971. Sir Gerald and a Corporal Land who had been in Tracy's boat were wounded, though neither very seriously. Sir Gerald's bleeding had stopped, and despite the agony in his leg, he had come to realize that the wound was not as bad as he had feared. Using his rifle as a crutch, he could hobble along and with his other hand use his .62 Harling if necessary. The corporal had a flesh wound in his left forearm, and after allowing a cursory examination of the application of dry bandages, he waved us away, saying that he had fought with wounds a hell of a lot worse.

We stopped in the shelter of a poplar grove a good hundred yards from the first building beyond the boathouse, unwrapped our weapons, checked them for dryness, and then got out our gas masks.

The corporal from the final boat sat his heavy pack on the ground and with the aid of Tracy's sheltered flashlight removed half a dozen gas grenades designed to be fired from our Enfields.

Kar-hinter had given us a weapon that had not yet been used in battle—at least not in this Line. It was a newly developed nerve gas, so we were told, and would stun and render unconscious for periods of two to three hours anyone exposed to it. It was claimed to be a British development, but I doubted it. I believed that Kar-hinter had it imported just for this one operation, though he had covered his tracks well. The grenades *looked* like British issue.

The corporal passed two of the grenades to me, two to Tracy, and kept two for himself. We each fitted one grenade onto our rifles, clipped the other to our belts. Then we all pulled our gas masks over our faces, cleared and checked them, and began moving toward the villa.

Halfway there, carefully concealing ourselves behind trees and bushes, we split into three groups: the corporal with the gas grenades and one man, Tracy and a private named Starne, and Sir Gerald, Kearns, the wounded Corporal Land, and myself.

"Okay," I whispered, "get yourselves into position, hold, and wait until you hear me fire. Then go into augmentation, and let them have it."

The others nodded, except for Sir Gerald who seemed puzzled at my reference to augmentation, and we moved apart.

Most of the buildings were dark. One of the servants' houses was lighted, two windows showing the yellow light of a gas lantern and the forms of two gray-clad Imperials sitting at a table, apparently playing .cards and drinking something —German beer, I guessed. The yard immediately before the villa was lighted by two gas lamps that bracketed the main entrance. A German staff car sat in the glare of the lamps, and two men sat in the car, one of them smoking a long black cigar. A single light burned on the second floor of the main house, off in what I thought to be the west wing. It was my guess that there we would find the count and his wife. They were my own special targets.

Kearns was at my side, Corporal Land assisting Sir Gerald a few feet behind us, as we slowly, carefully circled the house, came in from the dark rear.

At last, within rock-throwing distance of the house, I signaled for Sir Gerald to sit down and wait until we had cleared the house. He made an effort to protest, then seemed to think better of it and slowly sat down, assisted by Land.

Giving the general a brief parting handshake, I signaled Kearns to circle back around the house. Land and I moved in closer.

I don't know why I hadn't thought of it before, but I had the second grenade on my belt, and it would probably do us a lot more good if it were on the end of Land's rifle. I slipped it off my belt, handed it to him, and pointed toward a window in the east wing, bottom floor. He got the message. We parted.

I wondered where the six bodyguards were sleeping, but I had no way of knowing. We would just have to hope that wherever they were, they would run into the gas once hell began to break loose in the villa. I figured they probably would. They wouldn't be expecting it.

Now I was at the window near the center of the rear wall and pressed my fact against the cold panes of glass and tried to peer inside. There was total darkness. I only hoped that I wouldn't be firing into a closed pantry.

It seemed that there had been plenty of time for the others to have got into position. Kearns would now be standing in the shadows a few feet from the staff car, the safety off his tommy gun, a full clip in it. Tracy would be near a window of the servants' quarters where a light had shown, perhaps watching the two Imperials playing cards and drinking beer and probably wishing that he could have a stein himself. I did too. But later. Much later.

The time had come. There was no point in waiting.

I stepped back a few paces to be clear of flying glass, aimed the rifle and its heavy grenade at the window, snapped off the safety, squeezed the trigger.

The rifle seemed to explode with a tremendous roar in the stillness, though I knew that the grenade had muffled its sound somewhat. And the breaking of glass seemed just as loud, as did the pop! of the exploding grenade.

I willed electrobiological circuits into operation. All my senses and responses increased fivefold. Sounds slowed and shifted toward the bass; what light I could see became redder. The world seemed to be moving with slow motion now.

For a long, dragging instant it was still again, but only for an instant. A man yelled, his voice a rumble, a rifle fired, its sound like a distant cannon's boom, and was answered by another rifle from the servants' quarters. A voice sounded inside the villa, guttural German, and a light on the first floor flickered on.

"Come on," I yelled as well as I could from inside the gas mask, leaping toward the door that was a few feet off to my right. I kicked at it savagely twice before the latch sprang and wood splintered and the door swung inwards. Then I leaped into the house; Land was behind me, moving as rapidly as I in his augmentation.

Now I could see the room from which the light came, down a long corridor; at the end of it was a parlor or sitting room. A half-naked bull of a man stumbled to his feet in slow motion like a character in a dream, clutching for his submachine gun, swearing, yelling.

He never had a chance. I squeezed the trigger of my Enfield, firing from the hip, and opened a great hole in the man's left breast. He seemed to float back, stunned by the impact, but hung onto his submachine gun, slowly fighting to bring it up. I worked the bolt of my rifle, cursing its awkwardness when my reactions were so fast, threw another shell into the chamber and squeezed it off as the submachine gun in the dying man's hand came to languid life, emitting a trail of bullets my eyes could almost see individually that chipped plaster from the hallway and ceiling. But the German suddenly lost his face as my bullet and Land's both plowed through flesh, bone, brains.

The gas was slowly drifting up around us, pale white in the light from the parlor, drifting down the corridor terribly slowly as a predawn breeze blew in from the open door behind us.

There was a second man in the parlor, wearing only the underclothing he had been sleeping in, and his eyes were still dazed by sleep when I jumped into the doorway—no more than a blur to his eyes—and put a bullet in his chest and another into his stomach. His dying gurgle was a deep, bass rumbling and his slow-moving hand tried to grab for the pistol that lay a few feet from where he fell across a heavy oaken table, his blood terribly red against the old, dark wood.

I felt almost sorry for the man. He had probably never even had a chance to see me.

There was a crashing from the front of the house as Kearns kicked open the door, cautiously sprayed the entrance hall with submachine-gun bullets, then came on in, yelling for blood. He had already left two men dead behind him.

Land and I met him in the huge living room, an oak-paneled, fireplaced stadium of a room.

I cut out my augmentation and signaled for the others to do the same. The world shifted back into normal time and I felt a sudden, brief weakness. A human body can't operate like that for very long.

"Where are the rest of them?" Kearns' muffled voice asked through his mask.

"Damned if I know," I said.

We split up, moved through the house, Kearns and Land searching for the remaining bodyguards, I for the stairs that would lead up to the second floor.

It didn't take me long to find them. Big as they were, they were hard to miss, even in the dark.

Right at that moment I should have augmented again, but I

didn't. I was too confident, I suppose.

I dropped my rifle on the sofa in the enormous hall at the base of the stairs, pulled a flashlight from its clip on my belt with my left hand, the heavy Harling with my right. I flashed the light up the huge, broad stairs—and stumbled back as a pistol bullet cut along my left ribs.

"*Halten Sie!*" a voice called from the darkness above me.

I flashed the light up, saw a naked man standing at the head of the stairs, and shot him down. The heavy Harling slug seemed to lift him upward and throw him backward.

I was reeling back, cursing the pain in my side, thinking that somehow I ought to know the man who even now was tumbling down the stairs, smashing against the rungs of the banister, grabbing for a handhold on them, stopping his fall, reaching for the pistol that had tumbled down the stairs with him.

Holding the light on him and trying to forget about the pain in my side, I went up the stairs two at a time and realized who he was. Count Albert von Heinen.

He lay still when I reached him, blood oozing from a wound in his stomach, looking up at me, fire and hatred in his eyes, foul German curses on his lips.

Out of my own pain I hit him across the mouth with the back of my left hand, still holding the flashlight, and wondered how many of his teeth I was breaking.

"Shut up!" I told him.

Somewhere a woman was screaming, shrilly, hysterically.

"Mathers?" Kearns yelled from the darkness below at the bottom of the stairs.

"Von Heinen's up here," I yelled back, pulling my gas mask off my face, letting it hang by its straps around my neck. "I shot him, but he's still alive. Watch him. I'm going on up."

I heard Kearns' heavy feet on the stairs below, but I didn't look back. I went on up to the room at the head of the stairs where the light shone and a woman screamed.

The door was standing open, and the woman was too terrified to try to stop me.

She stood with her back against the wall near a rumpled bed that was virtually surrounded by mirrors. She was as naked as

Von Heinen, short, beautifully rounded, with the dark skin and dark eyes of the people of Mediterranean France. Lovely as she was, she certainly wasn't the count's blond American wife.

"Don't move," I told her and then repeated it in both German and my broken French.

She didn't, other than to sob hysterically, her hands at her throat, making no move to cover her exposed body.

There was no one else in the room, but then I hadn't expected there would be.

I slipped the flashlight back into my belt, crossed over to where the woman stood rooted in fear, grabbed her hands away from her throat, and slapped her twice with all the force I could muster.

"*Sei ruhig, stille!*" I told her. "*Wo ist Gräfin von Heinen?*"

"Here!" a voice said in English from behind me.

I spun, looked into the barrel of an Imperial automatic, calculated my chances if I went into augmentation now, shrugged and let the Harling drop from my fingers. I wasn't worried.

Sally Beall von Heinen was a beautiful woman, dressed in a thin, revealing gown that hid very little of her and I could not help wondering why the hell von Heinen wanted to bundle with the sobbing girl near me when he had a wife like this one.

Heavy feet had come up the stairs at a run, were now slamming down the hallway. Countess von Heinen turned, found herself facing Kearns' tommy gun, faltered for a moment, fired wildly, hitting nothing.

I jumped, my fist coming down heavily on her right arm, grabbing her waist with my left arm, pulling her to the floor. I didn't need augmentation for this.

She struggled, fought, spat, scratched, clawed for my face, cursed, grabbed for the gun she had dropped, her gown tearing open. I didn't have time to appreciate the view. I threw a fist into her jaw, snapping her head back. She barely moaned as she lost consciousness.

"You okay?" Kearns asked after he pulled his gas mask off.

"I'll live," I said, rising to my feet and gingerly touching my injured side. "Von Heinen?"

"He needs attention, but I've seen men live for days with worse."

Gunfire rattled from below.

"Land's found the rest of 'em," Kearns said.

"Stay here. Watch them."

I grabbed up the Harling from the floor, jerked out my flashlight, and headed back down the stairs, pulling my gas mask up and switching back into combat augmentation.

By the time I reached the ground floor the firing had stopped, but I could still hear the low rumble of movement. I ran down another hallway, into a room where a gas lantern sputtered feebly, its glow red. Land leaned against the wall, his uniform dripping blood, his chest a series of ragged holes, a grim, bitter smile on his face. He had lost his mask somewhere.

He feebly pointed toward the four men in the room, sprawled across the bloody beds and floor. One had the top of his head blown away, and the other had a great hole where his stomach should have been, and both were very dead. I couldn't see the other two very well, but they weren't moving either.

I cut out my augmentation and Land quit grinning and slid down the wall, leaving a wide red swash, and then he lay still. I didn't need to feel his pulse to know that he was dead too. I just wondered how he had lived as long as he had cut apart as he was.

As I turned and went back toward where Kearns was guarding the count and his wife, I heard a few ragged shots from outside the building, but by the time I had climbed the stairs and pulled my mask off again they had all ceased. I just hoped that the last shots had been fired by our boys.

Kearns and I found a robe to put on Countess von Heinen, covering her body and the torn gown, and then we tied her hands behind her back. Leaving her to regain consciousness as she would, we carried Von Heinen himself back up the stairs and laid him on the rumpled bed.

"Put a compress on that to try to stop the bleeding," I told Kearns. "I'll tie her up," pointing to Von Heinen's mistress who was returning to wide-eyed, fearful consciousness after having fainted during the fracas.

After tying and gagging the dark-haired girl—I hadn't

57

bothered to find anything to put on her—I sat her in a corner and began searching for clothing for Von Heinen. We couldn't take him out naked as he was.

By the time we had finished dressing the count there were sounds coming from below.

I grabbed my pistol, moved cautiously to the head of the stairs, peered down. There was just enough light in the hallway for me to see three figures, two of them supporting the third between them.

"Hold it there," I yelled, fairly sure who they were.

"Eric?" Tracy's voice, muffled and distorted by his gas mask, called back.

"Up here."

"It's me, Starne and Sir Gerald."

"We've got Von Heinen and his wife. Come on up," I told him.

"Just let me rest, old chap," I heard Sir Gerald say.

They lowered him to the sofa where I had dropped my rifle earlier—now it seemed like hours—and came up the stairs.

"What about the others?" I asked.

"Not sure," Tracy answered, loosening his mask. "Dead I think."

Then I could see his face. He had a nasty gash across his cheek that ended where his mask had covered his mouth and nose. There was a rip down his left leg that looked painful, but not serious. Well, he and three others had wiped out nearly a full company of elite troops.

"You hurt?" he asked.

"Side grazed. I'm okay, just got careless. Land's dead, but Kearns doesn't have a scratch on him."

"He wouldn't."

We entered the bedroom where Kearns was pulling the German officer's boots on the count's feet.

"Is he—" asked the man named Starne who wore a British private's uniform.

"Stomach wound," I said. "He'll live, long enough at least."

Then Tracy noticed the naked girl tied and sitting in the corner.

"Who's she?" he asked, a wicked grin on his face.

"The Graf's playmate," I said. "They must have been at it when we came busting in. At least they were both naked and. . . ."

"Let's get the hell out of here," Kearns said suddenly, reminding us all of why we were there.

We did exactly that, though Tracy looked almost wistfully at the dark-haired girl one last time as we started down the stairs.

8

AMBUSH

It was darker than ever when we carried the unconscious count out of the house. His wife, bleeding at the mouth, was walking with Tracy's pistol pressed into the small of her back. Sir Gerald, limping, assisted by Starne, brought up the rear.

The earlier drizzle had increased to a steady, soaking downpour, but we hardly noticed it.

"You're a lucky bastard," Tracy said to Kearns, who was carrying the German across his shoulder fireman fashion.

"No luck to it," Kearns said. "Just cautious."

"You didn't sound cautious," I said, "when you hit those two in the staff car."

Kearns laughed that odd laugh of his. We all laughed, even Sir Gerald. It was over, thank God, and the sudden release of tension brought us all easily to the point of laughter.

Von Heinen's wife did not speak; she only moved silently, mechanically as we forced her on. I would have expected a woman to yell, scream, go into hysterics as the dark-haired girl had, but Sally von Heinen did just as she was told, but nothing more. Then I reminded myself that she was the daughter of an American rebel leader and had probably been exposed to violence most of her life. In a way I was grateful to her. I think I would have knocked her teeth out had she behaved any differently.

We were a little more than halfway to the river when we saw the airship. It came down slowly, its propellers softly cutting the air, its engines muffled, its running light out. We could see it only as a black cigar against the slightly lighter sky. Had it been day, though, we would have seen the Imperial German insignia along her gas bag, the flag of Franz VI that she flew. But that's the way it had been planned. Kar-hinter's plan.

The airship touched ground a few yards from the river, and men leaped out, driving pegs into the wet earth, hooking cables to them. Other men moved to the rear of the gondola, opened huge cargo doors, slid ramps to the earth, began rolling out a huge squashed sphere.

All of us, except for Countess Sally von Heinen and her unconscious husband, were familiar with the shape of a skudder, though it must have appeared very alien to her: a huge glasslike bubble mounted on a small, dark base, a craft never designed to move in space, only across the Lines of time.

"Mathers?" a voice called from the group of men who now stood around the skudder.

"*Natl*," I answered in Shangalis.

"The skudder's ready. Want me to warm her up?" the man asked in the same language.

I glanced at Kearns in the rain and the darkness. He nodded.

"Yes," I called.

"You're not Englishmen!" Sally von Heinen said, sudden horror in her voice. Maybe she was used to violence, I thought, but not to being kidnapped by men who spoke a language that was not of her world.

"We're not," I said. "Go on. Get in." I pointed her toward the skudder.

In a few moments we were all inside the craft and I pulled the hatch closed behind me. The man outside yelled, "Good luck," and I yelled back my thanks.

"Have you ever skudded before, Sir Gerald?" Tracy asked in English.

"No," the injured British general said breathlessly.

"Then brace yourself," Tracy said, laughing. "You're in for an experience."

"Everybody ready?" Kearns said harshly.

"We're ready," I said, glancing over at the still-unconscious count.

By this time it dawned on me that his wife had shown absolutely no concern over his condition, but then he had been in bed with another woman when we burst into the villa. And I remembered Kar-hinter's having said that theirs was a marriage of politics. It made a little more sense to me now. Virgin wife? I wondered. And thought that if she were, it was a terrible waste.

Kearns' hands moved across the controls, making final adjustments, bringing the generators up to full potential, setting the destination indicators for about a dozen Lines to the East, one where gas and bacteriological warfare had nearly extinguished life in Europe before the Kriths and Timeliners could enter to alter the course of that world's history.

"Okay," Kearns said. "Here we go."

An invisible hand came up and grabbed my genitals, jerking down, then snatching at my guts, moving up to stir my stomach with a lumpy club.

Flicker!

For an instant I saw lights in the direction of the villa and perhaps men moving there in this next-door world, but I wasn't sure.

Flicker!

Total darkness.

Flicker!

"It's far more interesting in the daytime," Tracy told Sir Gerald, who was too busy being sick to listen.

Flicker!

A dozen times that hand inside my abdomen jerked and pulled and twisted. Sir Gerald once muttered something I couldn't understand and Von Heinen groaned in his unconsciousness.

Flicker!

Then it all stopped, and I sat still for a minute trying not to be sick myself. Skudding sometimes got me that way too.

The night was still as dark was ever, the same clouds lay over this world as lay over the one we had left behind us; the same rain fell; the same trees grew on the same riverbank a few yards away; the same villa stood on the rise above us—or almost the same villa. The one in this world was not as well cared for as the other, inhabited only by rats and the bones of the very last Earl of Kent and his family who had died of a bitter, flesh-rotting disease as biological war swept across Europe.

But it wasn't the villa I was looking for. It was rather a prefabricated hut that stood no more than a dozen yards beyond the villa, a larger version of our own hut, one designed to carry cargo as well as passangers.

"Everybody out," Kearns said. The skudding didn't seem to bother his stomach.

I rose to my feet, trying to pull Von Heinen erect. Kearns came back to help me.

I don't know what it was that bothered me. I can't even now put my finger on it, but I had the strange, uneasy feeling that something was very wrong. Maybe it was the fact that no one had come out of the hut to greet us, but that shouldn't have bothered me. Maybe it was the fact that everything was too quiet, even for Here. I'm not sure, but I know I *felt* something.

Tracy opened the hatch, jumped to the ground. Starne followed him, and they waited while Kearns and I maneuvered the unconscious Imperial count into position and then took his weight between them as we passed him down. Then we followed.

"Tracy," I said, "you and Starne help Sir Gerald and go on. Kearns and I will bring these two."

Kearns hefted the count onto his shoulder, while the others, supporting the British general between them, started toward the hut.

They didn't get halfway.

Suddenly the whole area was illuminated.

"Son of a. . . ."

A voice said very loudly in English, "Hold it where you are!"

I shoved Countess von Heinen back toward the skudder with a savage gesture, grabbed for the pistol on my hip, switched into combat augmentation. Kearns unceremoniously dumped the count, unslung his tommy gun. Starne broke into an augmented run toward the hut, and Tracy lowered Sir Gerald to the ground before going into augmentation.

Rifles chattered from behind the lights. Starne fell in midstride, clawing at his chest. Tracy staggered, cursed in Shangalis, jerked up his own pistol, fired, staggered toward the hut, and then fell in his own blood.

Whoever was firing at us had reactions just as fast as ours and that was a little frightening.

The whole night was ablaze with gunfire. *We* aimed for their spotlights. *They*, whoever they were, aimed for us.

Sir Gerald, perhaps unnoticed by our attackers, rolled over in slow motion, languidly pulled his pistol free, and fired off two shots as quickly as a nonaugmented man could—one put out one of the lights and the other brought an agonized yell—and then took a bullet between his eyes. He'd died in the old tradition. I wonder if he went to school at Eton—"The battles of Britain . . ." or however that goes.

Then a barrage of automatic-weapons fire splattered against the dome of the skudder behind me, some ricocheting away, some penetrating. Though the bullets seemed slow to my accelerated sense, they weren't, but I didn't stop to think about the damage done. There was no time.

I grabbed Sally, momentarily cut out my augmentation. "Get him in the skudder!" I pointed toward her husband.

She looked at me defiantly.

"Get him in the skudder, or I'll kill you both."

Most of the gunfire from the ring of lights was now aimed at Tracy and Kearns, who had crawled toward the meager cover of a bush a few feet away. Tracy was trying to pull himself up against the hut, very weakly, and he seemed to be on the verge of losing consciousness. But none of the bullets was coming in my direction now. They seemed afraid of hitting von Heinen or Sally, or both—whoever the hell *they* were.

I was back into combat augmentation and yelling, "Hold your fire or I'll shoot Count von Heinen," and wondering if they could understand my accelerated voice. I put my Harling to his head so they'd know I meant business. It may have been a poor maneuver, but it was the only thing I could think of at the time. And it worked.

They stopped firing.

"Kearns, get Tracy."

Kearns got up warily, looked around, then walked out into the

64

lighted area, his tommy gun held at the ready.

He stopped for a moment where Sir Gerald lay, then rose, shook his head. He repeated the same action above the unmoving form of Starne and then went on to Tracy.

In a few moments he had Tracy on his feet, half carrying him, and together they staggered back to the skudder.

"Get him in," I said, then, with exaggerated slowness, gestured for Countess von Heinen to follow. A moment later I jerked the still-unconscious count up and somehow threw him into the craft.

"Don't any of you try anything," I yelled, "or they'll pay for it."

I slammed the hatch shut and told Kearns: "Get our asses out of here!"

"Where?"

"Back to where we came from, I guess," I said, suddenly at a loss. "Maybe the airship's still there."

"Okay," Kearns said, dropping into the pilot's seat, snapping switches.

Then we flickered out of that universe, the inside of the skudder smelling of ozone and burning insulation.

I cut out my augmentation and fell back, gasping for breath. I was totally drained of energy.

9

PURSUIT

The airship was gone.

Up in the villa and the outbuildings the same lights still burned, and all was silent. There was no movement. In the short time that we had been gone there had been no change, save that the airship was gone. But it would be dawn soon, and someone would come. Imperials, of course. And we couldn't be there when they arrived.

I turned back to Kearns who still sat in the pilot's seat, cursing savagely.

"What is it?" I asked.

"This goddamned thing," he said, gesturing toward the skudder's controls. "It's just about had it."

"We've got to get out of here."

"Not in this skudder we won't."

I'd been afraid of that, afraid that each time we flickered from one Timeline to the next we might not make it, that the skudder's drive would break down. I suppose we'd been lucky to get as far as we had.

"It won't move?" I asked without hope.

"Not one more jump," Kearns said.

"Up in the stables," Tracy said weakly. "There're supposed to be motorcars."

"Kearns, go see," I said quickly.

"What's wrong with the one sitting in the front of the villa?"

"Nothing, unless you put a bullet through the block."

66

"I didn't," Kearns said coldly. "I was shooting at men, not motorcar engines."

"Then get it."

Kearns nodded agreement, climbed out of the seat, opened the hatch and jumped to the ground.

I glanced at Von Heinen, his wife and then at Tracy, who lay back on the seat, blood flowing down his left leg from a wound above the knee.

"How bad is it, old man?" I asked in English.

"Bloody painful, old top," Tracy said, trying to force a smile onto his face.

I knelt in front of him, felt the leg. The bone was broken and jagged.

"I could have told you that," Tracy said.

I pulled a knife from my pocket, snapped open the blade, cut a slit up Tracy's trouser leg, and then cut away the cloth above the wound.

"I'm going to put a tourniquet on it," I said. "Think you can manage with that?"

"I'd bloody well better."

"We'll bandage it and put a splint on it as soon as we can."

When I was finished, I turned back to Von Heinen, who was making the sounds of a man returning to painful consciousness. Opening his shirt, I checked the compress that Kearns had applied to the stomach wound. It was soaked with blood, but the blood was beginning to dry. Externally, at least, the count had stopped bleeding.

"He's not going to do us much good dead, old boy," Tracy said.

"He's not going to do us any mucking good at all unless we get him back behind British lines."

"How do you suggest we do that?"

"I don't know," I answered slowly. "We'll take the motorcar and see ifmmaybe we can get back down into Beaugency. It may be that the attack has broken up the German lines enough for us to get through."

I stopped for a moment and listened. The staff car that sat in front of the villa coughed to life, sputtered, then began to run smoothly. From a great distance, to the south, I could hear the infrequent boom of a howitzer, occasional small-arms fire, but from the sounds the real battle was over. Exactly what the British had accomplished, I couldn't even begin to guess, other than get *us* through the Imperial lines. But unless we could get back through, even that wasn't going to do us much good.

I turned back to Sally von Heinen.

"Who were those men?" I asked her slowly, coldly.

"What men?" she asked, her face showing nothing but hatred for me.

"Those men who tried to rescue you and the count."

"How should I know?" she asked. "I don't even know where we were."

"Shit!"

"What do you mean, Eric?" Tracy asked.

"There shouldn't have been anybody there but out people," I said, "in that Line. According to Kar-hinter, there wasn't supposed to be another human being alive within a hundred miles—and the surviving natives of that Line don't have spot-lights, rifles, and combat augmentation."

"Then you mean they were Timeliners?"

"You got any other ideas?"

"No, but—*Timeliners*, Eric?"

"It has to be. I don't know who or why, but—hell, you've heard stories of renegades who steal skudders and go off plundering backward Lines. Maybe it was some of them."

"I've only heard stories."

"I know, but who else could it have been?"

Sally might have had something like a smug expression on her face. I couldn't be sure, but before I could question her, Kearns pulled the staff car up next to the skudder and jumped out, leaving the motor running, but without headlamps burning.

"Ready?" he asked.

"Get out," I said to Countess von Heinen.

She did, but carefully, facing the deadly little Imperial pistol that Kearns now carried, the same gun she had tried to kill him with back in her husband's bedroom.

I helped Tracy over the hatch and lowered him down to Kearns. Holding Tracy with one arm, the other leveling the pistol at Sally, Kearns helped the injured man into the back seat of the car.

"You wait right there, ma'am," Kearns said, then turned to assist me with the groaning count.

We would have got him out of the skudder—but we ran out of time.

A dozen yards up the slope toward the villa the air shimmered for a moment, sparkling like arcing electricity; then a shape formed out of the shimmering, a flattened egg of metal and glass—a skudder that didn't look like any skudder I had ever seen before.

I thought about going into augmentation, but didn't know whether my body could take it again just yet. I'd wait and see.

Pushing the count's wife back toward our skudder, Kearns jerked up his diminutive pistol and fired into the developing shape.

"Get back in there," I yelled to the woman, crouching in the open hatch, leveling my Harling at the new craft.

Our bullets, roaring loudly in the predawn stillness, ricocheted off the flattened egg. A hatch opened and first one, then two weapons began to answer ours.

"Get Tracy," I yelled to Kearns, who stood midway between our skudder and the motorcar.

"I'll never get him back in," Kearns gasped.

"Get in the car then," I yelled suddenly. "Get out of here."

"You're mad."

A bullet rang shrilly as it struck the metal base of our skudder. I thought about the energy pistol that ought to be stashed inside our craft and wondered if I could get it.

"Do it," I yelled back to Kearns at the same time. "Turn on your lights, make all the noise you can. Maybe they'll follow you."

"Crap!"

"Go on!"

Cursing again, Kearns jumped into the car, snapped on the electric headlamps, and finally, firing across the hood as he did, he started the motorcar into motion.

"Stay right where you are," I said to Sally.

Turning back to the count, I saw that his eyes were open at last. "*Sprechen Sie*—Hell, do you speak English?"

He nodded weakly.

"Then listen very carefully. I will kill you and your wife on the spot unless you both do exactly as I say."

"Very well," he gasped.

"Can you sit up?"

He struggled awkwardly, but finally was able to pull himself up into a half-sitting position.

I turned to look out the hatch. The woman was still standing where I had told her to, perhaps fearful of the pistol I carried, but more likely just wary of the rifle fire from the strange skudder that was aimed at the dwindling taillights of the German staff car.

Then something happened that I couldn't quite believe at first. The thing that I knew to be a skudder, knew to carry the men who had attacked us on that Timeline a dozen universes away, rose slowly from the ground, turned in the direction of the staff car, and began flying a few feet above the ground.

A skudder that flew? I had always been told that it was impossible. I don't really know why a jet engine or an antigrav couldn't be used in conjunction with a skudder, but that was supposed to be one of the laws of the energies that allow passage across the Lines. Something about the nature of a probability field and its interaction with other forms of energy. It just wasn't supposed to be possible for a skudder to do anything but skud. But apparently what I had been told was wrong. I was seeing a skudder fly, though I couldn't determine what kind of propulsion it was using.

You know, I think that was the first time I had ever really had a doubt about the omniscience of the Kriths. But just the first.

Once I got over my astonishment I felt relief. It was a weak ruse—the staff car—but it seemed to be working. The men in the alien skudder must have assumed that we had all been able to get into the motorcar and they were going after it. I hadn't expected it to work at all, much less this well—the *whole* skudder chasing down the dirt road after the car.

"Stay where you are, Countess," I said, then gestured for the count to come after me.

70

"I don't know that I can do it, old boy," he said in excellent, British-accented, if gasping, English.

"You'd better, *mein Herr*, or I'll blow the top of your head off."

Before leaving the skudder, I went to its controls, opened an obscure panel and adjusted a dial and pushed a red button. You don't just leave inoperative Outtime devices lying around in a world where your presence is supposed to be unknown. We had about five minutes to get out of range before the skudder destroyed itself.

I reached under the control panel, pulled out the energy pistol that was hidden there and shoved it into my belt; then I clambered out of the hatch, dropped to the ground beside the woman, said, "Help me. Both your lives depend on our getting away before your friends come back. If they come back, I'll kill you both before they get me. I promise."

I don't know whether I really meant it. I'm not very good at killing in cold blood, but I suppose I thought I would do it at the time. Maybe I would have. But they believed me and that was the important thing.

The woman seemed to feel some repugnance at touching the man who was, technically at least, her husband, but she did, struggling with his weakened body to the best of her ability. We finally got him to the ground, where he stood, leaning against the side of the skudder, gasping for breath.

"That wound's going to start bleeding again," I said, "but I don't suppose we can do much about that." I paused. "We're going to the stables up there." I pointed with my Harling. "There'd better be motorcars in there."

"I don't think he can make it," the woman said.

"He will if he wants to see the sun rise," I said, noticing the beginning of a glow along the horizon in the east. It was going to be daylight in a few minutes. Again time was running out. That seemed to be a habit of mine.

"Let's go," I said, supporting one side of the wounded man, while his wife supported the other. Together we staggered toward the stables, our feet slipping in the mud.

The destruction of the skudder, which took place before we were halfway to the stables, was unspectacular, even in early

71

dawn. There was a flash of light and a subdued roar as the metal base and probability generator it housed were consumed. The paraglas dome crystalized and shattered and fell in tiny fragments onto the slag. There wasn't enough left for anyone ever to be able to tell what it had been, no one from this Line at least.

We went on, the three of us, toward the stables.

I had had little time to think of my own wound, but I became increasingly aware of it and of the exhaustion of my body from running under augmentation as we carried the man between us. With probing fingers of my free hand I found the flayed flesh, raw and burning when I touched it, the dried, crusted blood under the sodden fabric of my shirt. As I had thought, it was only a superficial wound and though it might hurt me some, unless it got infected, it wasn't going to be any real trouble. I'd worry about infection later. Once I was sure I was going to live long enough to have an infection.

It was halfway to broad daylight when we finally reached the stables. Von Heinen had lost consciousness again and the last few yards I had somehow carried him alone, keeping both my eyes on his young wife, suspecting that she would take the first opportunity I gave her to run like hell. I didn't give her the opportunity, so she didn't.

I lowered von Heinen to the wet ground, pulled the Harling from its holster, told his wife to stay at his side and went up to open the nearest doors.

At first I thought the cavernous stables were empty, but farther down I found three motorcars, all decked out with the flags of von Heinen's rank. A *Feldmarschall*, he was. And he had come to the villa in style, though I was afraid that he wouldn't leave it in the same fashion. Not this time at least.

Going back to where the woman stood beside the unconscious man, I slipped the pistol back into its holster, jerked him up, pulled him across my shoulder, took a deep breath, and said, "Go on. Get in the first car."

With resignation on her pretty face the young countess preceded me along the front of the stable to where the cars were parked.

"Can you drive?" I asked.

"No."

"I don't believe you," I said. "Get in front. Are the keys in it? Don't lie again."

"Yes, they are."

I dumped Von Heinen in the back seat, climbed in beside him.

"Okay, let's go."

The motorcar started at once, which was a pleasant surprise, considering the state of the art of motorcars in this Line.

"Wait a minute," I said. "Shut it off."

She did as I ordered while I jumped out of the car, grabbed up a large tarpaulin that lay on the stable floor a few feet from where the car was parked.

"Now let's go."

The motor started again, though it coughed a couple of times first. She shifted into gear and slowly pulled out of the stable into the driveway that led back around the villa's main house.

"Head toward Beaugency for the moment," I said, and then had the strangest feeling that I was being watched. I peered back over my shoulder out the car's rear window, and for a moment I thought I saw a figure standing in the stable, back in the deepest part of the shadow. It seemed to be a man, but beyond that I could tell nothing about him. I reached for the Harling, but when I looked again, I could see nothing. The figure, if it had ever been there, was gone now. Perhaps it was just my fatigued mind playing tricks on me. I wasn't sure.

"What is it?" Countess von Heinen asked.

"Nothing. Go on. Drive slowly." I forced myself to try to forget about the figure, but I still felt uneasy about it, though it was a strange sort of unease I can't quite define. "Be careful," I went on, "and don't do anything foolish. You've only got a few inches of stuffing between you and the barrel of this pistol. I'd hate to make a big hole in your lovely back."

"I know," she said slowly. "I'll do as you say."

"I'm sure you will."

We passed the main house where Kearns had casually dumped the bodies of the two sentries who had once occupied the staff car he now drove. I wondered where he was, and I didn't mourn the dead Imperials. If I were going to mourn anyone, it would be Sir Gerald Asbury and Land, who had been

73

cut apart by a submachine gun inside that big house, and Starne, who lay dead in another universe near Sir Gerald, and a British sergeant and three other men dead in the river and men who. . . . Hell! I didn't have time to mourn anyone. Not yet. I had to stay alive now and try somehow to get Von Heinen back across the British lines to Kar-hinter.

We had no more than hit the main highway outside the villa's grounds when I saw Imperial German troop movements in the direction of the city. Battered veterans of last night's fighting, moving back to regroup and refit and wait for replacements. They looked tired, but they didn't look *beaten*.

"Turn around," I ordered.

"Here?"

"Now!"

She slowed the car, made a U-turn in the road and headed north.

"The first road you come to off to your left, take it."

"Where are we going?"

"How the hell should I know?"

10

CONTACT AND REPORT

For most of the morning we traveled west in the falling rain, the feeble windshield wipers hardly allowing Sally vision to drive. We stayed on back roads, little more than muddy ruts between farm lands that had lain fallow as war swept back and forth across this part of France. The ruins of a village here and there, a pile of cold embers that had once been a house, a series of bomb and shell craters and sodden, abandoned trenches, and little else. It was my intention to stay far enough north of the current German lines to avoid much investigation.

Only once were we stopped by a roadblock: two gaunt, tired soldiers in Imperial gray, soaked to the skin by the night-long rain, manning a barricade across what once might have been a paved road, but was now hardly more than a muddy path.

"Go slow," I told my driver, wondering what the sentries would think of a lone woman dressed in a robe driving an Imperial staff car that flew the banner of a *Feldmarschall*. We'd see. "Smile and wink at them, but don't let them look too closely in the back seat. And remember, if anything goes wrong, neither you nor your husband will live to talk about it."

"I understand," Sally replied coldly.

Then I pulled the tarp over the still unconscious Von Heinen and myself, pushed the pistol against the back of the driver's seat and waited, the air under the tarp hot and damp, smelling of hay and horseshit.

"Halt, bitte," I heard a distant voice say. It may have had an Austrian accent; I wasn't sure.

"Guten Morgen, Zugsführer," Sally von Heinen answered.

"Guten Morgen, Fraülein," the Imperial sergeant replied.

In German, she asked him to let her pass, please. She was really in a great hurry. Her husband was expecting her by one o'clock this afternoon.

"Wie heissen Sie, bitter?" the sergeant asked politely.

"Gräfin von Heinen," Sally answered simply. She was playing it straight. She knew she had to.

"Graf von Heinen! Möge er lange leben!" the sergeant said patriotically. *"Jawohl! Vorwärts, bitte, gnädige Frau."*

"Danke," Sally said, forcing friendliness I suspected.

And that's all there was to it.

As we pulled away from the sentry post I began making plans. Before too much longer we would have to find a place to hide the car, a place of comparative safety where I could leave the count and his wife for a few minutes and try to contact Kar-hinter and bring him up to date. He was going to have to get in and pick us up soon, or the whole thing would have been so much wasted effort and wasted British blood.

That much settled in my mind, I turned my attention back to Sally and tried to get her to talk, but she was unwilling to speak to a man who had kidnapped her, shot her husband and God-alone-knew how many other Germans who were her allies.

At last I sat back in the rear seat, checked Von Heinen's bandage, wondered how long he would last, pulled a soggy cigarette from an inside pocket, lit it, felt my bladder demanding to be emptied, wondered how much longer I could stay awake, and looked across Sally's shoulder at the ravaged French countryside.

And I thought about the world in which I now found myself, a world very, very remote from the one in which I had been born.

As I said before, I am from a Europo-Macedonian Line and this one was a Romano-British Line, Anglo-European Subsector; to be exact RTGB-307. Our Timelines, Sally von Heinen's and mine, had split apart a long, long time ago. In my world Alexander III of Macedonia, called "the Great," had created the first and greatest world empire, an empire that before his death at the age of sixty-one had spanned all the civilized world and had survived its founder by more than a thousand years.

In the world of Sally Beall von Heinen, Alexander had died young and his empire had never really come into being. In her world the Greeks had gradually declined in power and influence, leaving only a great cultural heritage. A little Italian village on the Tiber River had picked up the pieces of the Greek world, adding a few ideas of their own, and from that built an empire, one not so great as my Alexander's had been, or quite so enduring, but a great one nevertheless.

The empire of this city called Rome flourished and grew, a new religion called Christianity had sprung up, the empire had fallen—ever read a fellow named Gibbon?—and the Western world slowly devolved into barbarism.

I guess us Greeks never really had a chance without Alexander. Funny.

Anyhow, ten centuries or so after the collapse of Rome the nations of Europe had formed and Western civilization reached a peak it had not known for a thousand years; ships sailed from Europe to India, China, Nippon, and eventually—there was an explorer named Columbus in these Lines—the two unknown continents to the west; here they're called North and South America.

Nations rose and fell; empires were carved out of the New World and the Old.

By about the beginning of the eighteenth century after the birth of the Jewish Messiah they call Christ, Europe consisted of Britain, France, Spain, Portugal, the Holy Roman Empire, and assorted nations of lesser importance. Britain, France, and Spain had come out as the greatest of the European colonial powers, though by this time Spain was already in decline and France was no real match for England on the high seas.

Britain took most of France's North American colonies away after establishing some of its own, battled with Spain, but never really got too much of a foothold in South America, looked east to China, India and south to Africa.

There is a crucial historical period in the Anglo-European and Anglo-American Subsectors in the latter years of the eighteenth century, local time. That was when the American colonists attempted to throw off what they called British Imperialism, for Britain was then the center of a burgeoning empire, threatening to surpass anything this world had ever seen before.

In many Lines the North Americans succeeded and the United States of America—as it is called in most Lines—was born. In many others they failed. This was one in which they had failed, Sally's world.

By 1775 the American Rebellion was in full swing in Sally's world, and for a while it also seemed possible that the American rebels could beat the British and gain the independence they wanted. And they probably would have, in her world, had it not been for a certain Major Patrick Ferguson, a British officer, who invented a new kind of weapon—one that loaded from the breech, rather than from the muzzle. It was a rather crude weapon at first, and for a while it seemed that Ferguson would get no help from the British lords—but in one of those curious twists of history that create the Lines of Time, aid was given him, resources were put at his disposal, and Ferguson went on to develop his breechloader.

By late 1780 the weapon was perfected, even beyond Ferguson's earlier dreams, a weapon with a rifle bore that could fire faster and more accurately than anything anyone had ever used before. It was a gun that could put the American rebel marksmen to shame. And it did.

By the summer of 1781 shiploads of the new Ferguson breechloaders were crossing the Atlantic, with men trained to use them. For once the innate conservatism of the generals was broken, and the bloody art of warfare leaped forward a hundred years.

In the next two years the Americans were on the run, their foremost leaders dead; Washington, a hero who made a valiant last stand at Yorktown, had died as he had lived. Half the American Congress was captured, tried for treason, hanged in the streets of Philadelphia.

Of the American generals only Anthony Wayne, "Mad Anthony," survived, to lead his battered, decimated troops across the Appalachians, where he held out for two more long, bloody years before he was finally pinned against the western Virginia hills and shot as a traitor, still cursing the British with his infamous eyes.

With the death of Mad Anthony Wayne the American cause collapsed, and Britain was again the supreme ruler of North America east of the Appalachians.

France, which had lent aid to the American rebels, feared an invasion by the British, but the lords in London, worn out by the war in America, let the French peasants punish the government.

The Peasants' Rebellion in France might have succeeded, very nearly did succeed, and failed only because the British, seeing that they had much to gain by supporting the French monarchy, finally came to the aid of the embattled Louis XVI, and with the still-further improved Ferguson breechloaders the redcoats shot down the French rebels as they had shot down the American rebels.

Its continental position secure with the first years of the 1800's, the crown sitting firmly on the head of the King of England, Parliament subdued and reduced in power, Britain went on to expand its holding in North America, sweeping as far west as the Mississippi River and down into Mexico to the isthmus of Panama. Indochina was British, as were North Africa, South Africa, and the islands of the Pacific. Britain was supreme on land and sea.

About this time, following years of decline, the Holy Roman Empire, ruled by Franz III, found a rebirth, a growth in wealth and importance on the continent of Europe as the Germans and their kindred finally united under their emperor. The specter of republicanism, which had haunted both Britain and France for so long, never bothered the Holy Roman Emperor. Republicanism was a dead issue in this world—the American Rebellion and the Peasants' Rebellion in France had proved that.

By the end of the nineteenth century most of the world was divided between four empires—British, Spanish, Holy Roman and Nipponese—and so it was into the twentieth—and the final clash between the British Empire and the Holy Roman Empire, in which I was now embroiled.

Well, I'm no historian, despite the ambitions of my youth. My facts and places and dates may be a bit confused, and I admit that even what I have told you is very sketchy, but basically that is how the world I was in had come to be the way it was.

By noon fatigue and the pain in my side were beginning to get the better of me. I knew that I could not go much farther without some rest, and I knew that I needed to talk with Kar-hinter.

At last, miles from any village or even any farm, I ordered Sally to pull off the road, drive back along a cowpath as far as she could get the car and stop.

It had finally stopped raining by now, though as yet we hadn't seen the sun. Still the day was getting quite warm.

"What are you going to do now?" Sally asked as she climbed out of the car.

I shook my head, trying to clear it of the fog that filled it, the cotton that seemed to be stuffed behind my eyes.

"Are you going to shoot us and bury us here?" she asked.

"Don't be stupid!"

"What's stupid about that?" she asked, standing outside the car, her hands on her hips, the robe she wore somehow making her look smaller than she was, a child dressed up in mommy's clothing. "You'll never get us to wherever you were trying to take us. So if you're going to save your own neck, you're going to have to kill us and go on without us."

"I'm not planning that."

"Then what are you going to do?"

"Arrange for someone to pick us up," I told her sharply. "Now you untie those lengths of rope from the tarp in the back seat of the car." When she did not move, I made a motion toward the pistol in my holster and said, "Go on!"

The girl went back to the car, and I stood there watching her, almost admiring her, thinking that she reminded me a little or Kristin or the way Kristin would have been if she had lived to be Sally's age. She had only been seventeen when she died. I tried not to think about her.

Sally pulled the tarp out, untied several lengths of rope, and brought them to me. She turned around, placed her hands behind her back, and waited silently while I tied them.

"Sit down, I told her, then knelt and tied her feet. "I'm going to have to gag you, y'know."

"I know. Don't tell me you're sorry. I don't want to hear it."

"Okay. Look, that robe you're got on, well, it's probably going to get warmer this afternoon. You'll be miserable if you leave it on."

"You want me naked, is that it?"

"I don't give a damn what you've got on," I said angrily. "I was just thinking about your comfort."

"Thanks!"

"Look, you've got that gown on under it. That's something."

"Not much." She paused. "Hell, take it off. You can rape me with the robe on if that's what you're after."

"I'm not going to rape you."

"Why not?"

"Oh, shit, woman!" Then I paused, looked at her, laughed. "I'm too damned tired, for one thing."

I knelt beside her, untied the rope, waited until she had unbuttoned the robe, and helped her slip it off. Then I retied her hands, carefully avoiding looking at her. She had the kind of body that was hard not to look at.

Then I took a fairly clean handkerchief from my pocket, knotted it, slipped the knot into her mouth, and tied it in place with another length of rope. Finally I pulled her back to where she could lean against a tree in what looked like a fairly comfortable position.

Von Heinen was sleeping or unconscious—I couldn't tell which—when I heaved him out of the car, carried him to within a few feet of Sally and tied and gagged him. I didn't particularly like the idea of trussing up a man as badly wounded as he was, but I wasn't in any position to take chances with his waking up and somehow freeing Sally.

"I'll be back in a few minutes," I told Sally, "and I won't be far away, so don't get any silly ideas about making noise. I'd hate to have to get rough with you."

Sally, of course, didn't answer, but she didn't have to. The way she felt about me was clear enough from her eyes. She'd have cut my throat laughing if she got the chance.

I looked one last time at Von Heinen, wondered how much longer he could live in his condition and then followed the path

81

on toward the stand of young woods that lay a few yards from the grove of trees where Sally and her husband lay.

The woods, which probably had been farmland not too many years before, lay a half mile or so from the road, what there was of the road. And there was very little likelihood of any traffic along it. It didn't look as if there had been another motorcar on it for days.

When I was satisfied that I was well out of the range of Sally's hearing unless I yelled very loudly, I stopped and doglike relieved myself against the trunk of a tree. I felt better when I walked a few feet away and began doing what I had come back there to do.

First I took off my coat and carefully spread it out on a fairly level spot of earth and then sat down on the coat. Taking what appeared to be a windproof cigarette lighter from my pocket, I pulled it apart. It wasn't a lighter. It was a block of gray plastic with three tiny jacks in one end.

Next I removed what looked like a British-issue knife from its sheath on my left hip, held the blade in my right hand, the handle in my left and gave the blade a counterclockwise twist. The handle popped free. Up inside the handle nestled several feet of exceedingly thin wire, a fingernail-size microphone, and an equally small earphone.

I unrolled the wire, plugged one end of it into one of the jacks on the block, and then looped it over a tree branch above my head. Finally I plugged the microphone and the earphone into the two remaining jacks and I was "on the air."

In this Timeline, operating radio was still in its earliest infancy, though the grapevine had it that the Kriths were about to help the British "invent" the vacuum tube. As it was, a few spark-gap transmitters and cat's-hair and crystal receivers were being used by experimenters who predicted the day when radio—or wireless telegraphy—would be used for communications all over the world. None of those wild-eyed visionaries had any idea that on earths other than their own radio had reached and far exceeded their most fantastic dreams.

This tiny unit was far from being the most sophisticated radio I had used, but it was the best Kar-hinter had seen fit to give me. It would do the job. Its transmissions would be received at the main Krithian-Timeliner base on this Line which was near the Butt of Lewis on the Isle of Lewis in the Outer Hebrides—most of it underground. And that is where Kar-hinter would probably be right about now.

Why code names were necessary, I had no idea. There was no one on *this* earth using this frequency. But Kar-hinter had required them should radio communications be necessary.

"Red mobile to red leader. Red leader, this is red mobile. Come in, red leader."

I felt like an ass sitting there on the soggy ground in the middle of nowhere, speaking code names into a little gray box, but that's the way the game is played.

"Red leader, this is red mobile. Red leader. . . ."

There was a crackle from the phone within my ear.

"Red mobile," said a voice that I didn't recognize, but thought was human, "this is red leader station. Stand by."

"Red mobile standing by."

There was silence for a long while. I assumed that the human operator had gone to get Kar-hinter.

I was right.

"Eric?" asked the Krith's voice.

"Yes, Kar-hinter. Late, but reporting."

"Are you safe?"

"As of the moment."

"Count von Heinen?"

"Alive, the last time I looked. I don't know how long he'll last, though. What about Tracy and Kearns?"

"Safe. They managed to get through the Imperial lines just after dawn. Hillary is in a field hospital now. He will be fine the doctors say."

"Good. Did they tell you what happened?"

"Yes, but they could give no explanations. Can you?"

I had the uneasy feeling that someone else was listening to me. I looked around, saw no one, felt foolish, and chalked it up to my imagination. I was just tired and getting jumpy. That's all.

"No. It doesn't make any sense. I've never seen a skudder like the one they were in."

"Nor I, from the descriptions." The Krith paused for a moment. "Can you tell me where you are?"

"Somewhere in France."

"I expected no more. We will be able to get a fix on you soon, Eric, but I do not know how soon we will be able to come after you."

"You can get a fix and then skud in from an adjacent Line, can't you?"

"We will, just as soon as a skudder is available to us. The one you used was the only one in this part of France on any nearby Line."

"The one at the station?"

"Damaged beyond repair."

"How?"

"A heat weapon of some sort, perhaps a thermal grenade."

"How long will I have to wait?"

"I cannot tell you as yet. Is your position exposed?"

"Not really, but I don't feel too safe."

"Do you think you can find shelter nearby?"

"I may. We passed some abandoned farmhouses a few miles back."

"That may do if there are no used roads nearby. Do you still have the motorcar?"

"Yes."

"Use it if you must to get to a place of shelter and then hide it so that no one is likely to see it. Then transmit to us again so that we can get an exact fix on your new location. Perhaps then I can tell you how soon we can come in to pick you up."

"Okay. Anything else?"

"No, Eric. Except, do what you can for Von Heinen. We need him alive."

"I know. I will."

"Very good, Eric. That is all then. Out."

"Red mobile, out."

I disconnected the radio, carefully stowed the component parts back in their hiding places and shook out my damp coat.

The trail I had followed from the place where I had left Sally and the count continued on through the woods, fainter, apparently unused in years, but it offered the slight possibility that it might lead to something, a house, a farm. I decided to follow it a little way.

A dozen times I very nearly lost the trail as it wound through the woods, obscured by the growth of trees and brush, but at last I passed through the wood and out into a meadow. On the far side of the meadow, on a slight rise that was topped by a grove of very old poplars, stood the ruins of what once might have been a nobleman's secret retreat.

The house had not been large when it had been whole, and now less than a third of it was intact. It did not appear to have been damaged by the war, only by time, for it had stood there alone for many years, perhaps unknown by any living person. The west end of the house—or rather, cabin—was still covered by a roof, and as I crossed the meadow, I thought that perhaps a room or two might still be habitable, for a short time at least.

I approached the house cautiously, the energy pistol in my left hand, the Harling still in its holster, and heard nothing save the sudden movement of some tiny animal as it made its way out of the back, darting into the brush. I peered in through an open door hanging on rusty hinges, looking as if it were ready to fall at the slightest breeze.

The single surviving room was filled with the litter of years: leaves, twigs, the droppings of animals who had passed through it. There was no furniture, save an old pallet in one corner that someone, perhaps a passing hobo or a teen-age couple looking for a place to make love, had made from old blankets and straw. The pallet too was covered with twigs and leaves and obviously had not been used for years. The fireplace, which must have been grand at one time, was cracked, falling apart, and its hearth was covered with ashes that had been cold for half a decade or more.

But it was a shelter, and it appeared safe enough. It would be as good a place as any to wait for Kar-hinter.

I went back for Sally and the count, not looking forward to carrying the injured man that far.

When I returned, Sally appeared to be asleep. I stood over her for just a moment, looking down at her lush body which was not really covered by the torn gown, and for an instant I thought about doing exactly what I had told her I wasn't going to do to her. She *did* look inviting. But, hell, I told myself, this certainly wasn't the time or the place—and certainly not with

Sally von Heinen, who hated my guts.

And, as I said, she did remind me a little of Kristin, and I remembered how she had been raped when she was seventeen by a gang of savage thugs, and I didn't think I could bring myself to act the way those bastards had.

I shook her gently.

"Wake up."

Her eyes opened with a start.

"I'm going to hide the car," I said. "Then we're going to take a little walk."

She just sat there and looked at me and hated me.

And I can't say that I blamed her too much.

11

THE CABIN

Count von Heinen was still breathing, if weakly, and his pulse was a faint, though steady, thump under my finger when we finally arrived at the ruins of the cabin. Once or twice as we made the short trip that seemed to me to be miles long, he had stirred, jerked fitfully as if attempting to awaken from his unconscious slumber. He hadn't quite made it, and I wondered if he would ever awaken again unless he received medical attention soon. The bullet had been in his stomach for something like nine hours now, and no aid had been given him other than Kearns' compress and bandages. If Kar-hinter expected to get him alive, he'd damned well better hurry.

Inside the cabin's single surviving room Sally brushed the accumulation of debris from the old, moldy, rotten pallet, and I carefully laid the count on it. Surprisingly enough the wound had not begun to bleed again during the time I had carried him to the cabin, and I was grateful for that.

As for myself, well, I didn't feel that I was in much better condition than he was. I ached in every muscle and joint, and the graze wound in my side was a burning flame, and I wanted nothing more than to lie down and sleep for a week or two. But that would have to wait until after Kar-hinter came.

"Sit down," I briskly told the count's wife and took a piece of rope from my pocket to retie her hands.

"Do you mind . . ." she started to ask, then stopped short.

"Mind what?"

"Well, I have to go to the bathroom."

"There's no indoor plumbing here," I told her, "but there's a big world outside. I doubt that anyone would mind your using it."

"You'd trust me to go outside alone?"

"No."

She sat there glaring at me for a moment, then asked, "You wouldn't take my word?"

"No."

"I'll wait."

"For what?" I asked her. "If you've got to go, you've got to go."

"With you watching?"

I shrugged.

After a while she said, "Okay," very bitterly, and I followed her outside the cabin where she squatted on the ground, filled with shame, and relieved herself.

"I hope you enjoyed that, you degenerate voyeur," she said as she rose.

"No, not particularly," I said. "It's just a biological function."

She spat on the ground in front of me.

Hell, even beautiful women are human beings. I learned that a long time ago. And at about the same time I learned that it's nothing to be ashamed of, being a human being.

When we got back into the cabin, I asked her if she'd like to put her robe back on. Maybe she'd be less self-conscious.

"What haven't you seen by now?" she asked.

"Not much."

"I'll leave the robe off for a while."

"Okay," I said, "I won't tie your hands, but you'd better just sit quietly on the floor. I have something that I have to do myself."

Clearing a space on the floor I removed my coat and quickly reassembled the radio. Before, I had still been wary of letting her see it, but now I felt safe enough. Barring a catastrophe I couldn't foresee, Sally would never tell anyone about this device that was alien to her world. Kar-hinter would come—soon, I hoped—she would be taken to an interrogation station, and during the painless mind probe her memories of this event, in fact, of everything that had happened since the predawn hours when we burst into the villa, would be removed. She would have no memories of strange men with stranger machines to spread to the rest of her world. Though by this time I already had the suspicion that Sally knew a lot more about Timeliners than she was willing to admit, maybe a lot that even I didn't know.

She didn't speak as I assembled the transceiver, nor did she speak as I began to broadcast in Shangalis.

"Red leader, this is red mobile. Come in, red leader."

"This is Kar-hinter, Eric," said a tinny voice from the earphone. "Have you found a place of shelter?"

"Yes," I acknowledged. "I believe we're safe enough here."

"How is the count?"

"Still unconscious," I told him. "He's in pretty bad shape. You'd better hurry."

"I am doing the best I can," the Krith said. "But I must wait my turn. Skudders seem to be much in demand across the Lines today."

"Don't you have priority?"

"A high priority, yes, but not the highest. There are more important Lines than this one, you know."

I halfway wondered whether he might be wrong about that.

"How soon?" I asked.

"As yet I do not know." He paused. "Keep broadcasting. We are taking a fix on you now."

Two, three, or more direction finders were now beaming in on my transmitter, determining the exact location of it in relationship to the base stations. With no other radio signals to confuse them and with the kind of gear they had, it shouldn't be difficult for them to locate my position quite closely.

"You are sure of your safety?" Kar-hinter asked.

"Fairly sure. No one seems to have visited this place in years."

"Very well. Leave your unit on. As soon as I know when we will be able to come in for you, I will let you know. That is all for now. Red leader out."

I sighed with frustration, but there wasn't anything more I

could do. It would have to be up to Kar-hinter now.

"Very well. Red mobile out."

I removed the earphone and laid it and the microphone beside the tiny block of the transceiver. I would leave it on for a while, then check back with Kar-hinter. The power cell inside the plastic block was good for hours of continuous operation.

Then I looked at Sally.

During the whole operation she had watched me with interest, but without astonishment, as if this were something she had rather expected.

"Who are you?" she asked as I found a fairly comfortable place to sit, pulled one of my few remaining cigarettes from my pocket, and lit it with a real lighter. I laid the energy pistol on the floor beside me; it was uncomfortable stuck in my belt when I was sitting down.

"Captain Eric Mathers, Royal British Army, Colonial Corps," I said flatly. I did not really expect her to believe it.

"No," she said, shaking her head. "You're no Englishman."

"I'm an American."

"American!" She almost laughed. "That wasn't English you were speaking just now."

"It was code."

"It didn't sound like code to me. It sounded like a formalized language."

"Have it your own way," I said, somewhat annoyed at her cross-examination, but also glad that she had finally begun to speak. Perhaps if she continued to talk, I would be able to learn a little of what she knew. I was damned curious. Maybe she was, too. Maybe that's why she was talking.

"Where *are* you from?" she asked.

"Virginia."

"Where in Virginia?"

"Victoria."

She smiled. "Do you know George Carter?"

The name meant nothing to me. It had been mentioned in none of the training tapes that the Kriths had fed into me when building my phony background, but still I thought I'd play it safe, though I had little hope of fooling her or little reason to, now. It was a game.

"The name sounds familiar. I'm not sure."

"Surely, if you're really from Victoria, you've heard of George Carter."

"I'm not sure. I've been away from home for a long time."

"Really now, Captain Mathers. George Carter served as mayor twice; then he was arrested for high treason in '64 or '65. It was a very big thing at the time. It must have been in the papers all over the Empire."

"Mike Trimble was mayor in '64," I told her. That was true.

"He was mayor before Mike Trimble."

"I thought Joe—ah—Joe Knight was." I was on shaky ground now.

"No, George Carter."

I wondered. I wasn't sure. The tapes hadn't been that detailed. Maybe a George Carter had been mayor of Victoria once.

"Don't you remember?" she asked, still smiling a sinister little smile. "He escaped from the provincial prison in Buffalo in '69. They've been searching for him ever since."

"No," I said flatly, deciding that she was inventing the whole thing to trap me into an admission. I was going to play the game all the way.

"Okay," she said, the smile fading. "I made it up. But I still don't believe you."

"Well, if I'm not an American, what am I?"

"That's what I want you to tell me."

"Okay," I said, giving her a smile of my own. "I'm a part of an invasion team from Mars. We're going to take over your planet next Tuesday."

"Do you really want it?" she asked, somehow returning my smile.

"It's better than Mars." And that was true, too. I've been there.

"You don't look like a Martian."

I can't say that I could really understand this apparent change of personality in her. Now she was talking to me on an almost-friendly basis, carrying on this joke. But then I wasn't too concerned about it either. A girl like Sally is nicer to be friends with than enemies.

"I'm in disguise," I told her. "Really I'm twelve feet tall with eight eyes and a dozen tentacles."

"I almost believe you."

"You might as well."

Von Heinen stirred, seemed for a moment as if he would awaken, then settled back, returned to the twilight state of unconsciousness.

"How bad is he?" Sally asked.

"Bad. A few more hours like this, and no one will be able to help him."

"You want to keep him alive, don't you?"

"That's my job."

"Were you calling for help just then?"

"Yes."

"Who?"

"My fellow Martians. They'll be landing in a flying saucer in the meadow out there in a few minutes."

"Flying saucer?"

"Forget it."

"I wish I could forget all of this."

"Maybe you will."

"What do you mean?"

"Nothing. You don't seem overly concerned about your husband."

"Should I be?"

"It's customary."

"He's a pig," Sally said slowly, bitterly. "But I don't want to see him die. We need him." She smiled a bitter smile. "Anyway, I suppose he's yours now."

"We'll give him back."

"Will you?"

"Yes."

"When?"

"When we're finished."

"Finished with what?"

"We want to ask him some questions."

"About the bomb?"

I nodded. Sally knew that we knew about the Baltic plant, so she was making no effort to hide it from me. How much more did she know? I was beginning to understand why Kar-hinter wanted her too.

"He doesn't know anything," she said.

"We'll find out."

"Your pleasure. But why me? You didn't kidnap me just because I happened to be there. You could have left me tied up as you did Françoise."

"Françoise?"

"Albert's bedmate."

"The dark-haired girl with the big—?"

Sally nodded, so I didn't say anything more about Françoise's very obvious physical attributes.

"I would have taken her along if I could have," I said, imitating a leer.

"Albert told me she was *good*," Sally said. "A better piece than me, he told me once."

"Is that why you hate him?"

"Because of her? Her kind's a shilling a dozen."

"Then why?"

"I'll hate people for whatever reasons I want. Why did you take me?"

"You're Archer Beall's daughter."

"Oh," Sally said, "you're also trying to find out just how closely the ARA is working with the Holy Romans?"

I nodded, though I wasn't really sure what Kar-hinter did want to learn from her.

"You don't have to force that out of me," she said. "Closer than I want, but not as close as the count and his friends would like."

"That doesn't tell me much, except that you don't like the Imperials."

"You didn't have to kidnap me to find that out."

"I think I get this much of the picture," I said. "You don't much like having the Imperials as allies, but they're the best available."

"They've got the only game in town," Sally said. "The Nippons don't give a damn about what happens in the Western world, and Spain doesn't have what it takes to try to buck Britain.''

''What happens when the war's over, if the Germans win?''

''That doesn't worry me too much.''

''Shouldn't it?''

''No,'' she said flatly.

''You mean to say that you think the ARA can defeat them whereas it can't beat the British?''

''The war's not over yet, one way or the other.''

''No, it's not,'' I agreed. ''But it seems to me that a world ruled by Britain would be preferable to one ruled by the Imperials.''

She laughed very bitterly. ''The only thing worse than an Imperial pig is a British pig. I'd shoot myself before I'd side with them.''

''You really hate the British that much?''

''I really hate the British—and anyone who works with them. Even Martians or whatever you are.''

''I'm sorry.''

''Like hell you are.''

''I am.''

''Shit!'' From her the word was startling.

She turned away, and we were both silent for a long while. I guess I'd blown that one.

Early afternoon was slowly changing into late afternoon, and shadows were lengthening across the meadow below. The warmth of the day was passing suddenly.

I got up, built a fire in the crumbling fireplace that filled the room with smoke, carefully moved Von Heinen closer to the fire, and checked his pulse again.

''He's still alive at least,'' I said.

''Good.'' There was little conviction in her voice.

I picked up her robe and held it out for her. ''You want this?''

She looked at me for a moment, then rose, took the robe from my hands, threw it across her shoulders, sat back down and muttered, ''Thanks.''

I went back to the radio, slipped the phone into my ear, and said into the mike in Shangalis, ''Red mobile to red leader.''

"Red leader station here," came an immediate reply, but the voice was not Kar-hinter's.

"Anything new?" I asked.

"Not yet. We have your position, but no skudder is available yet. Please be patient."

"I'll do my best, but I can't guarantee how long Von Heinen's going to live."

"I'll pass that on to Kar-hinter when he returns."

"You do that."

"Red leader station out."

"Red mobile out," I said with disgust and then added in English, "Screw you, Jack."

"You sound unhappy," Sally said as I pulled the phone out of my ear.

"Just getting impatient." I looked at her for a moment, decided that she was ready to talk again. "I don't suppose you happened to bring a box lunch with you?"

"No one told me it was going to be a picnic."

"Sorry. An oversight on my part."

I fished my last cigarette from my pocket, lit it with an ember from the fire, and felt very annoyed with everything.

"I'm tired and I'm hungry and my side hurts like hell and I'm on my last cigarette and I think one of my patients is going to die on me," I said slowly, "so, Countess von Heinen, I do wish you'd give me some straight answers."

"About what?"

"For example, who were those men?"

"What men?" The innocence on her face was thin, transparent. She knew exactly who they were.

"You know who I mean. The ones who tried to rescue you and the count."

"I have no idea."

"You're lying."

"Are you going to beat it out of me?"

"If I get annoyed enough, I just might."

"I wouldn't like that."

"I wouldn't either."

"You'd probably rather try to rape it out of me."

95

"Is that an invitation?"

"I thought those were standard tactics."

"Rape? What do you mean?"

She shrugged.

"Just tell me," I said.

"You know," she answered slowly, "my father was called a traitor all his life, and I've been called that more times than I can remember, but so help me God, Captain Mathers, I'm an amateur at the game of treason compared to you."

"Now what are you talking about?"

"You and your kind." She paused. "I've fought against the rule of a foreign nation imposed on my land, and I'm called a traitor for it. But you—you and your kind are selling out the whole human race. What do you call that?"

"I don't know what you're talking about. Wait—you don't *believe* what I said about Martians?"

"No, not Martians, something infinitely worse."

Did she know about the Kriths? Was that what she meant? It didn't seem possible. That was the most carefully guarded secret on this planet. But then. . . .

"I'll be glad when they get you into interrogation," I said. "Then maybe I'll find out whether you're really crazy."

"I doubt that you'll ever find out very much that way, Captain Mathers. And I strongly suggest that you keep your hand away from both your weapons."

"Stay right where you are," a masculine voice said slowly in English, and it was a voice that wasn't Von Heinen's. "Don't turn around."

Then I heard a swishing in the air—and the universe exploded in the back of my head. The last thing I remember was the look of triumph on Sally's face as I slumped forward and lost consciousness.

12

CAPTIVE

Mostly there was redness and flickering lights and pain from the back of my head, and the universe had an unpleasant, nauseating tendency to spin. Somewhere a long, long way off I heard a voice speaking.

". . . got the radio on the air it wasn't much trouble to find you."

"I was wondering if you'd ever come," replied a voice that I recognized as Sally's. The other voice I tentatively identified as that of the man who had slugged me.

"I'm sorry it took so long." His voice spoke Sally's English with an odd, almost intangible accent that wasn't German. Like me, English wasn't his native tongue, but I couldn't tell what was.

"That's okay. What about Albert?" Sally asked.

"Mica says he stands a good chance of living if we can get the bullet out soon."

"Where are we going?"

"Staunton."

"*Here?*"

There was an odd accenting to the way she said the word as if she were referring to some special kind of "here."

"We'll stay in this Paratime," the man said. "We won't shift Von Heinen unless his condition gets worse. But Mica believes that Sol-Jodala can fix him up in Staunton."

"I hope so," Sally said.

"I thought you hated him."

"We still need him."

"I suppose we do."

By this time I had worked up the courage to open my eyes. I was lying on a floor—or deck—of some kind of craft, behind a row of seats. Metal walls extended up about waist-high, then fused into a transparent roof that formed a dome above. Through the dome all I could see was a purplish evening sky, and though I had the sensation of motion, I could not be certain that we were actually moving.

My feet and hands were tied, and the rope that bound my hands was in turn lashed to a cargo ring set into the metal deck on which I lay. I could move, but not much.

By lifting my head up as far as the pain would allow, I could see the tops of two heads above the seats in front of me. One was Sally's blondness, the other dark. The man, I assumed.

I could not see what was behind me, but I had the feeling that I was near the rear end of the craft—and I assumed that the craft was the egg-shaped alien skudder that I had seen before.

Where was von Heinen? I wondered. Were Sally and the man the only other people in the machine? But then, I supposed, they could have been traveling in more than one.

"What are you going to do with Mathers?" Sally asked after a long silence.

"I don't know yet," the man answered. "Take him to Staunton with us now. We'll let Mica decide what to do with him then."

"You don't expect to get any information out of him, do you?"

"Him? No, not really. I've seen his kind often enough before. He's tough enough to stand up under just about any physical torture and the sort of mind blocks the Kriths put on their hired hands are impossible to break without killing the subject. No, if he tells us anything—if he even knows anything we don't—he'll only give it to us because he wants to."

"Do you expect him to want to?" Sally asked.

"Not really. But you can never tell. Some of them will listen to reason, but not many."

"And if he doesn't cooperate?"

"I suppose we'll kill him," the man said matter-of-factly.

"I hope you don't have to," Sally said.

"For God's sake why? He shot von Heinen and kidnapped you."

"He wasn't unnecessarily brutal about it. He just talked mean."

"You're getting soft, girl. Is that what love does to you?"

"Love?" Sally asked.

"Yes, you and Mica . . ." The man let his voice fade away as if he were realizing that he was making some kind of mistake that he really didn't understand.

The craft lurched slightly as if hit by a gust of wind, and then I was sure that we were in motion, physical motion. We weren't skudding, I was sure of that. You don't mistake *that* flickering for anything but what it is.

"No," Sally was saying, going on as if the man hadn't made his last comment. "I don't think he knows what he's doing. I mean, I believe he's sincere."

"Most of them are," the man said, "but the Kriths have them so brainwashed that they'll never come around. I'm sorry if you've taken a liking to him, Sally, but we'll probably have to kill him."

"Okay, old top," I said to myself, "you've just made yourself a dyed-in-the-wool convert to whatever brand of the One True God you're selling. I'll play your games if that's what it takes to keep me alive." And I meant to stay alive long enough to find out what the hell was going on.

"Do you think I'd better check on him?" Sally asked.

Where had all the hatred gone? I wondered. Was she one of those people who hate the enemy with a purple passion until he's beaten and then knock themselves out being kind to him when they've got him down? Okay, that would be all the better.

"No," the man was answering. "He'll be fine. I didn't hit him that hard. Just enough to keep him dazed for a while. Let him be. You'll have plenty of time to nurse his wounds when we get to Staunton, if that's what you want."

"Okay," Sally said.

"You just sit here and keep me company. We've got a long flight ahead of us. Care for some coffee? There's a flask and some sandwiches in the hamper there."

"Thanks," Sally answered. "I'm starving."

The sky above the flying skudder was growing darker by the minute, turning from purple to red, and it looked as if stars would begin to appear soon. I wondered where we were and where we were going.

None of it made any sense yet. Sally and the man seemed to know about the Kriths and Timeliners. But who were they, Sally and the man? Timeliners themselves? Of a sort, I gathered. But who? And why? And what were they doing here? And where did this machine come from? And why did they call me a traitor? Didn't they know what the Kriths were doing—trying to save humanity, a hell of a lot of humanities on various earths, from an invasion in the future?

They must have known, I told myself. The man had spoken of encountering others like me, of trying to convince them of something. Surely they would have told them why the Kriths were spreading across the Lines, why we Timeliners fought for them.

But, since they must have been told, they apparently hadn't believed it. And what could I be able to say or do to convince them? Nothing, probably. So, when the time came, I'd put up a few feeble arguments to whatever it was that they were going to try to sell me, then pretend to go along with them. That might give me a chance to stay alive a while, learn something and then maybe get back to Kar-hinter with what I had learned.

If it worked out—which seemed sort of unlikely at the moment, what with my lying trussed up on the floor of some alien kind of skudder—if it worked out, it would prove to be a lot more than Kar-hinter had ever bargained for when he sent us out to kidnap the count and his wife.

Just what had I stumbled into?

I figured that was enough thinking for the moment. My head still hurt like hell, and my empty stomach was more than a bit uneasy, and I was exhausted. The only logical thing to do was get a little sleep.

So I did.

When I awoke, rain was splattering against the dome above

me at a high velocity. I couldn't really see it or hear it well, but I knew it was rain. The dome was pitch dark, and I could see nothing beyond it.

In the front of the craft faint panel lights glowed, reflecting from the dome. The craft was quiet except for the hum of whatever propulsion it used and it was something I couldn't identify. It seemed to be nothing I had ever encountered before—and I had driven or ridden in just about everything from goat carts to grav cars to spaceships.

I heard a feminine sigh from the front and then the sound of motion, a body rising, straightening itself.

"I guess I fell asleep," Sally said.

"You needed it," the man answered. "You should have slept longer."

"How long has it been?"

"Oh, a couple of hours, I guess."

"Where are we?"

"Mid-Atlantic. We ought to be in Staunton by midnight."

"We've run into a storm," Sally commented.

"Not a bad one. Radar says we ought to clear it in ten minutes or so. I think your friend back there is awake."

"Mathers?"

"Yes, you want to go check on him?"

"Okay?"

Again the sound of movement, then a flashlight bobbing as Sally walked the few feet back to where I lay. For an instant I could see her silhouetted against the panel lights, dressed now in what looked like a form-fitting flight suit. I hoped that I would be able to see it in better light.

Then the beam of the flashlight was in my eyes, and I had to blink.

"How are you?" Sally asked, kneeling beside me.

"I'd be okay if I could find the rest of my head," I said.

"Scoti," she said, calling back over her shoulder.

"Yes?" the man replied.

"I'm going to untie him and bring him up front. Is that okay?"

"Do you have a gun?"

"The one you gave me."

"Make sure he knows it and that you'll use it."

"I know," I said.

"Okay, Mathers, but watch your step. Sally's a good shot. And if that isn't enough, you can remind yourself that I'm just as fast as you are, maybe faster. Augmentation, you people call it."

"Yeah," I said.

Sally knelt, placed the light on the deck beside the ring around which my ropes were tied, and quickly loosened them. She then slipped the flashlight into a pocket, but I could see her silhouette as she rose, pulled a small pistol from another pocket, and said, "Get up slowly. Do exactly what I say."

"Yes, ma'am," I said, awkwardly stumbling to my feet, then biting my lip against the pain that throbbed in the back of my head. The way I felt I doubted that I could have gone into augmentation even if I'd wanted to.

"That way," Sally said, gesturing toward the front of the craft with her pistol. "Take the seat behind Scoti."

Scoti turned out to be a stocky, dark man with almond eyes, apparently an improbable blending of Italian and Nipponese, but then he could have been anything from any When for all I knew.

"Remember," Scoti said as I sat down behind him, glancing over his shoulder, "Sally won't hesitate to put a bullet between your eyes if you do the slightest thing out of line."

"I'll remember," I said, and I wondered whether she would. She might.

"Are you hungry?" Sally asked, taking a seat opposite me, leveling the small pistol at me.

In the light of the control panel I could see the cream-colored outfit she wore a little better. It was some sort of flight suit, as I had thought earlier and apparently one made just for her unless the material from which it was made adjusted itself to whatever body wore the suit. It fitted her like a second skin, and that certainly wasn't bad on her.

"I think I could eat something," I said.

Sally nodded and, always keeping an eye on me, went forward to a hamper, extracted a thermal flask, a cup, and a plastic-wrapped sandwich. She came back to where I sat, loosened the ropes that still held my hands together, and handed me the sandwich. Sitting down again, she placed the pistol in her lap and poured me a cup of coffee.

"Thanks," I said.

There was no talking in the craft while I wolfed down the sandwich and coffee.

When I was finished, feeling more nearly alive, Scoti looked back at me for a moment, then said, "Let me spell it out, Mathers, so there's no mistake. We know who you are, what you are and why you're here. Kriths, skudders, Timeliners, we know it all. So you don't have to play any silly games about hiding it from us. Okay?"

"Who are you?" I asked coldly, looking across the top of my coffee cup.

"My name is Scoti Hauser Angelus," the craft's pilot said in the same tone. "I am from what you would probably call a Romano-Albigensian Timeline a long way to the Parawest of here, and I am here to prevent you and your masters from accomplishing your ultimate goals."

Well, I thought, he *had* come straight to the point. From the West, he had said. That was possible, perhaps even probable and why I hadn't thought of it before, I didn't know. The Timeline we presently occupied was about as far West as we and the Kriths had ever come in force. Of course there had been some explorations farther into the Temporal West, but not very far to my knowledge—there were hardly enough Timeliners and Kriths to do the job now, much less expend manpower exploring. Yes, for all we knew there could be another civilization with cross-Lining capabilities farther to the T-West, but why they should feel as they seemed to feel about Kriths and Timeliners I still had no idea.

I looked over at Sally.

"She's a *local*," Scoti said.

In a way I was relieved.

"Can you explain all this to me?" I asked.

"I think it's better if we don't even try for the time being," Scoti said. "Just wait until we get to our destination; then you can ask all the questions you want."

I finished my coffee, sat back in the seat, glanced at the ugly little pistol in Sally's pretty little hand, then looked up at the dome that covered the craft and at the stars that were beginning to break through the layers of cloud and tried to remember what I could of a place called Staunton.

The name, after I thought about it for a while, seemed to have some special significance. I was sure that I had heard of it before. It had been in the training tapes. A tiny, many-legged creature scuttled through my mind, knocking around pieces and bits of ideas, concepts, memories—and the proper pieces fell into place.

Staunton: (1) a town in Virginia, Shenandoah Valley or that area, that had been the rallying point of the American Republican Army during the uprising of the 1920's. In '28 or '29, I couldn't remember which, British regulars surrounded Staunton, boxed in the rebels and held them under siege for thirty-seven days. Finally the town caught fire; the rebels, half-dead of starvation, made an attempt to break through the British lines and were slaughtered. The British kept the town surrounded until the fire had burned itself out and nearly all the inhabitants had perished. The cream of the ARA died in Staunton, as did several thousand innocent civilians who were caught in the town. It was a bitter memory for the rebels and one that they weren't going to easily forget.

But that wasn't all there was to the name Staunton. There was something else and I slowly dug it out.

Staunton: (2) rumor had it that somewhere in West Florida the rebels had begun building a secret city. The stories first began in the late fifties, as well as I could remember from the training tapes, and were quite common for a few years. Most of the rumors were something to this effect: somewhere back in the wilderness of southern West Florida the ARA and the Mad Anthony Wayne Society were building an underground city where they would store arms, train troops and in general prepare for the great uprising that would one day free America from the British Empire.

Countless aerial searches had been made by the British with absolutely no luck. Soldiers had gone into the West Floridian forests and marched across hundreds of square miles without finding any trace of this new Staunton. Finally, in disgust, the

British gave up and attributed the whole thing to gossip, rumor, and just plain American madness.

So there it stood.

But now I was ready to believe that there really was a secret city, a hidden, unknown Staunton that was a hell of a lot more than the British had ever imagined, that was a base for Outtimers who were assisting the American rebels and the Holy Roman Empire.

Okay, I said to myself, we'll find out for sure soon.

Outside the craft the night was as dark as ever with no sign of a moon, though the stars shone brightly now that we had left the clouds behind us. Below, the Earth was a mass of unrelieved blackness, a nothingness. Then, very faintly, off to my left, south of the craft, I saw lights, a city on the horizon.

While I watched the lights, my mind still turning over all the information I had gathered since returning to consciousness, Scoti began angling the craft more to the south, in the direction of the city.

"I was a little off," he said to Sally. "That's Charleston down there."

Sally looked up, startled, as if she had been deep in thought. "Oh," she said, "I didn't realize we were so close to land."

"It's not as far as it was," Scoti said.

We passed directly over the mass of lights that was the chief harbor city of southern Virginia, Charleston, and lay near the borders of the provinces of Virginia and Florida, the way North America was laid out and subdivided in this Here and Now. Off to the right and left small masses of light lined the coast, revealing the shape of the shore where the sea ended and the American land began.

Soon, however, the coastal cities dwindled behind us and the darkness of the great and mostly undeveloped North American continent lay below us. We moved south and west, toward the forests of West Florida and the secret city.

I wondered what I was going to find there. And maybe I was a little bit frightened.

13

STAUNTON

I have no idea what time it was when we arrived at our destination. Earlier I had heard Scoti say something about midnight, but I'm not sure that's what time it really was when we got there. Whatever time it was, it was quite dark, though the night was pleasantly warm and crickets, frogs, things I couldn't identify sounded in the distance as I stepped down from the craft, Sally and Scoti each holding a pistol on me.

The grass-covered field itself was quite small and irregular in shape, perhaps a hundred feet long by twenty-five feet wide at its widest, but then it hadn't been designed for use by any conventional type of aircraft. One end of the field ended in a clump of trees, some real, some apparently artificial, that sheltered the hangar. Inside the hangar were two more craft something like the one in which I had just arrived. It was then that I realized that the craft I had been riding in was not the skudder that I had seen before, but a smaller one. The skudder that had carried the men who had tried to rescue the count and Sally was sitting inside the hangar, two or three yet unpatched bullet holes in its hull still revealing the battles of the night before.

I didn't have much time to look around right then. Scoti prodded me forward as half a dozen men and women, all dressed in the same sort of cream-colored flying suits that Sally and Scoti wore, came out of the hangar and toward us, flashlights in their hands.

"I am glad you made it, Scoti," said a tall, cadaverous-looking man when we were within speaking distance. He nodded to Sally, a strange, proprietary smile on his face. "I hope your ordeal was not too unpleasant."

"What about Von Heinen?" Scoti asked without waiting for Sally to reply to the other man.

"He is in the hospital," he answered, then turned to look at me coldly, clinically as if I were a bug under a microscope.

"How is he, Mica?" Scoti asked.

"Very close to dying. Trebum is standing by with the other sautierboat in case he doesn't make it. Sol-Jodala will then cold-sleep him and try to revive him in Altheon."

"Don't you think you should go on and transfer him now if he's that bad?" Scoti asked.

"Sol-Jodala says to wait," the tall man said, "and in this case I must defer to them." Then he turned and looked at me again, something that I interpreted as contempt flickering across his face for a moment. Then he smiled, but it was a very artificial kind of smile. "Good morning, Captain Mathers. I trust that you had a pleasant trip."

"I'm afraid that you have the advantage of me, sir," I said with the same fake cordiality.

"Yes, in more ways than one," he said, his smile shifting to one of satisfaction, "but please forgive me. I am called Mica."

"Are you in charge here?" I asked.

"Yes, in some respects I am," Mica answered, the cold, bitter smile returning to his lips. "Why do you ask?"

"Just wondering."

Mica nodded to me, then turned to Sally.

"You must be exhausted, my dear," he said. "Go on to bed. You can fill me in on the background tomorrow." Without waiting for her to answer, Mica gestured to one of the men with him, who took Sally by the arm and led her off through the trees beyond the hangar. From the look on Sally's face the man was an old friend; she was home now, safe among those she knew and trusted.

Mica turned and whispered something I couldn't understand to another of the men.

While this was going on, I was looking over one of the women in the group, who returned my gaze without lowering her eyes, an almost-smile playing across her lips. She was tall and fair-skinned and wore one of those form-fitting suits that showed off her enormous breasts and lovely figure to excellent advantage. Well, maybe things at Staunton weren't going to be all bad at that, I thought.

"Scoti," Mica said suddenly, "take Captain Mathers to his quarters. G'lendal can check him, if that will satisfy her inquisitive urges, but I will wait until after breakfast to talk with him. I need some rest before dawn." He looked at me again. "It has been a very long day for us all, do you not agree, Captain Mathers?"

I nodded, but didn't speak. It was a rhetorical question anyway.

Pointing with a pistol toward a path that led into the woods in a direction opposite from the one that Sally had taken, Scoti told me to get moving. A second man followed close behind, a flashlight and another pistol pointed at the back of my head.

"Do you know where we are, Mathers?" Scoti asked.

"I have a pretty good idea."

"And do you know what this place is?"

"Your base, I suppose."

"Our major base in this Paratime."

I walked on, waiting for him to say something more, but apparently he had decided that there was little point in talking about it now. Time for that later, maybe.

"Take the next path to your right," Scoti said after a while.

In the darkness I could hardly see the path until I was on it, but Scoti had apparently known where it was long before we neared it. I had the feeling that Scoti knew his way around here pretty well—and that I would be a damned fool if I thought I could escape from him in the dark.

"Okay, hold it," Scoti said.

I stopped, looked in front of me. The man with the flashlight stepped around Scoti and me and illuminated a small structure in the darkness. It was a concrete cube, perhaps four feet high, concealed in clumps of bushes and trees that grew high above it, dark, heavy, towering longleaf pines. In the side of the concrete structure was a metal door. The flashlightman opened the door by pressing his hand in a shiny spot and stood back, waiting.

"In," Scoti said, gesturing with his pistol as the door opened.

Ducking down, almost on my hands and knees, I entered the dark opening that immediately became lighted as my presence triggered some kind of mechanism. A staircase led downward from the door to a landing fifteen or so feet below. Beyond the landing I could see nothing.

"Go on," Scoti said, "but not too fast."

I went down the stairs, straightening up as soon as the ceiling got to a decent height and at the bottom waited for Scoti and the other man.

Now I was standing at one end of a pale-green corridor that extended as far as I could see, finally dwindling in the distance to a vanishing point. Every few feet a bluish-white light burned in the ceiling, more than sufficient to illuminate the corridor. Off in the distance I heard or felt the operation of machinery, but what kind I could not even guess.

There was a door every fifteen or twenty feet on both the right and left, each carefully labeled with characters of an alphabet that I had never before come across in all my cross-Line travels, and I was struck again by the fact that I was dealing with people whose existence was not even suspected by Timeliners and Kriths. If I ever got out of it, wouldn't I have a report to turn in!

"Move," Scoti said, "straight ahead."

Since Scoti's gun looked as mean and ugly as ever, and since my head still hurt like hell and since I didn't know what else to do anyway, I moved as I was told, down the corridor to whatever it was that Scoti and Mica had in mind for me.

At regular intervals, which I guessed to be about a hundred feet apart, other corridors branched off this one to the right and left at 90 degrees. These other corridors were painted the same pale, hospital green and seemed to extend to the underground horizon. This was an enormous place here under the earth.

When we came to the third intersection, Scoti told me to turn left and keep going. I did, counting my paces as I walked.

At first we seemed to be the only ones in the vast, subterranean burrow, but when we had gone a hundred feet or so down the branch tunnel, a door opened before us. A pale blond young man stepped out, nodded to Scoti and the other man, and walked down the corridor in the direction from which we had just come.

The fact that he was stark naked except for a wide green belt and a cap of the same color on his head aroused no comment from my captors and seemed to cause the young man no embarrassment. I shrugged.

We stopped for traffic at the next intersection. A man and a woman, both blacks, were coming down the corridor that crossed ours. They wore short, white, sleeveless gowns that reached to their knees. They stopped when they saw us, raised their hands in greeting.

"Good morning, Sol-Jodala," Scoti said.

"Good morning to you, Scoti, and to you, Nardi," the man said with a clipped accent that sounded British but wasn't. "A prisoner?"

"Yes," my captor said. "A Krithian Timeliner working with the British."

"Not the man who kidnapped Sally and the count?" the woman asked, her voice almost identical to the man's.

They all seemed to act as if I weren't there or at least couldn't understand them even though they were speaking English.

"The same," Scoti answered.

The two peered at me for a moment with an animal-in-the-zoo-behind-bars look, then seemed to realize that I was a human being who was aware of them, nodded abruptly and turned back to Scoti.

"How is Sally?" the man asked.

"The poor girl's exhausted," he said, "but other than that she's okay. A few hours' rest will fix her up."

"We just looked in on the count," the woman said. "We believe that he will pull through. The crisis seems to be past."

"I'm glad to hear that," Scoti replied.

"Excuse us, please," the man said. "Morning meditations, you know." Again that pseudo-British accent, but it seemed natural.

"Of course," Scoti said. "Good day, Sol-Jodala."

"Good day," they answered together.

As they turned and started down the corridor, the oddness of it all struck me. The whole time they had not looked at each other or even seemed to recognize the existence of each other, yet they had alternated in speaking, first one, then the other, and now as they walked away I saw that their steps, the swinging of their arms, every motion was perfectly synchronized. Odd, I thought.

"Let's go," Scoti said. "It's not much farther."

Two intersections or so later we finally stopped. The door before which Scoti told me to halt was no different from any of the others and labeled in the same unintelligible alphabet.

Scoti fished a small metal cylinder out of his pocket, peered at one end of it while he twisted a movable band, then seemed to be satisfied and pressed the cylinder against a small white disk on the door. The door hummed and began to swing open.

For half an instant I had my chance. When Scoti stepped back to allow the door to open, it came between us. I stood more beside than in front of the other man and he was watching the door, not me, his gun lax in his hand. Augmentation or no, I'm sure that I could have grabbed the gun from him, shot Scoti before he realized what was happening and then the second man. But what if I did? Killing or escaping from these two just wouldn't have done me a whole hell of a lot of good. In less time than it took to think it, I decided to play along with my original plan. I'd do as they said and pretend to accept whatever they wanted me to accept, and with my Krithian training and conditioning I believed that I could fool any lie-detection equipment anyone ever made or ever would make. Okay. Play it safe.

"In," Scoti said to me. Then to the other man, "Nardi, you keep an eye on him. I'll go tell G'lendal he's here, and then I'm going to get some rest. I don't think I've slept in three days."

To my surprise Nardi spoke. I had almost come to think he was mute. "Okay," he said. "You look beat."

"I am," Scoti said. "See you later." Then he turned to me. "Watch it, Mathers. I know you're no fool, but don't even think about acting like one."

"Thanks for the advice," I said and stepped through the open doorway, wondering just what was waiting for me inside.

The room was not small and ill-lighted and fitted out with torture devices as I had expected. Just the opposite. The room was a good twenty by twenty feet, pleasant and comfortable-looking. The furniture consisted of a bed, two easy chairs, a sofa, two unusual-looking lamps, two low tables, three land-scapes on the wall, and a device that looked like some kind of intercom. Off to the left a door opened into what appeared to be a bathroom and another door led into a closet. A rather comfortable dungeon, I thought.

"Sit down, Mathers," Nardi said, gesturing toward the chairs and sofa. "Just take a load off your feet until G'lendal gets here."

I did as he said, realizing that despite the sleep I had got in the skudder, I was still pretty well worn out.

"You wouldn't have a cigarette on you, would you?" I asked.

Nardi, still standing in the center of the room, reached into his breast pocket, pulled out a partially crumpled pack of cigarettes, Players, local origin, and a book of matches. He tossed them on the sofa beside me.

"Go ahead," he said.

"Thanks. You want one?"

"No," he answered, sitting down on the bed, keeping his eyes on me.

"Who's this G'lendal, anyway?" I asked.

"She's our chief interrogator."

"Interrogator?"

Nardi smiled. "Oh, don't worry. We don't use rubber hoses and thumbscrews. She'll just ask you a few questions and see how you react to them."

"And if I don't react right?"

"Look, fella, Scoti didn't bring you here to torture you. Tomorrow, I guess, Mica will explain the whole setup to you. If you listen to reason and if G'lendal believes you, then you'll probably be put on probation. If not . . . well, if you're too damned hardheaded to see the truth when it's shown to you, that's your tough luck." He paused. "But as for right now all G'lendal's going to do is feel you out."

"Feel me out, huh? Okay."

On the table beside the sofa where I sat was an ashtray and three worn books stacked on top of each other. I picked them up and glanced at their paper covers. The top one showed the picture of a Krith, a particularly ugly and unpleasant-looking

Krith at that, and the book's title was *The Greatest Lie*, by Martin Latham, subtitled *How Uncounted Human Beings Have Been Duped by the Kriths into Assisting Them in Their Conquest of Paratime*. The back cover, embellished with a full-length portrait of a naked Krith standing over a huddled man, went on to say something like: "Here, for the first time in a single volume, is Martin Latham's full story of the Krithian plot to conquer humanity. How their lies are created and how men are led to believe them. How Krithian lies are reinforced by distortions of reality. What some men will do in the name of Krithian domination . . ." and so on like that.

The second book was smaller than the first and not as badly worn. On its cover were only four words in letters at least an inch and a half high: *What Is a Krith?*

Good question. I'd like to know the answer to that one myself.

The final volume showed a full-color holograph of a beautiful nude woman standing against a background of Eden-like surroundings. It was called *Paradise in Paratime* and was subtitled *Rewards for the Ultimate Treason*.

Propaganda, all of it. And I realized that I was just beginning to encounter it. These people obviously believed, or wanted to believe, that the Kriths—and we Timeliners too—were a menace, and I knew that I was going to be pelted with it until I yielded or at least appeared to yield. I supposed that reading these books would be a part of my indoctrination. Okay, I'd read them.

Even though the cover of *Paradise in Paratime* intrigued me the most, I put it aside for *The Greatest Lie*. That one looked like the chief propaganda work—and as I later found out it was virtually the bible of the Paratimers—so I figured I'd better read it first and try to get my own lies in order.

I hadn't got beyond the title page when the door opened.

G'lendal, too, was a very pleasant surprise. I had expected a middle-aged, stocky, hard-faced policewoman type. She was anything but that.

At least twenty years old, but certainly no older than twenty-five, G'lendal was a diminutive ebony statue of Aphrodite straight from one of the more sensual cults of my own Line.

About five feet tall, skin the color of black satin, hair long and black as interstellar space, a figure only partially hidden by the shimmering gown she wore, a figure whose proportions would have been impressive on a woman a foot taller than she was.

God, she's beautiful, I thought. Maybe the most beautiful woman I've ever seen in my life.

In her hand she carried a black case about the size and shape of a large overnight case.

"Good morning, Nardi," she said smiling.

"Hello, G'lendal," he replied, stumbling over his words as if he were as stunned by her as I was. "This is Eric Mathers."

I stood up.

"Good morning, Eric Mathers," she said, smiling, setting the case on the floor beside one of the chairs. "That's not your real name, is it?" There was no trace of an accent in the American English she spoke.

"No," I said as she sat down in the chair and I returned to the sofa.

"That's a name the Kriths gave you," she said. "There aren't any Kriths here. You can be honest with me. In fact, you must."

I looked at her for a long while without speaking.

"You know why I'm here, don't you?"

"I think so."

"Then let's be honest. You can start by telling me your real name."

Why not? I asked myself. There wasn't much point in pretending to be a British colonial when everybody knew I wasn't.

"Thimbron Parnassos," I said at last, and it was the truth.

"I think I shall call you Eric. It is easier to say."

"It's up to you."

"Now listen to me, Eric," she said earnestly. "We're not your enemies here unless you make us be. I only want to help you. Your whole life has been a series of lies and you had no way of knowing that you were being told lies. If you'll merely be open-minded about it, you'll see the truth."

"And what is this truth you want me to see?"

"That the Kriths are monsters determined to enslave the human race," she said slowly.

114

"That's kind of hard for me to swallow," I told her. "I've only seen them helping us."

"In due time it will all be explained to you. All I ask, all that any of us asks, is that you listen."

"Okay," I said. "I've been given to understand that if I don't, I'll probably get my head blown off."

"Probably," she said and smiled. "Now I'd like to run a few tests on you just to establish some reference points."

"Tests?"

"To establish truth indices, you might say. Will you cooperate?"

"Would it matter if I didn't?"

"I would prefer to use as few drugs as possible."

"Okay, let's get on with it."

G'lendal smiled again. "Very good, Eric."

She rose from the chair, placed her case on the table beside the sofa. So far she had a damned good bedside manner, and I couldn't help wondering what her manner was like *in* bed. She had that kind of look about her.

"First I'd like for you to take your clothes off and give them to Nardi," she said. "Then you may go into the bathroom and shave and shower, if you like. I'm sure it would make you feel better."

I didn't see much point in asking stupid questions and playing modest. The girl had spoken clearly enough—and Nardi had a gun in case I didn't do as she said. I undressed.

"Everything," she said, smiling when I got down to my shorts and paused for a moment. "I'm sorry if it embarrasses you, but it's necessary."

I nodded, unsnapped the shorts, and let them drop to the floor. I stood there as bare-naked as the day I was born, and it didn't seem to bother anyone but me. I suppose I'd been around the British too long.

"Roll them up and hand them to Nardi, please," G'lendal said, neither looking at me nor ignoring me as she opened her case and reached inside. "Your personal possessions—if you have any left—will be inspected and returned to you." She glanced over her shoulder at Nardi. "I assume that Scoti checked him," she said.

115

Nardi nodded. "He got all the dangerous stuff off him while he was unconscious." Nardi didn't look at me while he spoke. "He's an Augie, of course."

"Of course," G'lendal replied.

She had taken several small objects from her case and now held them in her hands.

"I assume that your augmentation control center is located between your shoulder blades?" she asked.

I nodded. I thought she could have found it easily enough even if I denied it.

"Hold still for a moment, please," she said. "This won't hurt at all, but it will render your augmentation controls useless."

She approached my naked back and pressed cold metal against it. There was a short shrill buzzing, and I felt something dying within me, electrobiological circuits being killed. As she said, it didn't hurt—at least not physically. I felt as though I had lost a part of me.

"That's all there is to it," she said, stepping away. "You're an ordinary man now, Eric. Try to remember that."

I didn't speak.

"You may go shave and shower now," she said. "The bathroom is fully equipped."

14

G'LENDAL

When I came back into the room, my body still damp and my face still tingling from the odd shaver that seemed to dissolve my whiskers, a wet towel wrapped around my waist, G'lendal was assembling something on the table that I took to be a lie detector of some sort.

"Feel better?" she asked.

"Yes, some," I said, "but I could use some sleep." Though my senses were dulled from lack of sleep, G'lendal had dulled them even more by removing my augmentation. As she said, I was an ordinary man now, though I didn't resent her having done it. I would have done the same to an augmented captive.

"This won't take long," she said. "Then you can sleep as long as you like. Please take off that towel and sit down in this chair." She pointed with a long-nailed finger.

"You need any help?" Nardi asked.

"No, just stay where you are," G'lendal answered. Then to me, "Your wounds need attending to."

"I wouldn't object," I told her, feeling the tingling along my side from the bullet graze and the ache in the back of my head where Scoti had slugged me.

"Very well," the black girl said, fishing another kit from her case. "Hold still."

She sprinkled a bluish powder on the graze wound on my side and then covered it with a transparent adhesive bandage that seemed to melt into my flesh. I suppose that she did about the same to the back of my head, though I was unable to observe.

"That feel better?"

"Yes, I think so."

"Good," she said. "Now I'm going to tape some electrodes to your body. Don't be alarmed. They won't hurt."

I didn't answer, but then it seemed that I didn't need to.

From the thing on the table she carried a bunch of thin wires to where I sat, laid them across the back of the chair and began attaching the wires to my skin with a silvery-looking tape. One to each temple. One to each side of my neck. One on each shoulder. One above my heart. One just above my navel. One on each hip. One to the inside of each thigh. Even though her motions were smooth and professional, the touch of her woman's fingers excited me.

After she was finished, G'lendal stood behind me for a moment, tinkering with the lie-detection device. Nardi sat on the bed across the room watching me disinterestedly as if this were something he had seen a number of times before and wasn't too excited by.

"Now hold still just a moment," the black-skinned girl said.

Then something cold touched my left shoulder. There was a hissing sound and a sudden moistness entering my flesh.

"What was that?" I asked.

"Don't be alarmed," she said—I wasn't. "It was just a mild relaxer. I know better than to try to use any of the so-called truth serums on you Timeliners."

"Okay."

"Now I'm going to ask you a few questions," she said. "You can answer them any way you like. Right now you don't have to tell the truth unless you want to."

I'm sure that G'lendal knew that my training and conditioning, independent of my now inoperative augmentation circuits, could fool the lie detector, but she was going to try anyway. Okay, I thought, let's play your silly game.

"What is your name?" she asked.

"Thimbron Parnassos." My mind and body automatically gave the device a truthful response. But then it would have if I'd said Hieronymus Merganthaler.

118

"How old are you?"

"Thirty-three." Truthful response.

"When were you born?"

"2294 as we figure it at home. 1938 local time." Truthful response.

"Where were you born?"

"Sibyl, North Ionnia." Truthful response.

"Please equate that with some location in this Paratime."

"West Cheshire, England, near Hoylake." Truthful response—which it was.

Then—I supposed at the time that the sensation I felt in my mind was caused by the drugs she had injected me with. I still find it almost impossible to describe the feeling. It was, maybe, as if the top of my skull had been painlessly opened and someone were tickling my brain with a feather or maybe a very gentle puppy were sniffing at my gray matter. It was not really an unpleasant sensation, but it was one that I did not understand and that disturbed me.

"How long have you been in the hire of the Kriths?" G'lendal asked.

"Fourteen years."

"And what is your present position?"

"Mercenary soldier, absolute rank roughly equal to that of a colonel in the British Army."

"What do you think of the Kriths?"

"In twenty-five words or less?" I asked.

"In as many as it takes."

"Okay. Personally, I don't care for them. I mean, as individuals. There's something about them that I just can't bring myself to like. But what they're doing is good. It isn't just altruism—I'd suspect *that*. They're looking out for themselves, but to do that, they've got to help us humans. They're acting in their own rational self-interest to prevent their destruction by alien invaders two thousand years from now—and they're saving mankind in the process. How's that?"

"That's fine."

"How many words?"

"I didn't count."

The feathery tickling inside my head had now become a

plucking, a chicken, gently at first, then with more force was pecking at my brain in search of kernels of corn. I didn't like it.

"Have you ever had doubts about their intentions?"

"Yes." Truthful response.

"Please explain."

"Well, I think anyone at at some time or other will have a few doubts about anything he believes. It's only human. And I've had some vague, random doubts, but there's never been any real reason for them. Everything the Kriths have ever told me has been, sooner or later, supported by objective fact."

"Everything?"

"Yes, everything I can think of."

"What about the Cross-Line Civilization in the far Temporal East?"

"What about it?"

"Tell me about it."

Suddenly I had a strange sensation of disassociation, as if I had left my body for an instant and were now standing or sitting to the rear of it looking at my own back. For less than a heartbeat I saw the chair in which I sat, the back of my injured head, my own naked shoulders, the wires from G'lendal's lie detector trailing across the chair to where they were taped to my body. Then it was over, and all I felt was a vague swimming in my head.

"What about it in particular?" I was asking. "There's a lot of ground to cover when you start talking about fifty Lines that have blended into a single civilization."

"No," G'lendal said suddenly. "Forget about it. We'll go on to something else." She paused for a moment. "Why did you and your companions kidnap Count von Heinen and his wife?"

"For information."

"What kind of information?"

"About nuclear weapons. We wanted Von Heinen so that we could probe him about. . . ."

It happened again. This time more definitely and for a longer period of time. I— the consciousness of *me*—was sitting in a chair—no, on the sofa beside the lie detector, watching the dials and meters and glancing frequently at the back of my head. There was another consciousness there with me, but I could tell

120

nothing about it, other than the fact that it was there.

I tried to will the eyes I looked through down at the hands of the body I wore, but before I could tell whether I was having any luck . . .

I was back in my own body.

"What the hell are you doing to me?" I demanded, leaping out of the chair and turning to face G'lendal.

"I'll stop," she said, her face just barely showing shock. Her hand snapped a switch.

"It's off now," she said, looking directly back into my eyes.

"What is that thing?"

"I can't tell you," G'lendal said. "I'm sorry. Please sit back in the chair, and I'll remove the electrodes."

I did as she said and a moment later felt her fingers on my temples and then sudden pull of hair as she jerked the tape away.

"It's a kind of mine probe, isn't it?" I asked.

"No, not really," she answered, pulling the electrodes from my neck.

But it was, I was sure. Not the kind of mind probes *we* used. Ours recorded the electromagnetic fields of the brain, interpreted them into words and symbols, recorded them on paper and tape, analyzed them with computers. Her machine, though, I thought, did something more direct. It actually entered the mind and dug for what it wanted, and in that way maybe it could bypass my conditioning. So it seemed to me at the time, anyway.

When G'lendal had finished removing the electrodes she had taped to my body, she packed all her gear carefully in the case and then turned to look at Nardi, who had sat quietly on the bed all this time.

"I'm finished with most of it, Nardi," she said. "You may go now."

Nardi looked doubtful for a moment. "You want me to leave you here alone with him?"

"Yes," G'lendal said. "I don't think he's going to harm me."

"You never know," he told her.

"I'm safe enough."

"Okay, you're the boss." He rose, slipping his pistol into a

121

holster somewhere inside the breast of the one-piece suit he wore. "You know where to call if you need me."

"I know," she said.

Nardi left the room, and I remained sitting in the chair, waiting for her to tell me what to do next.

"It's all over, Eric," she said. "I just want to talk to you for a few minutes if you don't mind."

I shrugged.

Nardi's cigarettes were still lying on the table where I had left them. G'lenda picked up the pack, drew one out, put it in her mouth and then offered the pack to me.

I had to get up out of the chair to accept and suddenly remembered that I was still naked.

"Look," I said, taking the offered pack, "I'd feel a damned sight more comfortable if I had something on."

"I'm sorry," she said. "They haven't delivered you anything yet, and your own clothes are gone. You could take a sheet off the bed and wrap that around yourself."

I smiled. "That would probably be more foolish than my nakedness."

"As you wish," she answered. "Your being unclothed certainly doesn't bother me. In my own Paratime clothing doesn't have the importance nor nudity the taboo it does here. We wear clothing or go nude as we wish. I am quite accustomed to seeing naked men."

I nodded, lit the cigarette in my mouth and threw the pack and the matchbook back to the table.

"You're a good-looking man, anyway, Eric," G'lendal said. "You shouldn't be ashamed of being seen naked."

I couldn't help smiling at that. "I'm not ashamed," I said. "It's just that I've adapted to local customs. I've spent time in more than one Timeline where birthday suits were the uniform of the day."

"Okay, then consider that you're in one of them now," G'lendal said. "In fact, just to make you more at home, I'll shuck this stupid thing I've got on. I usually don't wear clothing unless it's required anyway."

For a moment I started to object, then realized the foolishness of it. If this girl wanted to be naked in front of me—and risk the possible consequences of it—who the hell was I to stop her? I'm no idiot. This interrogation might turn out to be more enjoyable than I had suspected at first.

The garment that G'lendal wore was, as I said, a very simple thing and was held around her by a single fastener down the front. A touch of her finger to the top of the fastener and the dress fell apart. A single, simple movement, a throwing back of her lovely shoulders, a shrug, and it slipped off her and fell to the sofa. She casually knocked it to one side. She didn't have anything on under it.

At various times and places in my life I've seen a lot of nude women, but I can easily and honestly say that I have never before seen one as beautifully constructed as she was, this black-skinned girl from some Timeline to the far West. Her breasts were large and high and full, tight mounds of flesh that needed no support. Her waist was thin, her hips were gently rounded and inviting, and she had the legs of a dancer. She was sensuality incarnate.

"How's your racial prejudice, Eric?" she asked smiling as she sat back down on the sofa and looked at me.

"No worse than the next man's."

"That's no answer."

"There are no racial problems in my Homeline," I said. "And I've been around enough to know that people are people, good or bad, regardless of what color they are. Really, it's something I don't think very much about."

G'lendal smiled. "That's good." She paused. "How about some breakfast?"

There was a big hollow spot in my stomach, though I had nearly forgotten about it. "Okay," I finally answered.

G'lendal rose with a gentle, graceful, flowing motion and walked across the room to the thing on the wall that I had assumed to be some kind of intercom.

My eyes followed every motion of her body and I hoped that things were going to turn out as I was beginning to think they were going to turn out. I wasn't *that* tired.

She punched a button and spoke a few words in a language that I didn't understand, though there may have been something French about it. Another voice replied. G'lendal spoke again, then smiled, apparently satisfied and then came back to the sofa where I was now sitting. She sat down beside me, lit another cigarette.

"This isn't such a bad place here, Eric," she said.

"The best damn prison I ever saw."

"This isn't a prison, Eric. And you're not our enemy unless you want to be."

"I don't want to be *your* enemy," I said, "but I'm not sure I can help it."

"Just be open-minded about it, will you?" she asked. "We'll do everything we can to show you the truth."

She dropped her cigarette into an ashtray on the table and turned to look at me, her hand gently coming to rest on my shoulder.

I looked into her deep, dark eyes for a long while, then placed my own hands on her shoulders.

"You know what you're asking for, don't you?"

"I know exactly what I'm asking for," she said, letting her eyes run the length of my naked body.

One of my arms slipped around her shoulder, the other around her waist, and I pulled her to me, her large, soft breasts crushing against my chest, her lips against mine.

There was fire in her mouth and in her body and in her hand that slipped down my back and to my hips and then around. I pulled her as tightly to me as I could, half swallowing her tongue as it came into my mouth.

We sat that way for a long while, the heat of our excited bodies mingling. One of my hands went between us, briefly cupping one of her breasts, then slid down her stomach.

Her lips broke away from mine, and she whispered softly, hoarsely, "The bed, Eric. The bed."

I picked her up effortlessly and carried her across the room, gently deposited her on the bed. For a moment I stood there above her, looking down at the dark, beautiful body. Her eyes were wide, eloquent, saying, Take me, Eric. God, take me.

Her mouth was open, her great breasts rising and falling heavily, breathing quickly, almost desperately as if her body were burning oxygen faster than she could breathe it in.

I felt one of the great, dark mounts of her breasts, pinching its nipple between my fingers, then lowering my mouth to it, nibbling with my teeth, then closing my lips around it. My other hand, the right, slipped down her body, down across the smoothness of her stomach to the clump of black hair that grew between her thighs, down to the soft, warm, inviting moistness of her.

"Slowly," she said. "We have all the time in the world."

15

THE GREATEST LIE

When I awoke, I was alone, and for a few moments I wondered if the whole thing had been a dream. Then I knew it hadn't been, smiled to myself and wondered what was going to happen to me next.

It wasn't until I sat up that I noticed the tray of food sitting on a table beside the bed and the clothing draped across the end of the bed. Well, someone was thinking about me.

First I dressed in slacks and sport shirt of the local Line and then ate the still warm and rather conventional, by local standards, breakfast of bacon and eggs, coffee, orange juice, toast and jelly that had been provided for me.

Then I lay back on the bed and waited to see what was next. I had a long wait.

Since there wasn't much of anything else to do, I lit a cigarette and picked up the three books that had been left in the room. After looking at the inviting cover of *Paradise in Paratime* and decided that G'lendal was even better looking than the lovely girl on the cover, I put it aside for *The Greatest Lie*.

The author, a fellow named Martin Latham, claimed to have been born in one of the Romano-Carolingian Lines where the Kriths had made their presence known quite some time ago. He told a little about his own Line—all of which seemed to be true since I had been there or to one very close to it—and then went on to tell how he discovered the "Lie," as he called it.

Since the "Lie" was one of the things that was stressed over and over again the whole time I was at Staunton, I might as well tell you about Latham's so-called discovery of it as well as I can remember it. I wish I had a copy of the book, and I'd give you this verbatim, but I don't. But it went something like this:

Latham showed an early inclination toward mathematics and technology. He had the soul of an engineer, but the mind of a pure research scientist and was ripe for the picking by the Kriths.

By the time he had finished the equivalent of secondary school the Kriths and their agents had already approached him about joining the Timeliners, with Academy instruction and training in skudder engineering. Latham jumped at the chance. And entered the Krithian Academy nearest his Homeline. While he was there, he showed such an amazing ability that he was allowed to do something almost unprecedented in the Academy: He took a "split major" in engineering—advanced electronics and skudder engineering—and graduated with honors in both fields.

The Kriths put him to work at once in one of their vast engineering labs in some unspecified, uninhabited Line. Latham loved his work. When he wasn't working on skudder design or tinkering with the most sophisticated electronic gear in all the Lines, he was spending his spare time reading anything he could put his hands on related to his fields and ultimately became interested in contratime communications. He requested that he be allowed to study the works of the Indus Line scientists who had actually established the contratime link that had informed the Kriths of the future menace of alien invasion. He was refused.

The story gets rather complicated and filled with cloak-and-dagger overtones along in here, but to simplify it, Latham's interest grew as he was more strongly refused the data he wanted. After a while he pretended that he had lost interest, though by this time he had become determined to learn everything he could about contratime communications, no matter what it took. Several years passed before he was able to lay his hands on the data he wanted.

One of his assignments led him cross-Lines to do some research in an area of the Lines through which skudders had always had some difficulty passing. On his way back to his base he was able to fake a malfunction in his skudder right in the middle of the Indus Lines. The defective skudder was examined by Indus technicians, and Latham was told that it would take some time to effect the repairs—his "faking" of a malfunction had been done well—and since no other skudders were available for his use, he would have to lay over for a few days—which is exactly what he wanted.

Latham managed to have dinner with one of his Indus colleagues and during the course of the dinner, by a stratagem I don't recall at the moment, he was able to steal the engineer's library access card, top-level. The next day Latham plugged into the planet-wide computer library and, pretending to be the engineer whose card he had stolen, asked for full data on the contratime experiments. The library produced a vast amount of data which Latham was given in the form of microdots which he hid on his person.

He secretly returned the library card to its owner, who had not yet discovered its loss, waited until his skudder was ready, and then returned to his base Line.

About half the information he had gotten from the Indus library was in Shangalis, while the remainder, and apparently the most important portion of it, was in the local Indus language. Before he could really get into it, he was forced to learn Indus in secret. This took him nearly a year, and more than once he was almost exposed, but finally Latham learned Indus and went back to his data.

According to his book, it didn't take him long to discover why the data had been kept from him. They were phony! The mathematics, while very complex and involved, led around in a circle and laboriously established nothing whatsoever. The experiments had been performed, the conclusions had been reached and the actual contact with the future had been . . . *faked*!

At first Latham didn't believe it. He checked and rechecked and re-rechecked his figures. And always came to the same final conclusions.

Stealing equipment from his own lab, he set up some of the experiments that the Indus scientists had performed—and their ultimate conclusions were validated. The whole theory of contratime communiaations fell apart. It just wouldn't work. Time was closed, forward and backward. The future could not talk to the past! It was that simple; the whole thing was a tremendous fraud!

Latham was in a quandary. What the hell was he going to do? Go to the Kriths? No, it was their plot, but for what reasons he couldn't even guess. Tell other humans? Who would believe him? And word would eventually get back to the Kriths—and then what would happen?

Finally, in desperation and fear, Latham stole a four-man skudder from the lab's skudder pool, removed the governor and the telltale from it, set its controls for the T-West and started out, intending to travel as far as the fully charged power cells would carry him, find men who had never been contacted by the Kriths, and tell them the whole story.

His skudder ran out of power in the Romano-Albigensian Lines, as he called them, far to the West of any Line that the Kriths and Timeliners had yet reached. There he found a civilization that had already developed their own skudders independently of the Kriths—and were moving East. He told them about the Kriths and the Timeliners and the "Lie" and that the Kriths were moving toward them.

The Albigensians began to prepare to meet the aliens—and save mankind from possible enslavement.

Well, in a large nutshell, that's the way the first part of Latham's book read.

Quite a story, but was any of it true? And if it was true, was that any proof that Latham was right? It seemed far more likely to me, giving it all the benefit of the doubt, that Latham had made an honest mistake—and had panicked. At least I saw no reason to believe one man whom I had never met, and who might not even exist, when all the evidence of my life pointed in just the opposite direction.

To hell with it, I said, and got out of bed and began to pace the floor and wonder what was going to happen next. I wished that G'lendal would come back for some more of her delightful "interrogation," but I didn't really expect *her* the next time. I was right.

The door opened and the tall, thin, corpse-white form of the man called Mica entered the room, dressed now in a gray business suit of this Line.

"Hello, Captain Mathers," he said.

I nodded to him, lit the last cigarette in the pack that Nardi had left, and sat down on the end of the bed.

"I hope you slept well," Mica said, "and that your breakfast was agreeable."

"Yeah," I said between puffs of smoke.

"G'lendal is very taken with you, you know."

"What?" I asked. "Did she tell you. . . ."

"Enough," Mica said, shrugging. "No intimate details, of course, but enough. Quite a girl, she."

"Well, did she get what she wanted?" I demanded angrily.

Mica laughed aloud, a hollow, humorless laugh. "Yes and no—er, should I call you Thimbron or Eric?"

"Call me whatever you like."

"Please," he said, spreading his hands, "don't be angry with us. As G'lendal told you, we are not your enemies unless you force us to be."

"Shit!"

"Come now. We can talk like rational men, can we not?"

"Okay, talk."

Mica was silent for a few long moments, his deep eyes scanning the room, then stopping at the open book on the table. "I see you have been reading Martin Latham's book," he said.

"Yes," I replied, thinking that if I were going to try to fool Mica and his gang into believing that I was swallowing their story I might as well begin now, but very gradually. It had better be believable. I didn't figure they'd be easy to fool.

"What do you think of it?" he asked.

"It's kind of hard to swallow, what I've read of it."

"How much have you read?"

"The first part, Latham's story of how he discovered the 'Lie' and you people."

"Ah," Mica sighed. "It is all quite startling to you, is it not?"

I nodded.

"It is as if, for example, an Englishman of this Paratime were suddenly told that there was no such place as China."

"Yes, sort of like that, I suppose."

"Let me go on," Mica said. "I would like to follow this analogy out. May I?"

"Why not?"

"Very well. Our hypothetical Englishman has been to America and the Continent, of course. He is a well-traveled man, and educated. He has met Chinese and seen pictures of China and knows fellow Englishmen who claim to have been to China—but he himself has never been there. *Still,* all evidence points to the fact that there is such a place as China. It never occurs to him to doubt for a moment the existence of China. Now what would happen," Mica asked, "if someone, in all seriousness, were to tell him that China does not exist?"

"He'd laugh in his face."

Mica smiled, nodded, then said, "Take this fantastic Cross-Line Civilization that you believe to exist far to the Temporal West. Have you ever been there, Captain Mathers?"

"No."

"Yet you know it exists. How?"

"Like your Englishman, I've seen pictures of it. I've spoken to people who have been there."

"Have you ever met anyone from those Lines? Any human natives, I mean."

I thought for a moment, honestly trying to rake up memories. "No, not that I can recall. I've met Kriths from there, though."

"No," Mica said, "let us ignore the Kriths for a moment. You have never met a human being who was native to those Lines. Now, the stories you have heard, the pictures, the tapes, the books you have read, could they have been faked? Could they have been lies?"

"Well, yes, I suppose they *could* have been. But it would have to be an enormous conspiracy to pull something like that off."

"Granted, but then, in the final analysis, all you have to prove that there *is* such a wonderful and beautiful Cross-Line Civilization is the word of the Kriths. Is this not so?"

"Yes, but not quite the way you mean it."

"Why not? Tell me, do you like the Kriths?"

"Yes and no."

"That is hardly an adequate answer, Eric. Do you know of a single Krith that you personally like as—well, as a person?"

"No, but then there are a lot of people I don't like either."

"Surely. But do you understand them? The Kriths? I mean, do they act from the same motives as human beings? Can you translate their thoughts into human terms?"

"No, not really. They don't think the way we do, I suppose, but then I don't think we should expect them to. They aren't people, but I trust them anyway."

"Why?"

"Well, they've never given me any reason not to."

"Ah," Mica sighed. "You're saying then that you have never *caught* them in a lie."

"I suppose you could take it that way."

"Then, in the final analysis, you believe in the Cross-Line Civilization simply because you have never caught the Kriths lying to you. That is hardly proof that they are *not* lying. All you can really be sure about is that, if they are lying, they are lying so well and so consistently that you have never caught them at it. Right?"

"I can't accept that."

"I do not expect you to at this stage." Mica paused. "Let us take Martin Latham. You have never met him, so you really have no reason to believe his words or even that he is a real person. He could be our 'Lie.' Is this so?"

"Yes, I suppose so."

"I have met him," Mica said, "and I believe him. Now you have my word that what Latham says is true, as opposed to the word of the Kriths that contratime communications exists. You must accept one of us on faith. Which will it be? You need not answer that yet. Not for a while, at least."

There was something almost sinister in his last sentence, but before I could comment, there was a gentle rapping on the door. Mica did not turn but called over his shoulder, "Come in." His eyes never left my face.

The door clicked, swung outward, and Sally and Scoti came into the room. They were both now dressed in the conventional clothing of this Line: Sally in a white blouse and a full green skirt; Scoti in a dark business suit. And more than ever Sally reminded me of Kristin.

"Good morning, Eric," Sally said. "How are you feeling?"

"Well enough," I answered, then nodded to Scoti.

"I hope you hold no hard feelings, old man," Scoti said. "For that bump on the head, I mean. I was just doing what I had to do."

I didn't answer.

"I have just been having a little chat with Captain Mathers," Mica said.

"And . . ." Scoti said expectantly.

"Calm yourself, Scoti," Mica said. "He is at least trying to be honest with us."

"That's all we ask, Eric," Sally said, sitting down on the sofa. "We don't expect you to give us any military secrets."

"I don't believe I have any you don't know about already," I said.

Sally looked so young and fresh and innocent that I found it hard to believe she was the same woman I had kidnapped—or tried to kidnap. She—well, I liked her.

"That doesn't matter," she was saying. "We just want you to listen to us and then judge for yourself what is true."

"Okay," I said. "I'll listen. I have a pretty good idea what will happen to me if I don't."

There was silence in the room for a few moments.

"Let me ask you a question," I said at last.

"Very well," Mica replied.

"Okay, suppose that what you're telling me is true. Suppose that there's really no Cross-Line Civilization and suppose that the whole contratime communications business is a fraud, then why are the Kriths going to all this trouble?"

Mica smiled, looked at the other two, then back to me.

"I was waiting for you to ask that, Captain Mathers," he said.

"So answer it."

"I wish I could."

That one sort of startled me. I had fully expected Mica and his gang to have a glib explanation of the Krithian logic behind the great plot they were postulating.

"I won't try to lie to you, Mathers," Mica said. "You are too intelligent a man for that. In all honesty we do not know why the Kriths are doing what they are doing. We know that they are telling the greatest lie in all history, in all the histories of all the Paratimes put together, but we really do not know why. We merely know that they are."

For a few moments I was at a loss for words. This wasn't working out as I had expected.

"Look at it this way, Mathers," Scoti said. "When you catch someone telling you a lie and you don't know why, you've got to assume that his purposes aren't good. It could be very dangerous to do otherwise, right?"

"Yes, I guess so."

"That is our assumption," Mica said. "We do not *know* that they mean mankind ill, but they are doing their best to profoundly alter the course of history in as many Paratimes as they can. They must have some reason, some logic of their own for doing it and all we can do is guess at what it is—and do what we can to stop it until we can learn why."

"Okay," I said. "If what you're saying is true, then I guess you'd have to act that way." For some reason I had the sudden feeling that Mica and Scoti honestly and truly did believe what they were saying. But then you never can tell about feelings, can you?

"We cannot tell you why the Kriths are lying, only that they are. And if you will let us, we will prove it to you," Mica said.

"Okay, prove it."

"That will take some time," Mica said, "but now I think you are going to let us have that time." He glanced at the watch on his wrist. "I have other responsibilities to attend to, but I'll see that additional books and tapes are sent to you. You can study them at your leisure. Is there anything else you would like?"

"Yes, some cigarettes, if you can get them."

"Of course," Mica said. "I will see to it at once." He rose. "Scoti, will you come with me?"

The other man nodded.

"I will see you later, Sally?" Mica asked.

"Yes," Sally said, glancing up at the tall, thin man, an expression on her face that I could not identify but that puzzled me. What was her relationship to him?

In a few moments the door closed behind the two men, and Sally and I were left alone in the room. It was a rather tense and awkward situation at first.

"I don't hold it against you," she said. "What you did. You were only doing your job as you saw it."

"I'm glad you look at it that way," I told her. "What about your husband?"

"Albert?" She smiled an odd smile. "He'll recover."

"You're glad of that?"

"I don't suppose it matters now. He won't be of much use to us anymore, it appears."

"Oh?"

"He was just a tool, as far as I'm concerned, and since it appears that the Kriths will find a way to destroy the Imperial nuclear project, we will just have to start another, without Albert."

I didn't go into it any further, either about Von Heinen or about the Kriths' destroying their Baltic plant. I was curious, but the answers could wait.

We were silent for a long while before I asked the next question.

"How long have they been here?"

"The Paratimers? Oh. . . ." She thought for a moment. "About fifteen years. They contacted my father when they first arrived. They've been working with us ever since."

"Who's this *we*?"

"The Mad Anthony Wayne Society."

"Uh-huh," I grunted. "What's their relationship to the Holy Roman Empire?"

Sally chewed on her lower lip for a moment. "Minor," she said after a while. "Only two years ago did they actually let them know who they were."

"Then the Holy Romans know about the Paratimes *and* the Kriths?"

"A little," she answered. "They haven't told them everything."

"Why?"

"They're on *our* side."

"Oh, and you believe everything they say?"

"Yes."

"Why?"

Sally smiled. "Now you sound like Mica interrogating one of our prisoners."

"I'm sorry, but I'm trying to learn what I can."

"I know. Yes, I believe them because, well, it makes sense to me, what I can see of it. They're human beings and the *things* you're working for aren't. That in itself seems reason enough."

"I suppose you've got a point there."

"Let me make another one, Eric."

"Go on."

"Our world is divided today between three, oh, call it four, if you want to count Spain—our world is divided between these empires and not a one of them is worth a damn. I suppose, if I could really be objective about it, maybe the British are no worse than the Imperials, maybe even a little better since there are a lot of British people, some in the aristocracy, who don't approve of the way the king has treated the colonies. But, all in all, ninety percent of the human race is in a state not much better than slavery and the rest rule them, except for a few of us, like the ARA and the Mad Anthony Wayne Society, who still believe that people have the ability and, yes, the God-given right to rule themselves.

"Okay," she went on, "now look at what is happening. Who are your Kriths supporting? The British Empire. The greatest slaveowner in the history of the world—my world, at least. And who are the Paratimers helping? Us, the rebels who want to see an end to *all* slavery—the fact that we're working with the Imperials right now is only incidental to the whole thing. We'll take care of them once we've beaten the British. The Paratimers will see to that. But honestly answer me: Whose cause is more moral? The Kriths'? Or Mica's and Scoti's and the other, Paratimers'?''

"On the face of it I suppose it looks right to you," I said. "But you can't see the whole picture."

"Can you?"

"Better than you can, I think."

"Then you tell me how it's moral to support tyrants. Or is your world ruled by a monarchy?"

I smiled. "No. My people are the ones who invented the republic in the first place, remember?"

"The Greeks?" Sally asked.

I nodded and then went on, "Well, if the Imperials are beaten by the British, your world stands a better chance of becoming free in the long run. If the Holy Romans win, you're in for a long period of tyranny and warfare that makes the present day look mild by comparison."

"How do you know?" she asked.

I paused for a moment. How could I answer her without falling back on the word of the Kriths? And, then, they hadn't figured on the Americans having an advanced technology behind them. Maybe my head was beginning to spin a little by then.

"You don't need to say it," she said. "You just have to accept the word of the Kriths, on faith, that that's the way it's going to turn out."

"Yes, I suppose so," I said defensively. "But I can show you the histories of other Lines where it has worked out exactly the way they said it would."

"That's still accepting their word. They wrote the books, didn't they, or at least supervised their writing?" She paused. "One of our great patriots was also something of a philosopher and once he said, 'A bird in the hand is worth two in the bush.' And at best your *bush* is only hypothetical."

"I don't suppose there's any point in trying to argue with you."

Sally smiled. "I don't want to argue with you, Eric. I want to be your friend."

"That's what everybody tells me."

She rose, smiled again. "I really must go. I'll come back to see you later."

"I'll be looking for you."

And then she was gone, and I was alone in the room again, and I wondered and wondered and wondered. . . .

16

AGAIN G'LENDAL

A short time after Sally left, a panel in the wall below the intercom slid back revealing a receptacle in which sat two cartons of cigarettes, a stack of books and video tapes, and a small tape player and monitor.

Lighting a cigarette, I placed the tapes and books and player on one of the tables and scanned the titles on the tape boxes. Apparently Mica was giving me the whole propaganda story in one lump.

Well, I decided, I might as well get into it. If I were going to fool them into believing that I had swallowed their story, I had better learn my lines well. I spent the rest of the day reading books and viewing tapes.

Two meals later, both of which arrived via the wall receptacle, I was beginning to feel a little sleepy and the healing wound in my side was giving me a little pain. I didn't know what time it was, but I decided that I wasn't going to have any more visitors that day and I might as well try to get some sleep.

I undressed, laying my clothes across one of the chairs, pulled back the bed's covers, and was about to snap off the light when there was a rapping on the door.

What does a prisoner say when someone knocks on his cell door? This prisoner said, "Who is it?"

"G'lendal," answered a feminine voice through the door. "May I come in?"

"Sure," I replied. "I don't think I could stop you even if I wanted to—and I don't."

The door buzzed open, and the beautiful black girl came into the room, this time without her case of instruments or very much else, except for the adjustable electronic key she was dropping into a skirt pocket.

This time Staunton's lovely chief interrogator was not wearing her shimmering gown, which I had taken for an odd and pleasant sort of uniform. Her clothing, if I can call it that, consisted of a simple red skirt that began well below her navel and ended less than halfway to her knees. And that was all she had on. Even her feet were bare.

I was sitting on the edge of the bed, naked, and reached for my pants.

"No," she said, allowing the door to close behind her. "Don't get dressed unless you want me to help you undress again."

I'm not sure that I approved of a girl being that forward about her intentions, but then, on the other hand, I didn't disapprove either. She was pretty damned honest about what she wanted, and that in itself was refreshing after the local girls I had met.

"I see you're about to go to bed, Eric," she said. "I won't bother you if you wish to sleep."

"I'd rather be bothered," I told her.

She smiled, crossed the room, sat down in a chair near the bed, and produced a cigarette from a pocket of her skirt. I got up to give her a light, slightly embarrassed at my nakedness, and then realized how foolish it was after last night.

"I wish I could offer you something to drink," I said.

"Let me offer it. Wine?"

"Okay."

She rose, crossed the room to the intercom, and spoke a few alien words into it. I may have caught something akin to the French words *vin* and *à l'aisa,* but I wasn't sure. She wasn't speaking French, but the languages might have been related.

Moments later the wall panel slid back, and a chilled bottle of white wine and two glasses appeared. The elaborate label bore Roman characters, but in a language I couldn't read, and—like the language she had spoken—I suspected it had evolved from Old French. That figures, I told myself. Romano-Albigensians, the Paratimers had said. I decided that I'd look into that a bit more when I had the time. Later.

G'lendal took the wine and the glasses and set them on the table near the bed. I waited until she had removed the cork and poured the wine into the glasses—then I grabbed her around the waist and pulled her to me.

"Wait, Eric," she gasped. "I want what you want and probably as badly as you want, but in my own good time. I'm not your sex slave."

"Am I yours?" I asked.

"Yes," she said, laughing, and handed me a glass of wine.

The wine had that kind of softness and mellowness that only good French wines can have, but it was warm in my throat when it went down, and I liked that too.

G'lendal broke away from my grasp, sat back down in the chair, and looked at me for a long while without speaking, sipping at her wine. I wondered what was going on inside her head and decided that I would probably never know.

"Would you like to talk for a while, Eric?" she asked at last.

"I had hoped you were here for pleasure, not business."

"I am, but I'm in no rush. I have all night. Do you have any appointments?"

I had to laugh at that even if it wasn't too funny.

She refilled our glasses, but still sat back in the chair apart from me.

"You're not from the same Line as Mica and Scoti, are you?" I finally asked since she seemed determined to talk.

"No," she said. "My home Paratime is nearly as far from theirs as is yours."

"Tell me about it."

"Oh, the divergence is a long way back, in the time of the New Kingdom of ancient Egypt, just after Ikhnaton was ruler."

"What happened, in your world, I mean?"

"No one is absolutely sure," she said. "My people had no written records then. Oh, there was a great folk migration, but what started it is still a matter of guesswork. My people came from central Africa, moved into the southern part of what was then Egypt, picked up the rudiments of Egyptian culture. After a while the D'hibas—that's what they came to call themselves; it means 'The Selected Ones'—set up their own kingdom and began a series of long wars with Egypt. They had infinite reserves to call up from Africa once a black nation had the sort of power it takes to fight against an empire like Egypt's and eventually, by sheer force of numbers, they destroyed the Egyptian culture. They drove the whites out of North Africa and established the D'hiba Empire.''

Empires, I thought, maybe with a little bitterness. Always empires.

She paused, smiled. ''I don't know too much history. That's not my field.''

''Go on, I'm interested.''

''Well, the D'hiba Empire expanded into the Tigris and Euphrates Valley and eventually engulfed the white civilization there as well. From then on there was constant warfare between the empire and the whites of the Mediterranean, but finally the blacks won and that pretty well ended white civilization in the Near East. The empire eventually expanded north and west into southern Europe, but left the far north to the white barbarians.

''Oh, it's a long story, Eric, and I don't want to try to tell it all to you. Just say that in my world things are reversed. It's the black people who built the world empires and established the first republics and discovered the western continents and colonized them and developed a technological culture—which the white north Europeans are just now doing.''

I smiled. Hers wasn't the only world in which the black races of Africa had dominated the Western world. Mostly, though, I thought, it was the whites who had done it—but that seems to have been an accident of time and location. The Near East and Europe are just better suited for high civilizations than is most of Africa—though I remembered the Trallian Lines where the first great city-state developed at the southern tip of Africa and its culture spread to dominate nearly half the world. But that was a hell of a long way off too.

''You could tell me about your world, Eric.''

"You probably know as much about it as I do by now."

"Not really," she said. "I know a little about it, but not as much as I'd like."

"Some other time."

"Okay."

By this time the wine bottle was half empty, though I could not remember having drunk that much. Still, there was a vague, not unpleasant spinning in my head.

When G'lendal emptied her glass and rose to refill it, I rose too, grasping her arm gently, taking the glass from her hand, and setting it on the table.

"That's enough wine, isn't it?" I asked.

She slowly turned to me. "Yes, I suppose it is."

My hand went to the buckle of her belt, fumbled awkwardly with it for a moment since I didn't understand its operation.

"This way," she said, guiding my hand with hers, placing my index finger into a tiny depression. "Push."

I did. The belt clicked and the skirt was loose around her waist. She shrugged, and it fell to the floor.

I stepped back for a moment, looked at her, still finding it almost impossible to accept a woman as perfectly built as she was. Those great, beautiful breasts of hers; the thinness of her waist; hips that were exactly the way hips ought to be.

"How do I look to you, Eric?" she asked.

"I've never seen anything more beautiful."

"Do you mean that?"

"I wouldn't be saying it if I didn't mean it, G'lendal," I told her. "I have never seen a more beautiful woman in my life. Never."

"I'm glad you mean it."

Yet I could not help wondering why this lovely creature was so desirous of me. My male vanity, of course, easily accepted the fact that she found me sexually desirable, but something above my ego told me that I certainly was but one man of the many available to her—and it didn't seem so likely that I was the only one she would want to go to bed with. And there was the fact that she was Staunton's chief interrogator and I knew very little yet of the Paratimers' methods of interrogation. My next

143

words came out almost against my will.

"G'lendal, is this standard procedure in your interrogation of new prisoners?"

"No, Eric," she said with slow deliberation and no trace of anger. "I don't make love with every male prisoner brought in."

I believed what she said, but I also believed that what she said was only part of the truth. She might not hop into bed with *every* male prisoner capable of carrying out the sex act, but. . . . To hell with it, I told myself. Did it really matter what her motives were, back down deep, as long as we both enjoyed what we were doing? Who did it hurt? Certainly not me. And at least she wasn't rationalizing love into what we had done the night before and what we were going to do now. It was pure and simple fun—"the friendliest thing two people can do"—whatever else there might be in her mind.

"What is it, Eric?" she asked.

"Nothing," I said, shaking my head and smiling.

"You still want to make love with me, don't you?"

I didn't speak. I let my lips and hands do it for me. She understood their language.

Something happened during that wild, exciting lovemaking that puzzled me, that disturbed me greatly and perhaps led me to understand a little better why G'lendal did what she did—though it certainly didn't do much to boost my ego.

While our bodies were locked together there on that bed, while the world quaked under the motions of our copulation, I again felt that strange sensation of disassociation that I had felt before, when she had been using that lie-detection device on me. Again I had the feeling that feathers were being brushed across my exposed brain, that something very soft and gentle was trying to find a way in.

Perhaps I could attribute it all to G'lendal's superb mastery of sexual pleasure, my sudden feeling that I was not just myself, but her as well, that I dwelt in both our bodies simultaneously and felt my own penetration as I penetrated her. But I don't think so. I think it was something very much more. And I think that

G'lendal's methods of interrogation were something rather more than the orthodox.

Before we reached our climaxes, the sensation left me, and I was again a man enjoying a very beautiful woman, nothing more.

And then, when the passionate storm was over and we lay spent, side by side on the bed, I wondered whether I had ever felt that gentle probing at all.

Then we slept.

17

MICA, SALLY, AND JONNA

The days that followed dragged by interminably. I read all the books and viewed all the tapes that Mica had sent me and even began some of them a second time. I felt that by this time I had pretty well absorbed the propaganda that I was supposed to absorb and could probably spout it back to Mica with the proper conviction. I was nearly ready to announce myself a convert.

During the day Mica, Scoti, and two or three others would visit me at intervals, mostly to answer questions, make suggestions, and point out avenues of thought I hadn't yet followed. At night there was G'lendal, though the previous sensations of "mind touching," of disassociation did not occur again—and I was able to nearly forget them as the nights went by in our passionate lovemaking.

I gradually pieced together the whole story of the Paratimers or at least that part of it made available for my consumption. In another nutshell, it was something like this:

In the Romano-Albigensian Lines from which Mica, Scoti, and about a third of the Paratimers in Staunton had come the European Renaissance that followed the fall of the original Roman Empire and the so-called Dark Ages had reached a full and early flower in early-thirteenth-century France under the religious heretics called the Albigensians, Arian Christians who denied the oneness of Jesus the Christ—the Messiah—and God the Father. After successfully resisting the persecutions of the Roman Church and finally raising an army of their own, the

Albigensians established their independence from both the emerging French nation and the orthodox church—and set about revolutionizing the world.

Despite the decades of religious war that finally led to the philosophical sundering of the Christian world, the Albigensians embarked on a serious program of learning. Their newly discovered and rediscovered knowledge spread like wildfire across Europe centuries earlier than it had in the world in which I now dwelt. The American continents were discovered in a steam-driven ship and fully colonized by Europeans within a century; a technological civilization evolved while Sally's people were still wondering what electricity was; world wars were fought; and finally, as the atomic age exploded across half the world and the first tentative steps to the stars were begun, the cultural descendants of the heretic Albigensians established a world at peace with itself.

Nearly a century ago, already with colonies on the moon and on Mars, with a starship abuilding in orbit around Earth, they discovered the parallel universes and set out on a cautious voyage of exploration. Then, less than thirty years ago, Martin Latham found them.

Under Latham's direction the Romano-Albigensian Paratimers explored eastward into Paratime, found that what he had said was true and set about undoing the work that the Kriths were doing.

By the time I was captured by them the Paratimers consisted of quite a large number of individuals from various Lines to the Temporal West, and all were devoted to the total and final destruction of the Kriths and all those who worked with them.

In the tunnels under Staunton better than a dozen Lines were represented, from Mica and Scoti of the original Romano-Albigensians to G'lendal of the D'hiba world.

There must have been a great deal of truth in these things, I told myself, as there is much truth in every great lie, no matter how well hidden and distorted it might be. I didn't doubt that in essence what I was told was true, for the most part, at least as far as it concerned the humans from the West, though I could not be so sure of their altruistic motives, as they denied the same motives on the part of the alien Kriths. And, of course, I was not ready to accept any of the things they said about the Kriths —though there were enough doubts in my mind by now so that I had some questions I was certainly going to ask Kar-hinter about when I saw him again—*if* I ever saw him again.

As far as Kar-hinter and the rest of the world outside Staunton were concerned, I was kept in total ignorance. What was happening in the war in Europe was unknown to me, though I could not force myself to feel very concerned. That had been a job when I was involved in it, but now I was no longer directly involved, and it didn't seem to matter too much. There were bigger things on my mind and, anyway, things would probably turn out pretty much as Kar-hinter had planned, though now he would have to do it without Count von Heinen and his American wife.

I wondered what kind of conclusions Kar-hinter had reached about my disappearance. He had known that I was waiting for him with the two captives, and he knew that we—Tracy, Kearns, and myself—had fought two short battles with men in an alien skudder. So, with very simple arithmetic, he would arrive at the conclusion that the man in the strange skudder had rescued the captives and had either killed me or taken me prisoner. I suspected that at that moment Kar-hinter was doing his damnedest to find out for sure. If I could only get a message to him.

Okay, then, I had decided early in my stay in the plush cell under the American earth, that was my sole objective: to get my hands on a radio and broadcast a message to Kar-hinter. But just how was I going to do that? Simple, convince the Paratimers that they had converted me, worm my way into their confidence, learn where there was a radio—and then do everything in my power to get a message out.

Simple. In a pig's eye!

When two weeks had passed—I assumed that it was about two weeks; I counted days in terms of G'lendal's violent, sensual lovemaking—I decided that I was ready to play the part of a convert.

Mica came in for his brief daily visit.

"How are you this morning, Captain Mathers?" he asked,

seating himself on the sofa, glancing through one of the books I had deliberately left there, several key passages underlined on the open pages.

"Well enough, I guess," I said.

"What's this?" he asked, noticing the passage I had underscored.

"What?" I asked in all innocence.

"This that you have marked," he said. Then he read aloud: " 'Despite their alien form, the Kriths have done surprisingly well in their efforts to win the confidence of humans. Their shrewd understanding of human psychology has enabled them to do this, playing on human vanity, while at the same time projecting a powerful father/hero image that even the strongest and most self-reliant men seem to find attractive. However, most humans cannot help feeling a basic animal revulsion to these creatures who, at best, can only be described as parodies of men.' "

Beside the passage I had put two or three exclamation points.

Mica smiled. "Is there a special significance to this, Mathers?"

"There is to me."

"And what is that?"

"I'm not really sure," I said. "It's just something that, well, puts into words what I've felt about the Kriths, I suppose."

"Few men *like* Kriths."

"I never said I liked them as individuals."

"But you admired them. Am I correct in using the past tense?"

"Hell, I don't know," I said. "You people have me so damned confused."

"Observe what you just said, Mathers, and keep it in mind. 'You people. . . .' We are people, human beings like you."

"That's hardly proof that you're telling the truth."

"We have been through all of this before."

"Yes, I know." I paused, wondered if I were going to be able to convince him. Maybe. I was about halfway ready to believe it myself. "Look, Mica, let me put it to you straight."

"I wish you would."

"Some of what you've been telling me is bound to be true,

149

and maybe all of it is. I don't know how much to believe of it yet, but give me time. I'll sort it all out eventually."

"What are you getting at?" Mica asked, the ghost of a smile flickering around the corners of his mouth as if all this were something he had heard before. Maybe so.

"I'm not sure. Except this. You damned people have put some pretty big doubts in my mind about the Kriths. Some damned big doubts. You've just about knocked the props out from under my world."

Mica smiled broadly at this. "G'lendal told me this two or three days ago, Eric," he said, using my first name, rare for him. "I have just been waiting for you to say it."

So I'd fooled G'lendal already. That was something.

"Damn it, Mica," I said, hoping this would convince him of my sincerity, "I'm not saying that I really believe you or that I'm ready to join you. All I said was that you've made me doubt."

"That is the first big step, Eric. The rest is downhill." He paused for a moment. "The world will never look the same to you again."

I'll be damned, I was thinking. He really does believe me.

"If I offered you transportation back to the place where Scoti picked you up, would you accept it?" he asked slowly.

"You mean set me free?" I asked, almost but not quite startled, then realized that it was an obvious trap that I wasn't going to let myself fall into. "I don't know. I mean, I'm not being treated badly here at all, but I would like my freedom. But as for going back with the Kriths right now, well, I don't think so. Not right now, anyway. I'd want to think about it and about what I'd do and about how I'd resolve these questions before I do anything."

"An appropriate answer," he said. "But do not worry. That is the last place you will be going, even if you were given your freedom. Excuse me for a moment."

He rose, crossed to the intercom on the wall, and spoke a few alien, French-sounding words into it. A voice that I tentatively tagged as Sally's answered back. Mica smiled.

When he turned back to me, he said, "This button will ring Sally's quarters."

"Okay."

"I just told her that you are to be given limited freedom in her custody. She requested that she be your 'guardian,' as it were, should you be put on probation. She will accompany you wherever you go outside your room, tell you about our little world here, and help you reach some further conclusions. I hope this is agreeable with you."

I smiled back at him. "Yes, quite agreeable."

"Now listen carefully, Captain Mathers," he said, his face suddenly becoming hard and cold. "You must remember that you are on a very limited probation. Sally has explicit orders what to do if you step out of line. I would hate for her to have to shoot you because of a stupid mistake. Ask her before you do *anything*."

I nodded understanding.

"Very well," he said. "She will be down before dinner to give you a Cook's tour, as they say, of Staunton. I probably will not see you again today." Then he smiled a halfway convincing smile. "Welcome to the human race, Eric."

When Sally arrived a couple of hours later, she was wearing tight shorts and an equally tight halter that matched the golden color of her hair and failed to cover her body very effectively. Though she wasn't the stunning beauty that G'lendal was, she was still a very attractive young woman and a person whose presence I enjoyed.

Yes, I told myself, I even *liked* Sally better than G'lendal. Sally was a fairy simple person. By this I don't mean stupid. She certainly wasn't that. But rather she was what she seemed to be, said what she felt, did what she believed to be the right thing to do. I could understand Sally and perhaps that was because I understood the culture in which she lived and where she had been formed. And she still reminded me of Kristin.

As for G'lendal—I understood absolutely nothing about her or about the world from which she had come. It really didn't exist for me. It was as unreal to me as the beautiful Cross-Line Civilization that the Kriths had told me about—and which, I suppose, I had even then begun to doubt.

But, back to Sally.

"Mica tells me that you're willing to listen to us," she said as the door closed behind her.

"Yes, I guess you could say that," I said, noticing the small bulge on her right hip under the shorts that obviously wasn't a part of Sally's anatomy—the bulge that could only be the shape of a very small handgun which I assumed was quite deadly.

"Would you like me to show you around?"

"Yes, I suppose so."

"Let's go then."

Staunton, I learned that afternoon, consisted of two major sections of underground burrows in addition to a dozen or so other tunnels separated from the two main ones. To my surprise I had been kept in the smaller one.

The Americans, the natives of this Line, dwelt and worked in the larger section that was, in reality, a small city built under the earth with a population nearing ten thousand. Here there were stores and shops and theaters and meeting halls and factories and machine shops and printing plants and weapons stores. And here the leaders of the American rebels directed the operations of their guerrilla war against the British overlords. This was, simply, the nerve center and store house of the American rebellion, A.D. 1971.

And I thought that Mica must have been pretty well convinced of my sincerity to allow me to see even that much—or pretty well convinced that I would never escape to tell anyone else what I had seen.

The other section, the smaller one where my cell was located, was devoted to the Paratimers' quarters and their Outtime devices. Most of this area was secret, and apparently even Sally didn't know all of what went on there, though she did show me what she was permitted to.

Unlike the American burrow city, that of the Paratimers consisted of little more than sleeping quarters, machine shops, laboratories, storerooms, one large cafeteria, and, of course, a few detention cells. For personal shopping and amusements the Paratimers visited the American section.

The Paratimers, as I said before, consisted of individuals from at least a dozen different Lines, and this was evidenced by the bizarre decorations and unusual costumes, or lack of cos-

152

tume, worn by the people in the Paratimer quarters. I learned later, however, that when visiting the American section they did their best to hide their difference. When in Rome. . . .

Sally officially lived in the American section, of course, but I somehow got the impression that she spent very little time there. This, added to the fact that I had already suspected that there was some kind of relationship between her and Mica, aroused an uncomfortable feeling of jealousy in me. But what reason did I have for feeling that? Sally certainly owed me nothing—and what did I owe her?

Other than my life, perhaps. . . .

No one, either in the American or Paratimer sections, showed us any special attention, though I got the impression that everyone knew Sally and they all were very glad to have her back with them and not across the sea in the Holy Roman Empire where she had spent the previous year as the wife—in name, at least—of Count Albert von Heinen.

The tour ended in the cafeteria in the Paratimer quarters, where we joined perhaps half a thousand people having their dinner.

When we had finished eating Sally told me that she would have to take me back to my quarters now. She had things she had to do that evening. She did not say that she was going to be doing those things with Mica, but I certainly got that impression.

I guess I got more impressions that day than outright information.

We went back to my quarters, and Sally locked me in.

For a while I paced the floor and wondered just where any radio equipment was located and glanced anxiously at my watch—which had been returned to me at last, having been found harmless—wondering whether G'lendal was going to come as she had come every night since I had been there.

Back to the radio question. I had not thought it wise to come right out and ask Sally about it, though I was sure that somewhere the Paratimers had radio gear, even though they must have used it sparingly to avoid detection by the Kriths and my own Timeliners. Well, I had to somehow find out where it was and learn to operate gear that I was sure would not be of any make I had ever seen before and would probably not even be labeled in any language that I could read.

Okay, I comforted myself, you're a damned sight closer to it than you were. Just be patient and take it easy and you'll find out.

Then I lit a cigarette and paced the floor some more and waited for the knock on the door that I had begun to doubt would ever come.

Finally it did.

"Come in," I said.

It wasn't G'lendal.

The girl—for it was a girl, if not the girl I had expected—was tall and fair-skinned in contrast to G'lendal's darkness, but her face was well formed, as was her body, what I could tell about it, for she wore a loose blouse and knee-length pants—though there was no doubt about what caused the protrusions that filled out the blouse. I thought I had seen her before, but I couldn't remember where at once.

"You are Eric?" she asked haltingly in an English flavored with an accent I didn't recognize.

"Yes," I said. "Come in." I was puzzled.

"I am Jonna," she said, smiling, though perhaps a bit ill at ease. "G'lendal could not come tonight. She, ah, asked me to"—she hesitated—"to visit you."

Despite the hesitancy of her speech, there was a boldness to her eyes, and that's what made me remember her. That night on the landing strip, the night I came to Staunton, she had been there with the others and had met my eyes with that same bold gaze.

"Why couldn't she come?" I asked.

"She said that she would be busy," Jonna said, still smiling, but the smile did not join the certainty of her eyes. "Do you wish me to stay?"

I smiled to myself and felt a little bit better, though I guess I really had no reason to. G'lendal was the Paratimers' chief interrogator, and now her *interrogation* of me was over. She would be spending her time now with another prisoner or perhaps with someone else just for the fun of it—and she and Mica were seeing to it that I didn't sleep alone. Oh, well, I thought, I knew all the time what G'lendal's game was.

"Yes, of course," I said suddenly, realizing that she had asked me a question. "Please stay."

I looked at her again, a little more closely this time. Her hair was light, almost but not quite blond. Her eyes were a blue that was almost green, and her lips were full and red. Her blouse swelled large in front, hugging her breasts, and narrowed to a thin waist where the blouse was tucked into her pants. She was a very, very good-looking girl, if not in the same league as G'lendal.

"Please stay, Jonna," I said. "Sit down."

She smiled warmly now, the hesitation gone from her face, and when she spoke, it was openly and honestly. "I came here to make love with you," she said. "G'lendal told me to tell you this since it is true." She paused for a moment. "I was not *sent*, Eric. I asked to come. Though I volunteered, someone else would have come had I not."

"Why?" I asked.

"G'lendal said I could tell you that too," she said. "I am one of G'lendal's assistants. It was my job to—to monitor you on the nights that G'lendal spent with you."

"Monitor?"

"Yes," she said, glancing up at the ceiling. "There are video cameras and microphones there. We did not trust you then."

I blushed. I couldn't help myself, though I can't say that I was too surprised at that either, their having "monitored" me.

"How much did you see?" I heard myself asking, remembering that G'lendal liked to keep the light on while we were making love.

"Everything," the girl answered simply.

"Everything?"

Jonna nodded, then looked frankly into my eyes. "That was my job." She paused. "But I came to envy G'lendal. I wished to be in her place. You gave her much pleasure."

I didn't know where this girl Jonna was from, but I had the idea that it was a Line without too many sexual inhibitions.

Jonna stood up slowly and began to unbutton her blouse. "I want you to give me that pleasure, and I shall give it back to you."

In a few moments her blouse was on the floor, and in only a

few more moments she had wriggled out of the rest of her clothing and stood naked before me for my admiration.

"Do you like me, Eric?" she asked.

"Yes," I said, then glanced up at the ceiling.

"Do not worry," she said. "The interrogation is over. We are not being monitored."

"I'm glad of that."

"Look at me, Eric. Do you want to make love with *me?*"

"With you? Of course." And I meant it.

I started to step toward her.

"No, wait," she said. "Let me undress you."

In her own right Jonna was a mistress of the arts of love. I slept very little that night, but I didn't mind that.

18

DEMOCRACY, SAUTIERBOATS, AND GUNS

The next four weeks went quickly, though my anxiety grew greater as I was continually frustrated in my efforts to discover radio equipment. I knew that there had to be some means of contacting the outside world, but I was unable to find it.

My days were full and interesting as I learned more and more about the world in which I found myself, as I learned more about the Paratimers who were beginning their secret war against the Kriths and Timeliners. And the nights . . . well, they were interesting too. Mica did not see fit to let me sleep alone a single night or even sleep very much. There was Jonna, of course, and even G'lendal, who came back to me a few times, and Deean and Suski and two or three others, all lovely and willing and fully experienced in bedtime pleasures.

I will not attempt to detail those four weeks, much of it would be repetitive and most of the details are, from my present viewpoint, unimportant, though I will hit on a few of the high points.

The American rebels of Staunton were self-governing and made a very big thing out of getting everyone involved in the democratic machinery that elected the governing council. The actual process—party meetings, speeches, nominations, campaigns, elections, and so on—was not unlike some other democratic processes that I had seen before. The outstanding thing was the fervor and dedication of these Americans. They not only believed in democracy—they loved it.

Every two years the five-man governing council of Staunton was elected and it so happened that the late spring of 1971 was the time of that election. Sally, who was an official of the Jeffersonian Party, invited me to attend the nominating convention of that party, which occurred one weekend, beginning on Friday evening and lasting through Sunday evening. As much as the rebels loved their democracy, they could not afford to allow it to interfere with their ordinary workweek.

Sally came for me after dinner on that Friday evening clad in a very conservative dress adorned with a large metal pin printed with a stylized picture of one of the rebels' heroes, the American patriot named Thomas Jefferson who was said to have been largely responsible for the writing of the American Declaration of Independence nearly two hundred years before and who had been brutally executed by the British after the collapse of the first rebellion.

"We'd better hurry," she told me. "It will begin soon."

We hurried.

One of the main features of the underground burrows of the American section of Staunton was a huge amphitheater cut from the stone and earth. My guess was that it would hold, when packed full, something on the order of four or five thousand people. And on this particular night, it was packed. There was hardly standing room for all the people who were attending, or rather attempting to attend, though Sally as a party official was able not only to get in, but to get us seats fairly near the front where we could see as well as hear the speakers on the stage. I wondered if the people in the rear of the theater could even hear despite the elaborate sound system of the theater—a Paratimer installation.

We had hardly got into our seats when music began to play, recorded, I supposed, since there was no visible band. At once Sally tugged on my arm, so I rose with her and followed her example of placing my right hand over my heart. I didn't recognize the music, but it was heroic and stirring, and I realized how much it must affect the people who knew it and the principles it represented to them.

Anyway I've always been a sucker for that sort of thing.

"Remain standing until I sit down," Sally whispered to me. I nodded.

A group of men dressed in antique costumes that must have represented the period of the first American rebellion paraded onto the stage. Three of them led the procession—one played a horn or whistle of some kind that I didn't recognize, one played a drum, and the man between the two carried a flag that I believe was one of the original flags of the rebellion. They were followed by ten more men dressed as farmers, clergymen, clerks, backwoods trappers, soldiers, and the like of that period. When the procession reached the center of the stage, it stopped, turned to face the audience, waited until the end of the music, and then the flag was carefully placed in a socket in the floor of the stage.

Two or three patriotic songs followed, one of them called "Yankee Doodle" or something like that. For some reason another of them stuck in my mind, and later I wrote the words down, with some help from Sally. It was about the man called Mad Anthony Wayne, one of their principal heroes, and the words went something like this:

> Bang! Bang! the rifles go; down falls the star-
>   tled foe.
> Aim! Fire! exclaim his eyes; bang! bang! each
>   gun replies.
> Ran-tan! the bugles sound; our force has still the
>   ground.
> Tramp! Tramp! away they go; now retreats the
>   beaten foe.
> Many a redcoat, the Continental scorning,
> Shall never meet the blaze of the broad sunlight
>   that shines on the morrow morning.
>
> His sword blade gleams and his eyelight beams,
> And never glanced either in vain;
> Like the ocean tide, at our head he rides,
> The fearless Mad Anthony Wayne.
>
> [This is followed by the Chorus:]

159

Bang! Bang! the rifles go; down falls the startled
   foe;
Many a redcoat, the Continental scorning,
Shall never meet the blaze of the broad sunlight
   that shines on the morrow morning.

Was e'er a chief of his speech so brief,
Who utters his wishes so plain?
E'er he utters a word, his orders are heard,
From the eyes of Mad Anthony Wayne.

Chorus

It is best to fall at our country's call,
If we must leave this lifetime of pain;
And who would shrink from the perilous brink
When led by Mad Anthony Wayne?

Chorus

Let them form their ranks in firm phalanx;
They will melt in our rifleball rain;
Every shot must tell on a redcoat well,
Or we anger Mad Anthony Wayne.

Chorus

Then they repeated the whole introductory chorus again before ending the song.

I'm not sure why that particular song impressed me so. It may
have been that its jingoistic fervor showed more than any other
the dedicated militancy of the American rebels which I was
coming to understand. I'm not sure. But the song did stick with
me.

When the song was finished, the costumed retinue retired,
and two men carried a microphoned rostrum to the center of the
stage. Moments later a clergyman carrying a huge black Bible
under his arm came out, placed the Bible on the rostrum, opened

it and began reading something from Moses that I can't seem to recall at the moment.

He then asked the Christian God for His blessing on this assembly and on the proceedings and asked His guidance in making the right choice of nominees for the council. During his prayer he alluded to men and events I was unfamiliar with, but which must have had some meaning to the native Americans. Then he retired from the stage, and the convention got down to business.

I won't try to relate the convention at all. There was too much of it, too many things happening at once, and I was never quite sure just what was really going on. In a way it reminded me of the way some elections are held back in my own Homeline —since we Greeks invented the idea, anyway—but there were a lot of differences too.

One thing I do remember, though, was when a man I didn't know got up and nominated Sally for a position on the city's governing council. Sally immediately rose, told them that she couldn't accept; she had been gone too long and was out of touch with things in Staunton, but she certainly did appreciate the gesture. She received a standing ovation.

Then there were other nominations and secondings and acceptance speeches, and sometime long after midnight on Saturday, when my eyelids weighed a ton each, the voting got started in earnest, with more yelling and cheering and calls to order and just about everything else you can think of.

I managed to slip away while Sally was making some parliamentary point and at last got some of the sleep I so badly needed— and I was grateful that Mica didn't send someone to keep me company that night. I wouldn't have been up to it.

"I don't think anyone before us really understood the principles behind the sautierboat, or skudder, as you call it," the gray-clad technician told me, pointing toward the huge craft that now occupied fully half of the hangar. "I mean, the Kriths could skud, but they never really knew how they did it. It was just something they did. I mean, men have been able to think for thousands of years, but we're only now really learning *how* we think.''

I nodded.

Sally had brought me to the hangar, introduced me to the technician, and then gone on her way, saying she'd be back later to get me. In the meantime, he was trying to help me understand how their Transtemporal sautierboats worked.

''Well,'' the technician said, ''when the Kriths had human beings start building skudders for them, they did it pretty much on an empirical basis. The human engineers learned the mechanics behind Krithian skudding and reproduced them in a machine without really learning the fundamental laws that govern this sort of thing. They didn't have to since all they had to do was reproduce a mechanical model of the skudding mechanism inside the Kriths. Follow me?''

''Yes, I believe so.''

''I don't pretend to understand it all myself,'' the technician said, gesturing toward a shelf of technical manuals and reference books above his elaborate workbench. ''I just know enough to repair these things when something goes wrong, but despite that I think I know a hell of a lot more about it than any of *your* people.'' The way he put an emphasis on ''your'' gave me the impression that he, for one, didn't really trust me, but he was going to give me a rundown of their sautierboats as Sally had requested and Mica had approved.

''I wouldn't doubt it,'' I said, hoping that would put him more at ease. ''I've seen your boats do things I thought were impossible.''

''That's exactly what I mean,'' the technician said. ''How about a cup of coffee?''

''Okay. I could stand one.''

While he dropped coins into the vending machine and waited for the hot coffee to come gurgling out, he went on talking. ''The engineers say that you can't really talk about sautiering in words; they say you need a special set of mathematics for it. And I guess that it's true, but I'm doing well just to follow the math when it's on paper and explained for me. I can't tell you much about it.''

"That's okay," I said. "I probably wouldn't understand any of it anyway. Cigarette?"

"Thanks," he said, taking my offered pack and knocking a cigarette into his hand.

I got the two cups of coffee from the machine, handed him one of them.

"Go on," I said. "Explain to me what you can."

"All right," he said, taking a light from my lighter. "It all has to do with what they call probability potentials and probability indices. It's as if nothing *really* is; everything is just *might be*. Like, ah, the universe can't make up its mind. Follow me?"

"Not really."

"That's okay. I don't think anyone does really. Well, they say that back when the universe first started there was just one Paratime, one Line, the Original Line, and it had a probability of 1.0000 forever. It was *real*. Then the first uncertainty happened. I mean, something came up that could have gone one way or the other. And the universe couldn't decide which. So both happened. Each new Paratime had a probability of 0.5000.

"Okay, so far?" he asked.

I nodded, sipped my coffee, puffed my cigarette.

"Well, when it all started, the Original Paratime had a probability index of 1.0000, like I said. When there were two Paratimes, one had a probability of -0.5000 and the other had a probability of $+0.5000$. The *plus* and *minus* represent what you call T-West and T-East. Well, let's say that the *plus* Line came to a fork and two new Paratimes were formed, each with a probability index of 0.2500. One was a $++0.2500$ and the other was a $-+0.2500$. Still with me?"

"I guess so."

"Okay. The *double plus* Line hit another fork, and the result was now a $+++0.1250$ and a $-++0.1250$. And this would go on and on toward infinity, with each new fork lowering the probability and increasing the number of signs. They figure that the probability of any given Line is now somewhere on the order of 10^{-85}."

I tried to visualize the number, but all I got was a string of

zeroes running across a sheet of paper and dribbling off the side.
I couldn't comprehend it.

"That's an oversimplification, way over. The way I understand it," the technician was saying, "is that the probabilities
don't break apart even. I mean, it isn't *always* a fifty-fifty
chance. You might come to a fork with, say, a thirty percent
probability one way and a seventy percent probability the other,
but that only confuses the probability values that much more.
But you get the basic picture, don't you?"

"I think so," I said. None of this was very new to me. The
Kriths had been able to tell me this much a long time ago.

"Okay, then, every Paratime had its own particular value in
pluses and *minuses* and its own numerical index. It's kind of like
a fingerprint; there's no two alike."

"I understand that."

"Well, that's how we travel across the Paratimes," the
technician said smugly. "The sautier generator, well, creates its
own probability potential. We adjust to it—well, to whatever
we want to adjust it to and then the boat and everything within
the field of the generator sort of seeks its own level."

"I'm with you."

"I guess that's the best I can do to explain it."

"That's good enough," I said, "but I still don't understand
how you can move about in space. The Kriths can't do that."

"Okay. As I said before, you and the Kriths don't really
understand what it's all about," he said. "Oh, they're right
about the relationship of probability generators and most other
types of machinery. You can't fly a sauteirboat with a jet
engine, but we've found out how to turn that into a positive
advantage.

"Now, the Kriths have a vague idea that there are two, well,
dimensions to sautiering, skudding, I mean plus and minus, but
what they don't understand is that there are three more. I mean,
as well as having Transtemporal plus and minus probability,
there are three spatial coordinates involved in probability. That
is, even within a given Paratime the probability of one thing or
place varies from all the others."

"You've lost me," I said. This was something new to me.
The Kriths had never talked about anything like this.

"Me too," the technician said, smiling. "Look, you're familiar with the mass displacement phenomenon, aren't you?"

"Yes."

"Okay, the Kriths know that an object entering a Paratime from Outtime cannot occupy the same place as an object already in existence in a Paratime. The newcomer, since it has a much lower probability within the Paratime, must give way to the one that's already there. Its mass is displaced in space a sufficient distance to avoid coming in physical contact with the thing that's already there. Right?"

"Right," I said. I guess if that weren't so, skudding would have been next to impossible.

"Well, whereas your people and the Kriths seem to accept this and go on, our people wanted to find out why, and when they did, they learned about probability interactions. The best I can tell you is that there are some kinds of interactions between the separate Paratimes. Some things are, well, more probable than others even in the same Paratime. Take Here and Now for example. Going *plus* and *minus* across the Paratimes, we'd find a number of worlds almost identical to this one, but each slightly different in some respects. Even though this hangar isn't native to these Paratimes and doesn't exist on any other, let's pretend that it does, okay?"

"I guess."

"Well then, if we were to take the nearest five Paratimes in either direction and built a composite picture of the hangar, we'd find some things identical in some, but different in others.

"All right, they all add together in a sense. Let's say, in the totality, that this building has the highest order of probability, then the tools on the bench, then me, then you with the lowest. Okay, then each item in this room has an order of probability in relation to each other item as a part of the total probability index of this Paratime because of the, well, interaction of the other ten Paratimes. Still with me?"

"I think so."

"Okay. Suppose the index of this Paratime is $5 + ^{25} \times 10 - ^{25}$. Now everything in this Paratime has varying potentials. If we assign 1.000 to the most likely thing, the hangar itself, the sautierboat might be, say, 0.7500 and the tools on the bench

0.5000 and me 0.2500 and you, say, 0.1250. Now each of these things here has a value, call it a field, that centers on the object itself, but extends outward, diminishing in force, still with a probability focal point."

"I'm getting a headache."

The technician smiled. "I'll cut it short. Take this sautier-boat. We can adjust the generator to take us to a given Paratime. Right?"

"Granted."

"Now within that Paratime we can subtly vary the sautier field, alter the probability potential just a little. Well, if we can move from Paratime to Paratime by seeking the level of the generator, it follows that within a given Paratime we can move from place to place by varying the field within that Paratime. Got me?"

I nodded. "That sounds awkward, though. How do you know which way you're going to go when you vary the field? And how can you be sure that you're not going to jump right out of this Line into another?"

"As I said, all this is oversimplification," he said. "We've got instruments that can detect the variations of probability within a Paratime. And these instruments feed into the boat's computer. I guess you know that most electronic devices, like most living organisms, don't seem to be bothered by probability fields. Don't ask me why. I don't know." He paused. "Anyhow, a human being never has to worry about any of these things anyway. All he does is set the controls to take him to a certain spot. The instruments gauge the probability potentials around the boat, find the levels that will take the boat where the pilot wants to go, and the computer varies the generator's potential accordingly."

"I see," I said, "and that would also prevent the boat from slipping into another Line by accident, I guess."

"Right," the technician said. "Say, if you can get permission from Mica, I'll take you for a ride sometime and show you how it works."

"I'd like that," I said, thinking that I had overcome the technician's initial distrust of me—and also thinking that his sautierboat would be sure to have a radio in it.

But I was sure that it would take some time before I could persuade Mica to allow me to take the offered ride, and I just might not have that time.

The arsenal of the Paratimers under the West Florida earth contained weapons of every imaginable type from crossbows to thermonuclear bombs big enough to sterilize half the planet. And I wondered why they had weapons that big and if they would really use them if it appeared that the Kriths were winning on this Line.

"Now this is one of my favorites," Scoti said to me, taking a well-oiled handgun down from its wall cradle. It was a big, heavy six-shot revolver that reminded me a little of the Harling that Scoti had taken from me. I wondered where it was now.

"This is from a fairly nearby Paratime," Scoti was saying. "And it's one of the most efficient pistols I've ever seen. It's called a .44 Magnum, and it packs one hell of a punch."

"Single-action, isn't it?" I asked to keep up my end of the conversation.

"Yes," Scoti agreed, "but I'm partial to them."

"They're dependable."

"This one sure is. Notice the construction of the cylinder." He snapped the weapon open. "Rugged as hell. There's virtually no way in the world to foul it up. And the hammer spring, well, it just won't wear out. That's the beauty of it—simple, efficient, and it's one of the most accurate big-bore pistols you'll ever find."

For an instant I wished that there were shells in the cylinder. Given half a chance, even now, I might be tempted to try to shoot my way out of here. Then I smiled and handed it back to him.

"If you can get Mica's permission," Scoti said, "I'll see if you can try it out on the range."

"That might be fun," I said, though again I doubted that Mica trusted me that much—enough to let me have a loaded weapon in my hands even on a target range surrounded by guards.

I just smiled again, and Scoti put the pistol back and started to show me another of his favorite weapons, an R-4 power pistol from his own Line.

It was two or three days later that Mica dropped his bomb.

We were sitting in his office one morning having coffee, discussing some of the Paratimes we had been in, when he almost casually mentioned his Homeline.

"It must be very interesting there," I said.

"Yes, I suppose it is," Mica replied. "You'll have a chance to see for yourself soon."

"How's that?"

"Next week Trebum and I will be going home to make a progress report to our governing council. We will be taking you along."

"Oh?" I said, unable to think of anything any more intelligent at the moment.

"Yes," Mica replied slowly. "The council would like to speak with you also. It isn't often that we get a Timeliner convert."

"How long will I be there?"

"I'm afraid that I cannot say. It will be up to the council. However, I doubt that you will ever be returning *here*."

I started to ask why, but decided against it. I knew why. They just didn't trust me that much, not enough to leave me here, this close to my "friends," though they trusted me enough not to kill me.

"I trust that you do not find that an unpleasant prospect," he said, a statement rather than a question.

"No, of course not," I told him. "It should be very interesting."

But I had already made up my mind about what I was going to do.

19

"RED MOBILE TO RED LEADER"

Mica told me that we were going to his Homeline on Friday. I acted on the Monday before that.

The Monday morning after a solitary breakfast I buzzed Sally's quarters on the intercom, hoping that I'd catch her before she left. I was lucky. She was still there.

"Yes, Eric," she said over the intercom.

"Are you busy?"

She paused for a moment before answering. "Well, no. Not really. I have a few things to do, but nothing urgent. Why?"

"Oh, no reason, really," I said. "I've just got a touch of claustrophobia. I'd like a chance to get outside for a breath of fresh air."

"We could have gone to the surface yesterday," she said. "There was a picnic, you know."

"I know, but I didn't feel like it then. How about it? Can you take me up for a few minutes, just to look around?"

"Okay," she answered at last. "Give me a few minutes. Then I'll come for you."

"Good. I'll be waiting."

Of course I'd be waiting. I still couldn't even open the door by myself.

It was nearly half an hour later when Sally showed up wearing bright yellow shorts, halter, and sandals. I was pleased to note the bulge of the small handgun that was still on her hip under the shorts. I had been fearful that their trust of me was enough for Sally to have come without the gun now. It wasn't. Good. I needed that gun.

"Ready to go?" she asked.

"Ready," I answered.

We followed the corridors to the stairs and took the stairs up to the surface, out into the bright springtime morning light. It was almost summer then all across the Lines.

When the door closed behind us; I took a deep breath of fresh air, looked up at the cloudless sky through the dark pine trees above, and then looked around and located the hangar off through the trees. That was my ultimate destination.

"Is there any place in particular you want to go?" Sally asked.

"No," I replied, "let's just walk."

So we walked away from the hangar across the flat countryside through the pine trees toward a small stream that cut through the forest, making its way toward the Gulf of Mexico less than fifty miles to the south.

"I'm going to be leaving soon," I said as I fished into my pocket for a cigarette.

"I know," Sally replied. "Mica told me."

"In a way I'll hate to leave here. I sort of like it."

"I envy you," she said.

"Envy me. Why?"

"You're getting to visit Mica's Paratime. I've never had a chance. It must be a wonderful place."

"Oh? You mean you've never been to where they come from?"

"No, very few of us have."

I wondered why, then dismissed the thought. It *might* have some kind of significance, but I doubted it. And it didn't matter. Not at the moment I had no intention of going there with Mica.

"I guess it will be interesting," I said, "but I'd rather stay here."

"What difference does it make to you? This isn't your Homeline. I thought that one Paratime was as good as another to you."

"Some are better than others. I've come to like it here."

170

"As a prisoner?"

"I've had freedom that's been a lot worse than this prison, and, hell, I've got such nice guards."

"You mean like G'lendal and Jonna?" Sally asked, a smile flickering across her face.

"Yes, like them and you."

"Me? What am I to you, Eric?"

"I don't know, Sally. I just like you."

"Guilt feelings?"

"Guilt? Oh, for kidnapping you and all? No, not really. Back then you weren't a person to me. Just a job. I don't have any reason for guilt, do I?"

"I'm not a person to you now either, Eric. I'm just a turn-key."

"No, more than that."

"I'm just your guard, Eric," she said, an edge to her voice. She had come to a stop near the base of a huge old pine. "I could never be anything else."

I turned to look at her, my hands going to her shoulders, memories of Kristin coming to me, beginning to hate myself for what I was about to do. "You could be a lot more than that, Sally."

"No, never, Eric."

"Why? Because you're married to Von Heinen? What's he to you?"

"Not Albert," she said, a strange mixture of emotions on her face. "You know—you must realize by now that I'm Mica's mistress. I'm. . . ."

That's when I acted.

I had never seen Sally draw her hip pistol while wearing those shorts. She must have had some easy access to it, though. I didn't know how and didn't have time to investigate. I just grabbed the shorts at the waist, jerked down and forward and hoped that the fabric or the stitches that held it together would tear. Something gave way.

Sally was as well trained in hand-to-hand combat as any woman I'd ever met, but fighting was my business, and I was bigger and stronger than she was. She fought back as I tore off her shorts, grabbed at the small holster strapped across her now-naked hips, wrapped my fingers around the weapon's butt and pulled it free. Then I shoved her away, jumped back and leveled the pistol at her, snapping the safety off. It was a small automatic of a make I didn't recognize, .22 caliber.

"Hold it, Sally," I gasped.

"Goddamn you!" she cried, on her knees and starting to rise, but then looking at the weapon aimed at her. "You lying, sneaking bastard. I trusted you. I. . . ."

"I'm sorry, Sally," I said as calmly as I could. "I hate to do this, but I've still got a job to do."

"You still believe them," she said, her eyes filling with fire and hatred, and tears. "You still believe those monsters are telling the truth. You traitor, you filthy. . . ."

"That's enough," I said sharply. "I'm doing what I have to do."

"Don't hand me that shit."

"That's not very ladylike."

"Don't mock me, you. . . ." What she said next was even less ladylike.

"Get up," I said. "We're going to the hangar."

"You're not stupid enough to think you can steal a boat, are you? You don't even know how to operate one of ours."

"I don't need to. Now get up and do as I say."

Sally came to her feet, clutching her torn shorts around her waist as well as she could with one hand turned in the direction I pointed with the pistol, started walking.

Well, I thought, I'm into it now. If I don't make it . . . Well, it's a bullet in the head for old Thimbron Parnassos if I don't pull it off this time. There'll never be another chance.

Sally did not speak again as we made our way back along the trail toward the hangar in which the Paratimers kept their sautierboats there on the surface, hidden from British airships by a thick cover of trees.

In a few minutes we were within sight of the hangar. Exactly as I had hoped, the big hangar doors were open, and I could see inside. Two of the alien skudders sat there, the big one and the smaller one, and inside the hangar, dark against the bright light outside, I could see two men, gray-clad technicians doing whatever technicians do when they don't have anything else to do.

172

"Don't make a sound, Sally," I whispered, knowing that we were still outside their range of hearing. "If you do. . . ." I let my voice trail off.

She turned to look at me, hatred still in her eyes, and for an instant—well, damn it, I loved her. I guess that's what it was. And damned if I knew why. And when that instant was gone, I knew that I couldn't trust her. She might—probably would—yell a warning to the technicians inside the hangar as soon as we got close enough. And I didn't think I would be able to kill her if she did.

I'm sorry, Sally, I said to myself, dropping the pistol, balling my fist and snapping my knuckles across her jaw in a single motion.

She looked startled for a moment, then collapsed quietly onto the soft, pine-needled floor of the forest.

I took off her halter, feeling guilty as I undressed her, and used it to tie her arms crudely to the trunk of a small tree. With my handkerchief and a strip of her torn shorts I formed a gag and hoped that she would be found soon. I didn't want her to strangle.

Looking regretfully at her for one last time, wondering whether I'd ever see her again, I left the now-nude girl behind me and began slipping through the thinning forest, around the hangar so that I could come up from the other side.

Standing only inches from the two huge open doors at the hangar's front, I could hear the two technicians talking, though I couldn't understand them. They were speaking that French-like language that was common to the Paratimers.

After a while I decided that I was gaining nothing by delaying. I might as well go on and do it before I was discovered. So I waited only until I thought I could pinpoint their locations from their voices, both together, standing not far from me near the hangar's doors.

Leaping out into the open, turning, and aiming the pistol, I said loudly, "Hold it! Don't move!"

The two technicians turned to face me, startled expressions on their faces, words cut off in mid-sentence.

One grabbed at the tool belt he wore, grasping at something

that vaguely resembled a flashlight, but might well have been some sort of laser device that could be used as a weapon. I pulled the trigger.

The technician staggered backward, grasping his shoulder, blood spurting between his fingers.

"Don't move again, either of you," I said, wondering if the report of the tiny pistol was really as loud as it had sounded to me in the stillness of the surface forest.

"Tie him up," I told the uninjured technician, the one that had explained to me the workings of their sautierboats a few days before. "And hurry. I don't have much time."

The startled technician seemed disinclined to argue with the tiny but effective weapon I held. Without speaking he bound his companion hand and foot and gagged him with black electrical tape under my supervision.

"Okay. Now drag him over there out of the way," I said. "And don't make a move toward any of those tools."

When he was finished, he looked back at me fearfully, or rather at the pistol. He could not seem to take his eyes off it even as he spoke.

"He'll bleed to death," he managed to say. "You hit an artery."

"Do both those boats have radios?" I asked. Right then I couldn't afford to care if the other technician did bleed to death. I was more concerned with my own life.

He was nodding.

"Which is the most powerful?"

"N-neither. Both are the same kind."

"Okay. The big one." I gestured toward the larger of the two craft. The technician didn't ask any questions. He just started across the hangar.

I wasn't foolish enough to believe that I could steal one of their sautierboats. I had no idea how to operate the controls, and I could not trust the technician to do anything that complex. The best I could hope for was one of the radios—if I could just get a message on the air and if Kar-hinter still had people monitoring and if I happened to find the right frequency and if. . . .

The technician opened the hatch of the large craft, stood for a moment waiting for me to tell him what to do.

"Get in," I said.

For an instant I had the same feeling I had had back in the stables of the villa near Beaugency, back when I was fleeing from the Paratimers in an Imperial motorcar with Sally and Von Heinen as captives, so long ago and half a world away. There was the sensation of another presence in the hangar, and out of the corner of my eye I caught the impression of a figure standing back deep in the shadows at the far end of the hangar.

I spun toward the image, leveling the small pistol, but when my eyes focused in the shadows, there was nothing there. Had there ever been?

I went on into the boat, feeling a strange chill on my back. Ghosts?

Inside the boat I recognized the controls as being basically similar to those of the craft that had brought me to Staunton, what I had seen of its control panel. The radio transceiver was easy enough to locate, though the lettering on the controls was foreign to me.

"Okay," I said, "tell me what does what."

The technician looked at me for a moment, perhaps wondering what he could get away with, then, gazing at the pistol, seemed to decide that he'd better play it straight and nodded. "This—this is the on-off switch. The receiver and the transmitter operate on the same frequency. That's controlled by this knob."

"What does that dial indicate?"

"Megahertz. Vernier control here and these—these buttons will select preselected channels."

"Go on."

"Yeah. This—this is your power amplifier tuning. The meter should register fifty percent when you're ready to transmit. This is. . . ."

In five minutes I thought I could operate it. Maybe the technician had given me the wrong information about the radio set, but I doubted it. He was too scared—and one VHF transceiver is pretty much like another when you get the basic idea of what it is supposed to do.

My worry was about the type of modulation this set was using, FM. And the Kriths mostly used AM in the VHF ranges.

175

Why, I don't know, but they did. And if I transmitted an FM signal into an AM receiver, even if I were exactly on frequency—well, they wouldn't get much out of it on the receiving end. I just hoped that the Kriths had planned for an eventuality like this and would be able to demodulate my FM signal.

"Sit down over there and stay quiet," I told the technician and began flipping switches.

Less than a minute later lights and meters said that I was ready to transmit. And if I were correct in remembering the Krithian emergency frequency and if the set were really transmitting and if. . . . Hell, worrying isn't going to do any good. Just try.

"Red mobile to red leader," I said into the microphone in Shangalis. "Red mobile to red leader. Do you hear me, Kar-hinter?" Then I realized how foolish all that was and decided to give it to them straight. "If anybody's listening, this is Eric Mathers, Timeliners, under Kar-hinter's supervision. I have been captured by invaders from another Timeline. I am held prisoner in a place called Staunton somewhere in West Florida. Lock in on my signal and triangulate. Inform Kar-hinter at once and tell him to get here fast. I've come across the biggest thing we've ever seen. . . ."

That was the gist of my message. I repeated it three times, then switched to another frequency and did it again.

I was on my fourth frequency when I heard the banging on the hatch.

"Who's in there?" a muffled voice called from outside. "What's going on?"

The technician looked at me for an instant, then back at the hatch.

"Stay still," I told him—but that didn't do any good. He was a brave man, that technician, to be as scared as he was and still do what he did.

Still looking directly into the barrel of my pistol, he jumped at me, a yell of pure hatred on his lips. I fired. There wasn't much else I could do. And then his face wasn't much of a face anymore.

The technician lay at my feet, his blood splattered over me

and the deck, and he was very still, and I hated very much that I had had to kill him.

The banging on the hatch had stopped, but a voice called, a different voice that I thought I recognized as Scoti's: "Mathers, we know you're in there. Come out and . . ."

"Come get me," I yelled back, switched to another frequency, and delivered one last frantic message into the microphone.

Outside, through the transparent dome, I could see a cluster of men in the hangar's open doors. Scoti came out from under the bulk of the craft, running and gesturing for the other men to clear out of the hangar. I only caught a brief glimpse of the weapon he held in his hand. But that was enough. He had showed it to me once before and told me a little about it. An R-4 power pistol. If I had been a praying man, I would have delivered my most heartfelt prayer at that moment. But all I could do was wait. There wasn't a damned thing else I could do.

Now the space in front of the hangar was vacant except for Scoti, who knelt with left elbow on left knee, left hand around right wrist, sighting across the barrel of the weapon he carried. I saw the muzzle flash. . . .

And I saw the universe explode. And I felt heat and flame and blinding light so bright that I could not see it. And that was all for a long, long time.

20

VOICES

The world is a very unpleasant place to be in when your face is a mass of raw flesh and your eyes won't open because they're sealed shut with blood and both your legs are broken and you've got internal injuries that are leaking blood into places where there shouldn't be blood and you're lying on a bed of broken glass and twisted metal and some damned fool is shaking the universe like a baby crib.

I couldn't see, but I could hear, and I really didn't want to do that, but I didn't have the strength to fight it.

"Is he dead?" a voice asked.

"No, but he ought to be," answered another voice, maybe Scoti's. "Don't worry. He won't last long."

"What about Joal?" That voice might have been Mica's. I'm not sure.

"He's dead. Mathers shot him in the face."

"Bastard. Kick him once for me."

He did. In the ribs. I passed out again.

The next time I heard voices the universe was holding a little more steady and the bed was just lumpy rocks rather than broken glass, but it would be hard for me to say that I was more comfortable. Maybe a little less painful.

"He needs a doctor," someone said from above.

"Screw the doctor," Scoti spat. "Let the bastard bleed to death."

"Okay."

"Have they found Sally yet?"

"I don't know."

"If he killed her. . . . If he killed her. . . ." Then Scoti's voice came close, right up to what used to be my ear. "Mathers, can you hear me?"

There wasn't much I could do to let him know. I couldn't even groan.

"Listen to me, bastard," Scoti said. "If you hurt Sally, I'll see that you live. You'll live so that I can slowly take you apart piece by piece. I mean slow, damn it!"

I think he kicked me again, but I couldn't really be sure.

I was somewhere between life and death, consciousness and unconsciousness when I heard a voice yelling, "Scoti, look up there!"

"What is it?" Scoti yelled back, his voice dwindling as he moved away from me.

"Airships," the other voice, or one of the other voices, said. "British airships."

"Call Mica! Full alert!"

I heard running feet and yelling voices, but everyone seemed to have forgotten about me, and that was okay. I just wanted to be left alone to die in peace.

There was a strange chill in the air, an alienness, an unknown quantity that I couldn't identify but knew was more than the feel of shock and pain, and all around me was the stillness you only find in a nightmare. I thought maybe I was dead and had gone to hell.

A voice was speaking to me, and the voice was that out of a nightmare, a masculine voice with a familiar ring to it, but my mind could not place the voice. It was saying, "Stay alive, Eric. For God's sake, man, hang on just a little while longer. They're coming to help you. The pain won't last long. You can stand it, Eric. *I did.*"

And then the voice was gone, and I floated down into a painful darkness, but I knew that I would try to hang on. Help was coming, the voice had said.

179

Later, how much later I don't know, but later I heard the whine of airship motors and another, different whine that ceased abruptly with a clap of air and it might have been the probability generator of a skudder—sautierboat—the other Paratime craft that had been in the hangar, because it was gone later. Then I heard small-arms fire from outside the hangar and a voice that yelled, "Fall back into the. . . ." And the chatter of a machine gun that cut off the voice and the sudden rasp of an energy pistol that had not been made on this world and a voice yelling in Shangalis, and I went black again.

Someone was bending over me, holding my head up, putting something to my mouth that was cold and wet and very welcome. I think I also got an injection of something, but I didn't feel the prick of the needle.

"Eric, Eric, can you hear me?"

It was a voice that I ought to remember. I thought I knew who it was. Sally? No, it wasn't Sally. She had a soft contralto voice. And this voice wasn't soft. It was harsh and rasping, and there was a British accent to it that was too pronounced to be real.

"Eric; for God's sake, old man," the voice said. "What is this?"

"Get Sally," I somehow managed to say to that voice that I ought to recognize, but didn't yet.

"Who?"

"Sally. Back in the woods. Save Sally. Don't let them get her."

"Don't let who get her?"

"*Them. Them.* Don't let *them* get her."

But who *they* were I wasn't sure, and I'm not sure to this day.

This time when I awoke the bed was softer still, but it was moving, upward, lurching, and I wanted to vomit all over the place because I didn't want to be moving. Not now. Not ever.

"Get us some altitude," the strange/familiar voice said.

"I'm doing the best I can," another voice answered, another one that had something to do with me, my past, that I ought to know. "This damned thing's no fusion rocket, you know."

180

"I know, but get us out of here. They're going to bring up their big guns soon."

"I know. We'll make it. How's Mathers?"

"Pretty bad. He must have been in that skudder we found."

"How in God's name did he live through that?"

"He's too mean to die."

"What about the girl?"

"I gave her a shot. She's still out."

"She ought to have some clothes on."

"I didn't bring a change. How was I to know?"

"Well, cover her up with something."

"Does that bother you, her being naked?"

"Yeah."

"I enjoy looking at her."

The other voice grunted and then said, "Man, is Kar-hinter going to be glad to get these two back."

"I am too."

"I know."

"Eric and I have been together for a long time."

"Tracy! Look down there!"

"What is—"

It was just one of those days when the universe wouldn't behave itself.

A great fist came up from below, aimed directly at the bunk on which I was lying, thumping it with such force that I was thrown into the air, out of the bunk, and onto the hard floor beside it. And then the BOOM! so loud and so terrifying that I thought it would shatter whatever was left of the world.

"They blew it up," one of the voices said incredulously. "They blew up the whole damned place."

Then I went back down into the darkness.

21

RECOVERY

It was a long, long while later before I had truly lucid moments.
I think I remember a long sequence of nightmares, most of them
false, some of them real. I remember strangely gentle hands
carrying me out of a British airship on a stretcher and across a
landing field to a horse-drawn ambulance and an unbelievably
bumpy ride across an infinite, pitted earth. And I remember a
fifty-foot-tall Mica, with skin as white as a parson's blessing,
but with eyes that were as dark and empty as interstellar space,
and he had an enormous knife that he used to probe my liver and
said over and over and over, "What did you do with Sally?"
And I remember the bright overhead lights of an operating room
and a doctor who said, "Easy, Captain Mathers. Rest easy.
You'll be asleep soon," in a voice of the archangels, and then he
started putting me back together again. And a bomb that kept
exploding across the Timelines, wiping out world after world,
destroying the whole complex of continua. And somebody
swabbing my hot forehead with cotton dipped in alcohol and
asking me to sip some kind of liquid and crushed ice through a
straw. And then G'lendal, naked and beautiful, her big breasts
pointed at me like twin cannon, standing before me, gradually
changing into a naked and hideous Krith with a wide, sneering
grin and a hungry look on its face. And a universe that consisted
of paper cutouts and a voice that I ought to know telling me that
this was reality, all the reality I would ever find.

Then, after a while, I woke up, and the nightmares were over, most of them.

At first I couldn't have said for sure where I was. Oh, it was a hospital room, of course: pale-green walls and a stark white bed and all the other paraphernalia that goes with a hospital, all with the overtones of a second- or third-level technology, just like the world in which I had been and where I still might be.

Above my head and to the right was a cord that I assumed rang for the nurse. I pulled on it, or rather tried to pull on it, and as I fought to wrap my weak fingers around it, I noticed the glucose drip that was plugged into my left arm, the bottle half full of colorless sugar. Finally my hand closed around the cord, and I tugged and thought that off in the distance I heard a bell ring, and then let my arm fall back to the bed and waited to see what would happen.

Five hundred years later, more or less, the door directly opposite my bed opened and a tall, thin man wearing a white smock and rimless glasses came in. I started to try to speak, realized that I wasn't sure what language to use, and waited for him to say the first words.

"Oh, you've come around, Mathers," the white-clad man said in Shangalis. He was a Timeliner.

"Yeah," I managed to say.

"You've had Kar-hinter worried," he said.

"I've had me kind of worried, too," I said in short gasps.

"Rest easy now," the man said, coming to the side of the bed, taking my right wrist in his left hand, feeling the pulse while he looked at his wrist watch, saying, "I'm Dr. Conners."

"Where am I?"

"Bakersville, South Africa," Conners answered when he had finished counting the beats of my heart. "You're still on the same Line, though, if that's what you mean. This is a hospital that the British have turned over to us. We're all Liners here."

"What happened?"

"I'm afraid I couldn't tell you," the doctor replied. "But Kar-hinter and two of your friends are outside if you feel up to talking with them."

"Yes, please," I said, then lay back on the bed and closed my eyes and rested and tried to gather what strength was left in my body. But before the doctor left the room, I was forced to ask, "Just how bad am I?"

"You'll be fine. Nothing's missing," Conners said, and for a moment I thought that was all he was going to say. "You had both legs broken and several ribs as well. We also had to replace your liver. Your face was pretty badly cut up, but plastiskin is going to cover the scars. You'll never know the difference. And, well, you ought to be up and walking around within forty-eight hours."

Thank God for the medical science we've picked up across the Lines! I wouldn't have lived if I'd had to depend on the local skills.

"While you were here," Connors went on, "we also replaced your augmentation control center. Apparently it was deactivated."

I nodded.

"And we replaced your missing fingers," he completed.

I looked down at my left hand and saw that I had a full set of fingers on it. The grafting scars were either already healed or very skillfully hidden by plastiskin.

"I'll send your friends in now," the doctor said.

"Thanks."

So I just lay there waiting for Kar-hinter and whoever else was with him to come in and thought and wondered: How was Sally? And, in fact, where was she? Had they really found her and taken her with me? And what had happened to Staunton? Had it really blown up? Or was that just a part of my nightmares? And. . . .

The door opened; and Kar-hinter, Tracy, and Kearns came into the room. The alien was naked, of course, and the two men were dressed in British uniforms.

"I told you that he was too mean to kill," Tracy said, smiling. "How are you, old man?"

"Bloody damned poorly," I said, trying to answer Tracy's smile.

"Hello, Eric," Kar-hinter said in his precise English that somehow reminded me of Mica's. "Feeling better, I trust."

"Damned if I know," I said. "I don't feel much of anything right now."

184

"You must have given them hell, Mathers," Kearns said, a strangely misplaced smile on his face.

"Not as much as they gave me," I told him.

"I don't know," Kearns said. "Tracy and I found at least two bodies that you must have killed."

"That was my limit for the season," I said, wishing they'd get over the small talk and that somebody'd answer some questions for me.

Kar-hinter must have sensed my feelings, for he said, "We have many questions to ask you, Eric, but first we will answer yours."

"Okay," I said weakly. "What about Sally?"

"Count von Heinen's wife?" Kar-hinter asked; something that might have been puzzlement in his voice. I wasn't sure. You can never be sure about a Krith. "She is well. Hillary and Ronald found her when they rescued you. She is now at an interrogation station on an adjacent Line."

Thank God for that, I said to myself. "What happened? From the beginning."

Kar-hinter gave me what passed for a smile, said, "As you know, Hillary and Ronald crossed the Imperial lines to safety on the morning of the raid on the villa. We then established contact with you. When your signal ceased abruptly, we investigated as quickly as possible, found that you and your captives were gone. We assumed that you had been taken by the people in the strange skudder you had fought earlier. We could do nothing but wait until you tried to contact us, though we were following up clues."

"You know who those people are, don't you?" I asked.

"We know now," Kar-hinter replied. "Countess von Heinen gave us that information under the first mind probe."

"Had you suspected?"

Kar-hinter smiled. "Suspected, but nothing more. But, to go on, we had nearly given you up for dead when your message was received at the Butt of Lewis."

"Then you did get my signal?"

Kar-hinter nodded in a very human fashion. "Yes, we have had continuous monitors on all frequencies with recording equipment attached. Computers determined that you were using

FM and demodulated accordingly. We came as soon as we could get a fix on your signal."

"How did you get there so fast?" I asked Tracy.

He smiled back at me and said, "Kearns and I were working out of Victoria, Virginia. Kar-hinter sent us there with a couple of platoons of men to investigate a resurgence of Staunton-rumors. He thought that they might somehow be connected with the—er—Paratimers who captured you. We didn't know who they were then, of course."

"What about Staunton?" I asked. "Did you get inside?"

Tracy shook his head. "We only got as far as the hangar where we found you. And we were damned lucky to get away from there. We lost most of our men. They blew up the place, y'know."

"I thought they did," I said. "I thought I remembered it." I paused, took a deep breath, then asked. "Was it with atomic weapons? They had quite a stockpile of thermonukes."

"No," Kar-hinter said. "The explosives they used were chemical. Their nuclear weapons did not go off, fortunately for this world. We are in the process of recovering them now. They will be shipped Outtime at once."

I nodded, looked back at Tracy. "How many sautierboats —skudders were in the hangar?"

"Just the one," Tracy said. "The ruined one you must have been in. Were there others?"

"One," I said. "Some of them must have gotten away in it."

"It would appear so," Kar-hinter said.

"Were there any captives?" I asked.

"A few," Kat-hinter answered. "But they were only locals and most of them knew less than the countess. By the time we were able to get another force in there most of the survivors had fled and gotten into hiding."

"Well, what about the Imperial Baltic plant?" I asked. "We didn't get the count for you."

"An alternate plan was used," Kar-hinter said, though he did not tell me what the plan was. "When we raided the plant, we discovered evidence of Outtime activities."

"But you've shut down the plant?" I asked.

"Quite completely," Kar-hinter said. "One of their experimental weapons went off 'accidentally' and totally destroyed the installation.''

Before I could ask anything more, Dr. Conners stuck his head in the door. "Gentlemen, Kar-hinter, I suggest that you let Captain Mathers sleep now. He needs the rest."

"Of course," Kar-hinter said, rising. "I will be seeing you again tomorrow, Eric."

And in a moment they were gone, and I drifted off into a long drugged sleep punctuated with hellish dreams of monster Kriths and equally monstrous Micas and Scotis; and I wondered if those two had escaped the destruction of Staunton.

When Kar-hinter came back the next day, accompanied by the tall, swarthy, black-uniformed Pall, his bodyguard, I was more nearly able to carry on a decent conversation, though now it was his turn to do most of the talking. Pall, as was his custom, said nothing at all.

Mind probes had been used on Sally, Kar-hinter told me, and her every memory was now recorded in tiny molly cubes that were being scanned by computer, extracting important data about the Paratimers and their operations. Already Kar-hinter knew more about them than I did, though he did ask me a few questions to confirm certain things that Sally had believed to be true.

"You have done us a great service, Eric," Kar-hinter said at length, "a truly great service to both mankind and Krith. We now know who our true enemies in this Timeline are."

I just nodded.

"Tell me, Eric," Kar-hinter said slowly, peering into my eyes, "you were there six weeks, under their eyes, constantly bombarded with their propaganda. What has that done to you?"

I had the sudden feeling of fear, as if Kar-hinter were about to uncover some deep, hidden guilt.

"What do you mean?" I asked.

"Sally von Heinen deeply believes that we Kriths are monsters involved in some great, elaborate plot to conquer and enslave mankind on all the Timelines. Has any of that belief rubbed off onto you, Eric? What *has* the experience done to you? Do you doubt us?"

187

"For God's sake, Kar-hinter," I said, trying to convince myself as much as him, "I sent those messages, didn't I? I called you there."

"I know that," Kar-hinter said, "but that is not the answer I want. Are there *any* doubts about us in your mind?"

"Run a mind probe on me," I said defensively. "Then you can tell if I'm lying."

"Eric," Kar-hinter said slowly, "you know that we cannot run a mind probe on you. You are a Timeliner. You are conditioned. A mind probe would kill you."

"Oh," I said weakly, foolishly. "That's right, isn't it?"

"It is, Eric. I will have to trust you. I will have to believe what you tell me."

Pall's dark eyes gazed at me with a cold look that seemed to cut through my skin. I didn't feel that *he* would trust me no matter what I said or did.

I looked back at Kar-hinter. "Then it's this," I said slowly and knew that I was lying even as I said it, but there wasn't anything else I could say, "I'm the same man I was six weeks ago. Nothing has changed. I still believe in what we're doing, we, all of us, Kriths and Timeliners. Those people—the Paratimers—have made some kind of terrible mistake. They're the ones who are wrong."

"I believe you, Eric, and I am glad of it. You are too valuable a man to lose." He paused. "Now tell me, what is this Von Heinen woman to you? We must assume that she is a widow now, if that helps you any."

"I don't know what she is to me, Kar-hinter," I said, and this time I was speaking the truth. "I really don't know. Maybe she just reminds me too much of someone I knew a long time ago." I shook my head. "But I can assume that she hates my guts now."

"For betraying Staunton?"

I nodded. "She trusted me. She thought I had been converted to their side."

Kar-hinter was silent for a few moments "We are finished with her," he said. "We have gained all the knowledge we can from her. You may have her if you wish. I am sure that our technicians could see to it that she, ah, felt differently about you."

"No!" I said vehemently. "Don't tamper with her mind."

"As you wish," Kar-hinter said, rising, his short tail lashing the air behind him. Pall rose with him. "You may decide whether you want her and, ah, as she is. Tomorrow or the next day you will be debriefed at length concerning your stay in Staunton. Routine formality, you understand. But when that is over and Dr. Conners releases you from the hospital, you may take a rest. I am sure that you have earned it."

"Thanks," I said.

"I thought that you might like a cabin in one of the Eden Lines," Kar-hinter said. "You and Sally."

"I'll think about it."

"Please do, Eric. A long rest is prescribed for you."

And I did think about it for the next few days.

22

WITH SALLY IN EDEN

I didn't really know exactly where the Eden Lines were located
Somewhere to the far T-West of RTGB-307, beyond the
Carolingian Lines. Why the worlds there were uninhabited I'm
not sure either. Chemical warfare seems to be the most likely
thing since the Earth there shows no signs of thermonuclear
craters, nor does its air carry any deadly bacteria. So, I guess, on
those worlds men had developed deadly gases which they had
used to destroy themselves. In a way I was glad of that since that
left maybe half a dozen Lines that the Kriths had taken over and
cleaned up, using automated equipment to transform them into
virtual earthly paradises. They were rest and recuperation stations for weary human Timeliners of rather high status. I was
honored in being offered a cabin in one of them.

Sally didn't feel quite so honored, though she accepted her
fate with stoic calm. She hardly spoke to me from the time we
boarded the airship in Bakersville, South Africa, to when we
stepped out of the skudder somewhere in North America in one
of the Eden Lines.

"Here you are, Captain Mathers," said the tall, dark-skinned
skudder pilot who reminded me a little of Pall. "Eden. You
know the rules. You're not allowed to bring in any Outtime
artifacts. Everything you will need is provided by the cabin."

"I know," I said.

"Then, ah, would you both please undress and give me your

clothing." He smiled awkwardly. "This *is* Eden, you know."

I remembered the Judeo-Christian myth that had given the Eden Lines their name.

"Yeah," I answered and began stripping.

Sally stood silently staring at us both, hate and defiance in her eyes. So must Kristin have stood when the governor's men approached her.

When I had removed my clothing and handed it to the pilot, I turned to her.

"Come on, Sally," I said. "You've got to play it by the rules."

"I'm your prisoner," she said. "I'll do as you say. I have no choice."

"I wish you wouldn't take that attitude," I said, trying not to look at the skudder pilot.

"Well, it's the truth, isn't it?"

"Only partly. Oh, damned it, get undressed."

Sally did, without expression, quickly and efficiently. In a moment her blouse and shorts and panties were a bundle wrapped around her shoes, and she handed the bundle to the skudder pilot.

It's funny. I don't think I've ever really described Sally to you. I suppose it's about time.

I had really only seen her naked once before, back when I was trying to get to the radio transceiver in the sautierboat in Staunton and then I didn't have time to appreciate the view. Now I did—not that I hadn't appreciated how she looked from the moment I saw her. But that's all beside the point, isn't it? I was going to tell you how she looked.

Sally appeared younger than her twenty-six years, fresh and almost innocent. She had blond hair and a funny color of green to her eyes; she was five feet five inches tall, and her measurements were something like 37-22-36. So much for statistics. What can they really tell you?

Maybe she didn't have the *tremendous* proportions of G'lendal or Jonna, but what she did have was perfect. Like her breasts, for example: high, round, firm, tipped with small round nipples, and if she had ever worn a bra in her life I couldn't imagine why. Her waist was slender, flaring out to perfectly rounded hips and the neatest set of buttocks I've ever seen. The clump of hair between her thighs was so pale and blond as to be almost invisible.

Her face was midway between being oval and triangular, and her eyes seemed almost too large for her face, but that wasn't bad at all. Her lips, even when she was angry, seemed to have a tendency to want to smile, and when she really did smile, she showed teeth that could hardly have been better formed. Her face was surrounded by the blond hair that was very long, though she usually kept it piled high atop her head, with bangs curling down across her forehead almost to her eyebrows, while another bunch of hair cascaded down her back to her shoulder blades.

If there were anything wrong with the appearance of Sally Beall von Heinen, I don't know what it was, unless you'd be foolish enough to say that she wasn't *quite* as beautiful as G'lendal. But then maybe G'lendal was a little bit too perfect.

And, as I said before, I thought there was more to my feeling for Sally then just the hot urges I felt below my waist.

"Thanks," the skudder pilot was saying as she handed him the bundle of clothing, and he looked at her with something in his eyes that wasn't hard to read. He'd like to have been in my place.

"I'll be back for you in a month," he went on. "You two have a nice time." He paused, then said, "Oh, by the way, Kar-hinter said to tell you that he'd probably drop in on you in the next few days, if that's okay with you."

"Yes, I suppose. Thanks," I said.

Moments later the pilot closed the skudder's hatch, waved to us through the bubble. Then a time-wrenching buzz filled the air. The skudder vanished.

"Let's go take a look at the cabin," I said to Sally.

"Let's get something straight right now," she said, holding still. "I know exactly what my status is here. I'm your prisoner, and you can make me do whatever you want. Because I know that I'm not going to put up a fight every time you tell me to do something. I don't have that kind of fatal pride. I'll do what you

192

say." She paused for breath. "But get this straight, Eric Mathers or whatever your name is, and get it straight right now. I'll only be doing what I do because I have no choice, because you and your goddamned Kriths can make me do it—and not because I want to. Do you understand me?"

There was no point in arguing at this stage of the game, so I simply said. "Yes, I understand. Now let's look at that cabin."

I took her by the hand and led her.

The field in which the cabin sat consisted of perhaps half a dozen acres of cleared land, green and gently rolling, each rise topped with fruit trees of different kinds, apples, cherries, peaches, oranges, you name it. Bushes grew in profusion, many of them flowering and all of them carefully trimmed. Paths ran between the trees and bushes, rock-bordered and lined with other types of flowering plants. The grass was a bright, rich green, closely cropped and soft as an expensive carpet under our naked feet.

The cabin itself sat just to the left of the center of the carefully tended clearing and reminded me of a brick and glass model of the planet Saturn, cut in half, or maybe half-buried in the earth. The ring was a low wall that circled the house and the planet was the brick and glass dome of the structure, a hemisphere sheltered by the wall that circled it and the trees that rose above it, shadowing the cabin under their leaves.

Inside was a single room, divided by low partitions into four roughly equal sections. One was the sleeping area, containing two big double beds, the second the autokitchen and indoor dining area, the third was a living area with library access console, video tape player, multichannel music gear and miscellaneous games and things. The final section of the house was a huge sunken bathtub and a toilet cubicle. It was done in soft pleasant earth colors, and sometimes it was hard to tell where the walls ended and the broad expanse of windows looking out into the gardens began. It was a nice place to be marooned with a beautiful woman, even one who wanted to see me dead.

"Sit down," I told Sally, gesturing toward the comfortable-looking furniture in the living area. "I'll see if I can get us something to eat."

"I'm not hungry," Sally replied, sitting, but refusing to look at me.

"Okay, then, I'm ordering you to eat."

She didn't protest, at least not out loud, so I went into the kitchen and studied the menu. The autokitchen had been programmed to suit the culinary tastes of men from hundreds of different cultures, everything from the obscure and involved vegetarianism of some of the Indus Lines to the cannibalism of the Dramalians, though in this case the "long pig" was synthesized. The Aegean squid appealed to me since it was one of my favorites and a delicacy I hadn't tasted in years, but I gave way to my concern for Sally and punched out something that her Anglo-Saxon upbringing would have found more tasteful: roast beef, baked potatoes, etc.

A few minutes later the plates popped out of the oven, and I wheeled the trays into the living room, where Sally sat in the same position, apparently having moved nothing but her eyes during my absence.

"Now here it is," I said. "I won't try to force you to eat, but you won't be hurting anyone but yourself if you don't."

I sat down across from her and began devouring my meal. After a while Sally began to eat as well, but without any great gusto.

"Pretty good, isn't it?" I asked between mouthfuls.

Sally nodded morosely.

After a while, having eaten perhaps half of her serving, Sally put down her fork, looked up at me, and said slowly, "Why did you bring me here?"

I looked back at her for a long while before I answered. "You know, I'm not really sure. Kar-hinter suggested it, more or less, and it seemed like a good idea."

"Kar-hinter?" she asked. "The Krith?" The way she said it made it sound like a dirty word.

"Yes."

"Hasn't he done enough to me?"

"Did he harm you?"

"You wouldn't understand," she snapped.

"Maybe I would. Try me."

194

"What does a man like you know about honor?"

"More than you might think," I said. When she didn't speak again, I went on. "I suppose you're referring to the mind probe he had used on you?"

"Of course."

"Okay; so he forced your mind to divulge everything you know about the Paratimers. You had nothing to do with it really. I mean, it's not as if you betrayed them voluntarily. Kar-hinter just. . . ."

"He invaded my soul!" Sally said angrily. "He raped my mind!"

"Now wait a minute. All he did was. . . ."

"I know what he did and you can't explain it away. He made me betray everyone and everything I love." She paused for a moment, fought with her emotions. "Why did you let him do it, Eric? I . . . I thought we could trust you. Mica did too. We all did. We. . . ."

"I'm sorry about that, Sally, but I did what I had to do."

"What you had to do! Why? I can understand your working for *them* before, when you didn't know any better. But . . . but how could you after you *knew*, after we told you what *they* are?"

"Just calm down for a minute and listen to me."

Sally crossed her arms below her naked breasts, her fingernails digging into her upper arms, her face a complex of unreadable expressions.

"All I had was the word of the Paratimers as opposed to the word of the Kriths. Mica was never able to offer me any real proof of his claims. I know that *you* believe what he told you, and I think he believed it too. But belief isn't proof, no matter how strongly the belief is held and no matter by how many people. It's just a belief unless there's objective proof—and I never saw any really objective proof that couldn't have been faked."

"Are you saying that Staunton and Mica and Scoti and all the others and the books and tapes and all that are, well, built on lies? Can you believe that's true?"

"Aren't you and Mica trying to tell me that everything I've seen in my own Lines is based on a Lie?"

"Yes, of course. . . . Oh."

"You see? It was easier for me to accept Mica and his world as a lie than it was for me to accept the experiences of my whole life as a lie."

For a moment I almost thought I had got through and that she was going to be able to see it from my point of view, but then she said, "How can you be so blind?"

"I could ask you the same thing. Just look around you. Does this look like the work of man-hating monsters?"

"It's just a part of their scheme to lull you into trusting them."

"Here we go again," I said, rising and looking out the vast expanse of window. "Our arguing won't convince either of us that the other is right. I spent six weeks in your world. Now you spend a month in one of mine. Maybe you'll see why I couldn't accept what I was told."

"No," Sally said. "You won't be able to brainwash me that easily. I know better. I know what the Kriths are, and I won't believe their Lie."

I suddenly wished that I knew what the Kriths were and what they wanted, what they really wanted from us. And I realized then, maybe for the first time, that Sally and Mica and Scoti and the others in Staunton had planted some serious doubts in my mind, doubts that I would, sooner or later, be forced to resolve.

In the garden behind the cabin was an enormous swimming pool, a great free-form thing some hundred yards long and maybe fifty yards wide at its widest point. One end was no more than a few inches deep, but the other, where the diving boards were, was at least fifteen yards to the bottom. And the water was a clear crystal, pure, reflecting the cloudless blue sky above.

Along the sides of the pool ran a wide strip of soft, spongy green material, a vast mattress for sunbathing. Here and there were reclining chairs and two extensions of the autokitchen for dialing meals and drinks.

We had been there for three days by then, and Sally had begun to relax some, at times even seeming to forget where she was and why and that she was, by her own definition, my prisoner.

We had been swimming in the pool, diving and splashing and even occassionally laughing at our own foolishness. Finally, exhausted, we had climbed out of the pool onto the sun-deck and lay dripping with water. I dialed us drinks and lay back looking up at the clear blue sky of this earth, a world uncluttered by the more obvious works of civilization.

"Eric," Sally said suddenly, a sharp edge of seriousness to her voice, "we can't go on like this."

How many times across the Lines have women said that and for how many different reasons?

"Why?" I asked in all seriousness.

"I'm beginning to like you too well," she said. "I really believe you're sincere about what you say." She paused. "Sometimes I even forget and just, well, enjoy myself and then I remember and. . . . Well, when I remember what I am and what you are and what this place is and why we're here, when I remember these things I hate myself for enjoying it and I hate you for making me enjoy it. And I think that sooner or later I will come to hate you enough to kill you."

"I wouldn't want you to do that," I said, jealously thinking about her relationship with Mica. Back in Staunton she had told me that she was his mistress. I somehow just couldn't bring myself to imagine her in bed with that cold fish, and I wondered just what it was that she felt for him. I couldn't believe it was love or even real sexual attraction to him.

Why then, I asked myself, had Sally been his mistress? Well, maybe you could attribute it to hero worship, gratitude for what she believed he and his Paratimers were doing for her and her people. If she could marry Count Albert von Heinen to advance the American rebel cause, couldn't she be bedding with Mica for just about the same reason? It seemed sort of likely to me—especially when she had never shown any real affection toward the Paratimer leader—and it did help my ego a lot to think it was so, as if I didn't have to compete with the man if I could show him up for what he was—whatever he was.

Then she brought me out of my thoughts.

"Listen to me," she said, sitting up. "One of us is right and the other is wrong. Do you agree?"

"Well, yes. There must be objective proof somewhere."

"Then if we learn what's true, can't we both accept it?"

"Yes, I'll accept it if we can find real proof."

"Can you call your Kar-hinter some way?"

"No, but the skudder pilot said that he'd be coming here to see us in a few days. Why?"

"Ask him about this Cross-Line Civilization you talk about. Ask him to take us there and show us that it really exists and that it's as wonderful as they claim it is. And then, if he does, I'll believe that the Kriths are really what you think they are and that the Paratimers are as mistaken as you believe."

Perhaps Sally and her friends had made me doubt the Kriths, I thought, but it also looked as if I had somehow made Sally begin to doubt what she had been told. We were both doubting the verities by which we had lived—but they could be proved, one way or the other. Kar-hinter could take us to the Cross-Line Civilization, show us how men and Kriths worked together to build a perfect world—and that would solve our problems, destroy my own growing doubts, and show Sally that everything I had told her was true. It was so simple. Why hadn't I thought of it before?

"Okay," I said. "We'll do that. We'll get Kar-hinter to take us there."

Four more days went by before Kar-hinter arrived.

It was night. The yard-tending robots had completed their work and the carefully controlled nightly rain had begun to fall. Sally and I were inside the cabin watching a videotape of the classic *Pirates of Avalon,* with English dubbed, when I heard a rapping at the door.

"What's that?" Sally gasped, almost leaping to her feet.

"I'll see," I said, rising and crossing to the door.

When I told the door to open and the cabin's light spilled through it out into the darkness, I saw the tall, naked form of a Krith.

"Kar-hinter?" I asked, not sure that I recognized him in the poor light. And all Kriths do look pretty much alike to a human.

"Hello, Eric," Kar-hinter replied, water running down his

face from the steady rain, dripping from his chin, trickling down his nearly olive-colored, hairless body. "May I come in?"

"Of course," I said. "We've been expecting you."

As Kar-hinter came into the room, shook water from his body like a dog, and found himself a chair, I cut off the video player and turned up the lights.

"Hello, Sally," he said. "I hope that you are finding Eden to be a pleasant place of captivity."

"There are worse prisons," Sally said, forcing herself to smile just a little despite the revulsion she must have felt. She moved back in her chair, trying to cover herself with her arms and legs as if there were some reason she should not let the alien see her naked, though I have never known a Krith to find any human being sexually attractive. I have the impression that their ideas of sex bear little resemblance to ours, but I don't know anything about them.

"I am glad you have accepted it," Kar-hinter said. "Eric is not an unpleasant jailer, I trust."

Sally looked at me, but did not reply.

"At least there is no open enmity," Kar-hinter said. "I had even hoped that perhaps you were lovers by now. Eh, Eric?"

"We get along," I said.

"Ah, but you sleep in separate beds, I think," the Krith said.

"Does it matter to you?" I asked, knowing that there was an angry, resentful edge to my voice. What business *was* it of his?

"I only want you to be satisfied, Eric," the alien said. "And you, Sally, do you still consider me a monster and Eric a traitor to mankind?"

"I've seen nothing yet to change my opinion of either of you," she said coldly. I wondered how much of it she really meant.

"You are doing a poor job of converting her, Eric."

"Is that my job?"

"No," Kar-hinter said. "Her conversion is of no importance to me. She can believe what she wishes. I only want to see you happy, Eric, rewarded, so to speak, for what you have done for us."

"Us?" Sally asked.

"Ah, yes, must I explain every plural pronoun I use?"

He was as close to being angry as I had ever seen him—him or any other Krith.

"By *us*," Kar-hinter was saying, "Sally, I mean allied mankind and Krith. We are partners in our own salvation."

"I wish I could believe that," Sally said.

"Do you really?" Kar-hinter asked. "That would be a beginning, at least."

"Kar-hinter," I said, "let's cut out this verbal fencing for a minute."

"Of course, Eric."

"I want to make a request."

"Anything that is within my power to grant is yours," the Krith said.

"I want you to take Sally and me to the Cross-Lines Civilization."

"Why, Eric?" He didn't seem surprised at my request, but then did anything ever seem to surprise him?

"Well, that's one of the cornerstones of the Paratimers' arguments against the Kriths," I said. "They say that the Cross-Line Civilization is one of the Great Lies, the other one being the Contratime signals. Well, if we could show Sally that the Cross-Line Civilization does exist, she would accept that *she* is the one who has been lied to."

"But, frankly, Eric, it is of no importance to me what *she* thinks is true or false."

"It's important to me."

"I see." Kar-hinter paused for a moment. "And you, Eric, why do *you* want to see the Cross-Line Civilization?"

"I just told you."

"Did you? Or, Eric, might it be that you too have begun to believe her and her Paratimers? Is *she* converting *you*, Eric?"

"Does it matter?" I asked. "If we can visit the Cross-Line worlds, neither of us would have any reason to doubt."

"But it does matter, my dear Eric," Kar-hinter said slowly, spreading his manlike hands. "You know as well as I that skudders are scarce this far West and must be used only for work of vital importance to the master plans. We just cannot call up a

200

skudder every time we want to take a pleasure trip, especially one so long as the one you propose.''

''Surely you could arrange it if you tried,'' I insisted.

''I could, Eric, I believe, but only if I were convinced it would be worth the while. I am not, not for *her*. She does not matter to me or to the plan.''

''Do I?'' I asked slowly, playing what I supposed was my trump card.

''Of course you do, Eric. You are becoming one of our most valuable operatives.''

''Then would you arrange such a trip to convince me?''

''Are you that near to defection?''

''I don't know,'' I said slowly, being more honest with him that I had been before and on purpose. ''I don't want to know.'' I paused, then said to him: ''I admit that I've been pretty shaken by some of what has happened. The Paratimers were awfully convincing. And I do have some doubts, not many, but some, and I don't like them. I want absolute certainty that I'm doing the right thing, that I'm fighting on the right side. And you can give me that certainty if you'll just take us to the Cross-Line worlds. If you don't. . . . Well, I don't mean to be threatening, Kar-hinter, but if you don't, I'll wonder why. And I'll suspect that maybe you didn't take us there because you couldn't, because there's really no such place.''

''Quite a speech, Eric,'' Kar-hinter replied at last. ''I did not know that it had gone this far with you.''

For the first time I felt fear of Kar-hinter and the whole Krithian machine. What if Sally were right? What if Kar-hinter were really the monster she believed he was? It would be the easiest thing in the world for him to bring in a squad of men and wipe us out here and now. No one would ever know, and my doubts would never have an opportunity to spread if he killed us both now. I wonder if my fear showed.

''So you might turn against us,'' Kar-hinter was saying slowly, but without antagonism. ''I would not want that to happen, Eric. Perhaps I should not have given you this woman.''

''She has nothing to do with my doubts at this point,'' I said.

"Can you convince me that what I am doing is right?"

"As I said, Eric, skudders are hardly available for pleasure cruises, but perhaps this is important enough. I will see what I can do. I will return tomorrow and tell you." He rose from the chair where he had sat. "I will leave now. Good night, Eric, Sally."

The not-quite-human smile on Kar-hinter's face faded into a look of intense concentration, and then he flickered out of existence, and Sally and I sat there quietly, looking at the place where he had been and wondering what he would do tomorrow when he returned.

23

ACROSS THE LINES

Kar-hinter appeared simultaneously with the skudder, both arriving in the middle of the garden before the cabin just a short while after noon on the day following his visit. The Krith waved for the skudder pilot and the black-uniformed Pall to remain in their seats and walked quickly up the path toward the cabin, smiling broadly in an almost human fashion and waving to Sally and me. We had just come out after hearing the unmistakable whine of the skudder's probability generators.

"Eric," he called, "I have been able to arrange the transportation for the two of you. We shall leave at once for the East. Are both of you ready?"

I looked at Sally.

"I didn't bring anything here with me," she said, "and there's nothing I want to take." She paused. "But, well, I would like to comb my hair and put on some makeup."

Since she had resigned herself to being nude while in Eden, Sally had taken to using body makeup from one of the Europo-Minoan Lines that was supplied by the cabin. Not that I thought she really needed it; her face and body looked fine without it.

"Very well," Kar-hinter said, still smiling as broadly. "There is clothing for you both in the skudder. I do hope that you have eaten."

"Yes," I said. "We just finished lunch."

"Good," the Krith said. "It is a long trip."

"So we've been told," Sally said, her voice suddenly doubtful, as if she were feeling the same sort of fear that I had felt the night before, as if she suspected that Kar-hinter was now arranging to have us both killed before we could express our doubts to anyone else.

"Hurry, then," the Krith said to Sally. "Fix yourself and we shall go."

She went back into the cabin, almost seeming fearful of leaving me alone with Kar-hinter.

It wasn't long before we entered the skudder and began the trip across the Lines.

The small skudder was crowded with the five of us in it, though neither the pilot nor Pall spoke, and Pall hardly even moved. Pall, if you weren't looking at him, was easy to ignore.

After a while you can almost become adjusted to just about anything, even the mind-wrenching, stomach-twisting sensation of skudding across the near infinity of parallel universes. Flicker. Flicker. Flicker. At least I seemed to become more adjusted than usual as the trip lengthened from minutes to hours and still we moved.

Sally, Kar-hinter and I talked very little after the first few minutes. Despite the adjustment, talking in a skudding craft seemed to be more trouble than it was worth.

There were two bundles of clothing for us, brightly colored, nearly transparent, form-fitting sleeveless shirts and knee-length pants, pointed shoes, and peaked caps. Kar-hinter assured us that these were the height of sartorial splendor in the first of the Cross-Line worlds that we were about to visit.

To pass the time, Kar-hinter had provided us with a stack of magazines from Sally's native Line, some of which I suppose she found interesting. I was left to boredom. A large thermal bottle of coffee sat on the floor between us and after our stomachs had more or less adjusted to the flickering, we each, Sally and I, had a cup.

What happened after my first cup of coffee seemed unimportant at the time, but in retrospect it loomed much larger, and I later thought it might be the key to the whole sequence of events.

When I finished my cup of coffee, I set the cup carefully on he floor beside me, picked up one of the magazines, a cheap olonial picture magazine devoted mostly to news, gossip, and umor about the British nobility, pictures of castles and of peers f the realm, subtle hints of what lord was sleeping with whose vife in articles written for a child's mentality. My eyelids began o grow heavy in the middle of a story about a party held by the arl of Something and attended only by the Duchess of Whatsit she was the complete guest list) and how neighbors and ser- ants later claimed that they saw them dancing in the nude in the arl's garden to the music of the fifty-piece orchestra the earl ad hired. I never did find out what happened after the nude lance, but I have a good imagination. I put the magazine down nd saw that Sally was nodding too. This didn't strike me as nusual: the skudder trip had now become dull and uninterest- ng, and sleep would be the best thing for us both until we got to ur destination. I shifted into a more comfortable position, losed my eyes and thought about as little as I could until a varm, comfortable drowsiness slowly settled over me.

My next memory was that of Kar-hinter shaking my shoulder, aying, "Eric, wake up. We are nearly there."

I shook myself, forced my eyes to open, and felt for an instant great sense of impending doom that I was now sure was njustified.

Can I say that things looked any different when I awoke? No. he skudder was exactly the same. My empty coffee cup still sat n the floor where I had put it. The magazine, its pages open, vas exactly where I had laid it. Sally sat in the seat across from ne, leaning against the wall, sleeping. Kar-hinter, the skudder ilot and Pall were as they had been, looked the same in every letail. Nothing had changed. Or had it? I felt that something ad, but I could not say what and chalked it up to my imagina- ion.

"I must have fallen asleep," I said, rubbing my face, feeling ny hands on my cheeks, knowing that I was doing exactly what was doing, but still somehow unsure of it.

Actually, even now, I'm not sure how much of this sensation f unreality I felt at the time and how much of it has entered my nemories since the events—which I have gone over in my mind

so many times that I have probably lost the original memor[y]
under layers of, well, remembering the memories.

"Awaken Sally," Kar-hinter said. "We will be there in les[s]
than five minutes."

"Okay," I said, fully awake now.

I shook Sally's shoulder. Her eyes blinked open; she looke[d]
up at me, shook her head, yawned, and nearly smiled.

"We're almost there," I said.

"Oh, good," she said. "I was having the most pleasar[t]
dream."

"Momentarily you shall have a most pleasant reality," Ka[r]
hinter said.

I became aware of the flickering of the skudder's probabilit[y]
force as it slowed and then stopped, and bright late-afternoo[n]
sunlight flooded the interior of the craft through the transparer[t]
dome.

"Everybody out," the skudder's pilot said, rising from hi[s]
seat, then pushing a button that caused the craft's hatch to open.

"I hope that your sleep has been sufficient," Kar-hinter sai[d]
as he rose. "We will be here several hours, and you will hav[e]
little opportunity to rest before we leave."

"We're fine," I said.

"Good," Kar-hinter replied. "Come. We are expected."

The place where the skudder had come to rest was a shallo[w]
circular depression in a wide field composed of what I thought t[o]
be concrete, though the substance was blue-green in color and [I]
discovered upon disembarking from the craft that it was so[ft]
under my feet. The field extended perhaps a hundred yards in a[ll]
directions, pitted every few dozen feet with other depression[s]
and in perhaps a third of them sat skudders like our own, thoug[h]
some were brightly decorated with designs that I didn't recog[-]
nize.

On our left the field terminated in a broad green meado[w]
which was apparently a landing field for another type of craf[t]
fragile-looking teardrops of metal and glass that I tentativel[y]
identified as some type of antigrav aircraft. To our right the fiel[d]
gave way to a gray concrete slab upon which rested a sli[m]
golden tower that reached into the sky perhaps a hundred fee[t]
On the top of the tower sat a transparent globe maybe ten feet i[n]

diameter or a little larger. I don't know what it was. Beyond the tower was another grassy field across which a number of people were strolling and playing a game that looked similar to the golf of Sally's Line. Beyond the field was the city.

It was a fairyland of towers and turrets and minarets and bright flags and streamers waving in the breeze, bridges and catwalks of spun glass connecting the towers, sparkling in the sunlight. Here and there in the air above them were the teardrop aircraft.

Two men and two women waited outside the craft, smiling, but not speaking until we had climbed down to the blue-green field and taken in our surroundings. Then Kar-hinter said, "Eric Mathers, Sally von Heinen, please allow me to introduce our guides. Dylla, Jocasta, Dicton, and Hallacy."

The first two were women and the other two men, all with the rich earthy features of south Europe, the kind of Latin beauty you can find in some of the Roman statues that still exist in Sally's Line. There was a similarity about them, as if they were all of a single family, brothers and sisters, though I never really knew for sure. They all smiled in reply, offered their hands and welcomed us to Calethon I in flawless, idiomatic English of Sally's Line.

Just a few words about these people and their clothing. Like Sally and me, they were dressed in sleeveless shirts and knee-length pants made of an almost transparent material, transparent enough so that their excellent bodies were quite visible. And every square inch of their skin was artificially pigmented in bright, yet pleasant colors.

Dylla, the larger and more sensual of the girls, was sky-blue: her face, her arms, her legs, her torso, even her hair was blue, but of a darker shade, and her thin clothing was blue as well. She had an almost round, though not moonlike face, with deep, dark eyes and full lips. Her breasts were fully as large as Jonna's and it seemed as if they were about to tear through the thin fabric of her blouse. My eyes were drawn on down her slender waist to the triangle of dark-blue hair that grew between her thighs. I tore my eyes away to look at the others.

Jocasta and her clothing were a canary-yellow. She was a shorter girl than Dylla by several inches, and the proportions of her body were a little less impressive, though not bad at all. She made up for this lack—if it can be said to be a lack—with one of the prettiest faces I've ever seen and a smile that was simple, friendly, ingenuous. She was like somebody's kid sister who had suddenly become a woman, but still had the innocent openness of a child. I liked her instantly.

Dicton was the largest of the four, a red man well over six feet tall and with the features and physique of an Adonis. He spoke rarely and then only in short sentences, and I didn't know whether that was because he wasn't too bright or because he was very bright and didn't want to waste time with useless conversation.

Hallacy was shorter, stockier, more bullishly masculine in all respects than Dicton—an orange Hercules to his red Adonis —and a loquacious fellow with a keen sense of humor once he got started. He was a likable person, but I suspected that he could be a hard man to deal with if you ever got his temper up.

These were our guides.

Calethon I, they explained, once the formalities of introduction were out of the way, was the most westward of all the Lines that made up the Cross-Line Civilization. To the East forty-nine more Lines extended, all interlinked and mutually interdependent, all differing phases, as it were, of the same "world." There were a dozen Calethon Lines, then five Matthen Lines, the sixteen Manshien Lines, and so on. Calethon I was, they told us, the Westward Terminal Line for the Cross-Line worlds, a transfer and processing world, in essence, though there was some light industry and a number of Transtemporal research centers and universities specializing in Timeline studies, history divergence and things of that sort.

"What will be first?" orange Hallacy asked. "A tour of Bershaw?"

"No, I think not," Kar-hinter said. "Let us save that until last. First I would like to prove to our friends that what we are saying is all true. Take us to the terminal head, please."

"Certainly," said Dylla, the girl of the big blue breasts. "We can take our aircar into Bershaw and leave it there." Turning to me and smiling a very warm—and was it inviting?— smile, she said, "That's the largest terminal head in this hemisphere, you know."

I certainly didn't know. I didn't even know what a terminal head was. But I smiled back, and then Sally and I followed the smiling foursome and Kar-hinter across the field to one of the teardrop aircraft. Pall, silent and enigmatic, brought up the rear, perhaps standing guard over us.

The crystal fairyland that I had noticed on arrival was the city of Bershaw, or as near to a city as these people of Calethon I had. It was a vast, intertwined complex of shops and open-air markets and government offices and amusement centers, though it was not a city in the sense of being a dwelling place for people. The natives of Calethon I lived in isolated houses scattered across the world, never in tight clusters like most of the Lines I knew. Someone, probably Hallacy, told me that the permanent population of Calethon I was somewhere in the neighborhood of eight hundred million, and there was plenty of room for everyone to have privacy. There were certainly no population problems here.

Jocasta, the little canary girl who piloted the aircar, set us down in another green field in the very center of the city, directly in front of a long, colorful building of glass and metal and stone that must have covered an area equal to a dozen city blocks in Sally's world. The front of the building showed a long series of doors through which a constant stream of people moved, in and out, many of them in costumes differing wildly from those worn by ourselves and our guides or in no costumes at all. It reminded me a little of the mixture of cultures I had seen in Staunton and seemed to remind Sally of the same. At least her face clouded, though she did not speak.

From the rear of the building or perhaps from a landing deck on its top rose dozens of large aircars, or perhaps airlorries would be a better term since they appeared to be cargo-carrying vehicles. An equal number came dropping out of the sky to replace those that rose, all moving easily, silently, even gracefully.

We all climbed out of the aircar, crossed the grassy field, and stepped onto a moving sidewalk that carried us effortlessly toward the gaping doors of what our guides had called a terminal head.

"Just exactly what is this place?" I asked Hallacy, who was standing at my side.

Before the orange man could answer, Kat-hinter interrupted, saying, "Wait a moment, Eric, and we shall show you. That would be more effective than telling you. Would it not?" he asked of Hallacy.

The orange Hercules nodded, and I said, "Okay."

"Where shall we go?" the lovely blue Dylla asked.

"You make the choice," Kar-hinter answered. "Merely make it interesting for our guests."

"Very well."

With Dylla leading us with her swinging buttocks, we stepped off the moving sidewalk just outside the building, stepped onto another; and were carried into the terminal head.

The building was interesting in the way that many public buildings are interesting, decorated with vast, colorful murals and exotic statuary, but all in all it wasn't too unlike many other buildings that I had seen before. Except, that is, for the *conveyors*.

The far wall of the enormous room consisted of rows of booths that extended dozens of yards in both directions, small rooms that reminded me more of elevators than anything else, and my first impression was that that was exactly what they were. People in the line ahead of us stepped into the booths, punched a series of buttons, and the doors closed. Moments later the doors opened and the booths were empty.

I noticed that just the opposite seemed to be happening at the booths at the far end of the row. People got out, but no one got in.

"What is this?" Sally asked, perhaps with a touch of fear in her voice.

And then we were entering a booth ourselves, all eight of us, and the doors were closing behind us as Dylla punched on the button panel. I had an instant of fear myself, the thought that perhaps Kar-hinter had taken us all this way to. . . . *Don't be foolish*, I said to myself. *He's only doing what you requested.*

"Calethon IV, I think would be a good place," the blue girl was saying.

Then flicker. Flicker. Flicker.

Exactly like being in a skudder, I thought. Then, by God, that's what it is. A skudder!

The doors opened and we were back in the terminal head. Or, rather, *a* terminal head. One very similar to the one we had just left, but differing in some respects, minor things that were hard to pin down. Except for the people. Most of them were lighter-skinned than those we had encountered before, and their clothing was of a different cut, more elaborate and decorative, though there was a liberal sprinkling of other costumes, not a few clothed as we were and with brightly pigmented skin like that of our guides. I still had not seen a single Krith besides Kar-hinter in the Cross-Line worlds.

"This is Calethon IV," Dylla said, "one of our heavy industry Lines. Let's go outside for a moment; then we'll go on to Matthen II."

Following the blue girl's swaying butt and then stepping onto a sliding sidewalk, we moved out of the terminal head and out into a city that looked more like what I thought a city should look like: regular streets, buildings of steel and stone and glass, moving vehicles that stayed on or near the surface. Beyond the city, from an observation deck located on top of the terminal head, we saw the dark structures of factories stretching toward the horizon, belching thin, filtered smoke into a sky that was still very blue. Somehow the factories had an esthetic charm of their own, but I would find it hard to describe. It wasn't at all unpleasant.

"There are more skudders produced here in a day than on all the other Lines combined," red Dicton said proudly.

Then, a little while later, after stopping for drinks in a luxurious lounge in the terminal head building, we reentered one of the conveyor booths and flickered again.

Matthen II was the spaceport Line of the Cross-Line worlds where huge, silvery, needle-thin spaceships rose silently into the sky, bound for the moon and Mars and Venus and the asteroids, there to discharge passengers and cargo and reload

211

with raw materials and a few finished products from the extraterrestrial colonies and return them to Earth. Space travel was comparatively rare across the Timelines; it was generally far more expensive than skudding, but even here in the Cross-Lines there were a few products that were cheaper to get from the Solar planets than to try to collect across the Lines.

Hallacy told me that a fantastically huge spaceship with a faster-than-light drive was being built in orbit around Earth. Soon it would carry a load of colonists across the light-years to a very Earth-like world that scouts had recently discovered some three hundred light-years away. And he said that he was sorry that we could not wait around an hour or so until it got dark and then have a chance to see the ship. Even though it orbited rather far out, it was large enough to be easily seen from Earth after dark.

I was impressed.

After that, just before we returned to the terminal head, Dylla whispered something to me about Manshein IX which I didn't fully understand, but left me with a pleasant, excited feeling of anticipation.

Our next stop was Matthen V, the "Sea World," they called it, where most of mankind had moved into the oceans, leaving the land little more than a carefully landscaped playground, a world where men talked with dolphins, had learned to live in their aquatic environment, breathing through surgically implanted gills. Together, men and dolphins, they were building a culture unlike any on any other Timeline known to the Kriths.

Manshein III was a Timeline devoted entirely to the arts. Here there were settlements of writers where the greatest literature of all the Lines was slowly coming into being, we were told: artists' colonies where painting and sculpture were reaching unparalleled heights; groups of musicians who were evolving new and exciting forms of musical expression; photographers and hoiographers, engravers and printers and lithographers and dancers. You name it. We had no more than a few minutes to glimpse something of each, though even then our senses were overwhelmed with the sound and color and beauty of it all.

I hated to leave there, and that may sound odd coming from a professional killer like me, but it was true.

Manshein IX—the one blue Dylla had hinted about—was a Line devoted to nothing less than pure sexual hedonism, a world of constant Saturnalia, a place to which people came from the other Lines to spend a few days—or perhaps years—in erotic escape.

It was here, in the city that occupied Berhsaw's place on this world, as darkness was beginning to fall, that our party became divided. And I was sure that it was by intent, though who engineered it I didn't know, nor did I really care.

Dylla and I found ourselves alone, wandering down a wide avenue filled with people and one or two Kriths. The humans wore the most exotic and erotic dress I have ever seen, and the evening air was filled with pleasant, sensual odors and sounds and sights.

"We have a few moments together," Dylla said, looking at me with an inviting smile in her eyes. "Shall we spend them in pleasure?"

I looked back at her, my eyes following the full length of her blue-dyed body, nodded, felt a familiar urge rising in me.

"Come then," she said, leading me across the wide street and down a narrower one into a great green park that consisted of labyrinthine hedges and soft, yielding grass and the odor of flowering plants. Around us were the soft, rustling sounds of body against body and subdued cries and moans of pleasure and excitement, though the producers of those sounds were hidden from us by the growth of hedges and flowers.

"Here," Dylla said after a while, leading me into a hedge-surrounded recess as large as a medium-size bedroom and covered by soft grass.

"Now, dear Eric, do you want me?"

"What if I said no?" I asked, teasing her.

"Then I'd probably call Dicton for you. They tell me he's good at. . . ."

"No, I like girls better."

She took a step away from me, pulled the thin blouse up over her breasts and head, slipped her shorts down her hips and legs, and then stepped closer to me again, lovely and naked. Her body, now totally revealed, though it had hardly been hidden by her clothing, reminded me of that of G'lendal. The two could almost have worn each other's clothing, though both seemed inclined to do without clothing whenever possible.

"Kiss me, then, Eric," she whispered.

I did, and it was a long, lingering, burning kiss that reminded me of the way G'lendal kissed.

"Take these off," she said softly as we broke apart, tugging at my clothing. We were both gasping for breath, hot in our excitement.

As quickly as she had, I undressed, and then together, my hands on her full, round breasts, we lowered ourselves to the grass.

"I don't like to rush," she whispered into my ear, "but we shouldn't be away too long, darling."

I didn't speak, and there was no need to. Dylla lay back on the grass and opened herself to me. I moved above her and entered her easily, finding her warm and moist and passionately ready for me.

Again, during those short minutes while our bodies thrashed together on the grassy bed surrounded by hedges in the falling dusk, she reminded me of G'lendal, and in a way I didn't like that. Not now. But everything else I did like—Dylla was damned good at it.

It just didn't last long enough—but then does it ever?

The universe shattered with our orgasms.

Then, after a while, we rose, dressed, and returned to find our companions near where we had last seen them.

Sally did not meet my eyes, though Hallacy had a smug, satisfied expression on his orange face, and I wondered just what the others had been doing in our absence—and I felt a little jealous of Hallacy, though I knew that I really had no right to be. No right at all.

Into the terminal head and then back out again—into Manshein XIV, the university world, an earth given over to study, research, contemplation, to vast library computers that cataloged and refined all the knowledge of the other Lines, where men sought the ultimate answers to the ultimate questions about the nature of time and space and man and Krith and the "what" and "why" of the universe—but for some reason I didn't think that even here they had found the answers to those questions, not really.

Manshein XV—again a Timeline where men sought ultimates, but here in dark robes and the quietness of cloisters; in meditation or the mind-expanding sensation of half a hundred kinds of drugs, a half million religious orders sought whatever it is that men called God in their own diverse ways—and I wondered if any of them had made it.

"Time is running short," Kar-hinter said at last. "Take us back to Calethon I. We shall eat and see the sights of Bershaw before we must leave."

Following the undulations of Dylla's blue hips we walked back to the terminal head and flickered across the Lines back to Calethon I and the city of Bershaw.

Bershaw—a city out of the *Arabian Nights,* though lacking the barbarism and cruelty of ancient Arabia. A pageant of light and color and sound, an orgy of food and wine and music under the stars and crystal towers, a symphony of beauty, a collection of all that is lovely from uncounted worlds.

Bershaw—the gateway to the Cross-Line Civilization.

Six hours or a little more had gone by when Sally, Kar-hinter, Pall, and I returned to our waiting skudder, Sally and I at least still stunned by what we had seen and experienced. We said good-bye to beautiful blue Dylla, to yellow Jocasta, to red Dicton, to the Herculean-orange Hallacy, and began our trip back to—well, back to an Eden Line that would seem more dull than it had before.

Flicker. And the Cross-Line worlds were behind us.

"Are you satisfied now?" Kar-hinter asked as we settled down for the trip back.

"They lied to me," Sally said, pain in her voice. "It was all a lie. They said that the Cross-Line Civilization did not exist. But it does.''

"Yes, it does," Kar-hinter said seriously. "It is exactly as we have told it. Is that not so, Eric?" I nodded. "And the Contratime communication is a fact as well, though I cannot prove it so easily."

"I don't think you need to, Kar-hinter," Sally said, apology in her voice. "We can accept that, too. Can't we, Eric?"

"Yes, of course," I said. "You've shown us more than enough, Kar-hinter. Please let me apologize for ever having doubted it."

"Don't concern yourself," the Krith said. "I am merely pleased that your questions have been resolved. Now we can go about our proper business of preparing for the future. Now, sit back, relax, for the trip ahead of us is long."

And I did, sitting back in the seat, letting drowsiness take me, feeling again that odd sense of unreality, that nothing was quite what it seemed to be, and somehow knowing that I was still lying to Kar-hinter, knowing that despite everything we had seen and experienced, I was still not really convinced.

Something was wrong, but damned if I knew what.

24

DREAMS AND NONDREAMS

Kar-hinter awoke us as the skudder came to rest in the Eden Line from which we had started.

"Give me your clothing," he said. "You still have over two weeks of your stay left. Enjoy it."

So we gave him our clothing, climbed out of the skudder, and in the darkness watched it flicker out of existence. Then we went into the cabin.

During the days that followed Sally gradually began to adjust to the idea that her life had been compounded of lies and dreams, that what the Paratimers had told her was false. One doesn't change a lifetime of belief overnight, but her strange, almost ambivalent feelings toward Mica slowly solidified into resentment, and he became the focal point of her growing anger; *in absentia* he bore the brunt of her disgust. And I, whom she had always wanted to like, became the pole to which she was attracted. She used me, I know, as a solace for her growing disillusionment with Mica and all that he represented, but I did not mind that use and still hoped that eventually her feelings for me would mature into something deeper. But even without this I had no cause for complaint.

On the night of our visit to the Cross-Line worlds we each slept alone. On the next night we went to our separate beds, though I had tried at least to persuade her to come to mine. She had resisted, though I thought I could feel that her resistance was weakening.

That second night I lay there in my bed, listening to the nightly rain as it began to fall, turning things over in my mind, things about Sally and Staunton and Kar-hinter and Calethon I and Dylla and other things that I couldn't quite put tags on —though in time I would come to, I knew. After a while, a long while, listening to the rain and Sally's distant breathing, I fell into a shallow sleep and was perhaps on the verge of dreaming when I felt a soft warmness coming up against me, a hand placed on my naked chest, a mouth suddenly pressed against mine.

"Sally," I murmured against her lips.

"Yes, Eric," she answered, moving her body closer still and then up over mine. She was nude, of course, and her soft breasts were crushing against me.

I pulled her mouth to mine again, and her answer was savage, demanding. I was almost gasping for breath when she pulled her lips away.

"Yes, Eric," she said again, still lying atop me.

"I want you, Sally," I said. "I've wanted you from the first time I saw you."

"I know," she whispered, then said, "Do you want to do it with me as much as you wanted to do it with G'lendal?"

"Yes," I gasped.

"As much as you wanted it with Jonna?"

"More."

"As much as you wanted it with Dylla?"

I did not speak again, but pulled her mouth back to mine and kissed her as savagely as she had kissed me. And as we kissed, her hips began writhing against mine, pushing herself down on me, demanding, almost begging.

Then suddenly she broke her lips away from mine and cried, "Now, Eric. I want it now."

Later our lovemaking settled into a comfortable pattern and we learned the intimacies of each other, the little ways of giving greater pleasure to each other, the sharing of our pleasure, and it was even better.

And never again did we speak of G'lendal or Jonna or Dylla,

and we never brought up Hallacy or Mica. They did not matter any more, not to either of us.

Eden was beginning to live up to its name.

But there were other things.

While the visit to the Cross-Line worlds appeared to have solved all the problems for Sally, it hadn't for me. The feeling of unreality had not left me but rather grew as the days went by. I could not have said why, but there was the feeling, the vague, deep idea, that what we had experienced had not been real.

Sally could accept it easily enough. She had not seen the work that the Kriths could do, how they could implant memories into the minds of men that were more real than the actual experiences; she did not know how the Kriths could alter men's personalities. I did. And I wasn't convinced.

Then there was the dream. I suppose that's what did it for me.

It was more than a week after our visit to the Cross-Line worlds. I had found it difficult to go to sleep that night. Sally had sensed something in me, had sensed that something still bothered me, though she had not asked me outright to tell her about it. She believed, I think, that I would tell her when I was ready.

So I lay there in bed beside her, waiting for sleep to come, and when it finally did come, it was a very disturbing sleep. The dream was like this:

We were in the skudder, Sally and Kar-hinter and the pilot and Pall and me. Sally and I were dressed in the costumes that we had worn in the Cross-Line worlds, and we had drunk our coffee and had fallen asleep.

Then the skudder stopped suddenly. My eyes half opened, then closed, and I could not force them open again, though I could hear the voices of Kar-hinter and the skudder pilot speaking in Shangalis.

"We're here," the pilot said.

"Good," Kar-hinter replied. Then I heard him move to a place beside me, felt him place his hand on my forehead, pull back an eyelid and peer into my eye. I could see his non-human face, though it was blurred and I could not focus on it.

Moments later the skudder's hatch opened, and other voices spoke, voices that I thought were those if Kriths.

"You have them?" one of the voices asked.

"Yes," Kar-hinter replied. "They are quite unconscious."

"Very well," replied one of the unnamed Kriths. "We will help you carry them out."

Arms came under my shoulders and knees. I was lifted, carried, handed down, carried again, then placed on some type of wheeled conveyance, and rolled for a long distance.

"The tapes are ready, I assume?" Kar-hinter's voice asked.

"Yes."

"Both identical?" Kar-hinter asked.

"Yes," the other voice sighed. "Except for viewpoint. They are self-programming, self-adjusting and interacting."

"Very good."

The other Krith gave a very human snort. "It is quite complex, you koow, the sort of interacting pseudo-memories you require for these two."

"I know," Kar-hinter's voice said. "But they must be convinced."

"They will be convinced. Of that I am absolutely sure. We worked all night on them. Six hours of tapes each, covering every human sense. There will be no reason for either of them to doubt their experiences."

"Are you sure?"

"Of course I am sure."

"Eric has a strong will. The Paratimers even tried telepathy on him, but it did not work."

"Yes, I know that, but when we are through, even he will be satisfied."

"I hope you are correct. You do not know this man as I do."

"I am correct."

There was a long silence, marked only by the faint squeak of the wheels of the thing on which I lay as it rolled along.

"Is this man really important?" the other voice asked.

"I believe he is," Kar-hinter said, "and the *Tromas* agree with me, though they seem to see even more in him than I do."

He paused for a while before he went on. "He has been of great value to us in the past. I believe that he will be of even greater value to us in the future, once his loyalty is established beyond question."

"In six hours it will be."

Then I heard doors open, close behind me, and moments later the motion stopped.

"I will return in six hours," Kar-hinter said.

"They will be ready then."

My eyelids were peeled back, then held back by tape. Two small, cold glass objects were placed against my naked eyes. At the same time I was stripped of my clothing and felt cold metallic objects touching my skin in different places.

"Is the woman ready?" one of the Krithian voices asked after a while.

"Yes, sir," a human voice replied.

"Very well, begin the tapes."

Suddenly I could see again, into the skudder, and a voice was saying into my ear, "Eric, wake up. We are nearly there." It was Kar-hinter's voice.

And then I relived the whole visit to the Cross-Line worlds!

The dream was just a dream, wasn't it? Or was it a real memory that had been suppressed by drugs?

But was that possible? I had been told that the Kriths were not able to tamper with a mind that had been conditioned as mine had. But, then, had they actually tampered with my mind? No, in the dream they had merely drugged me, and then, while I was drugged, they had fed me false sensory data. They had not tried directly to manipulate my mind or to alter anything that was already in it. Yes, I supposed that it was possible.

Okay, I thought, suddenly convinced, this whole damned thing was faked. As I sat up on the side of the bed, my thoughts went on: I was never in the Cross-Line worlds. Kar-hinter took us a few Lines away, drugged us, and then planted the false memories. Why?

Well, that was pretty simple. There was no Cross-Line

Civilization after all. Mica had been telling the truth about it. I was all an enormous plot.

I lit a cigarette, looked down at Sally, who still slept soundly. What the hell was I going to do about it?

"Sally," I said, shaking her shoulder. "Wake up."

Her eyes opened. She looked up at me with a startled expression on her face, recognizing the urgency in my voice.

"What is it?"

"I've got to talk to you."

"Okay," she said, sitting up and accepting the cigarette offered her.

I dialed for coffee on the autokitchen extension, lit myself another cigarette.

"What's bothering you, Eric?" she asked as the coffee arrived.

"Listen to me carefully, Sally," I said.

"I will. Tell me."

"It's all a lie just like Mica said it was. There is no Cross-Line Civilization."

"But, Eric, we were there. We saw it."

"We only thought we did. It was all faked. False memories."

"How do you know?" Sally asked, something on her face saying that she almost doubted my sanity.

I told her about my dream, about how I thought I remembered all the preparations for implanting the false memories.

"But maybe it was just a dream," she said.

"No."

"How do you know? How can you be sure?"

"I don't know, but I'm sure. You don't know the Kriths the way I do, Sally. They can do things like this. I've seen it done before."

"But would they do it to you, Eric, knowing that you know they can do it?"

"They did it," I said. "They must have a lot of faith in it."

"But it's fantastic."

"Hell, it's all fantastic. That's as easy to believe as any of the rest of it."

"I don't know, Eric. I mean . . . I don't know what to believe now."

222

"There's truth somewhere," I said. "And we've got to find it. And I know that we won't find it with Kar-hinter's help."

"Then how will we find it?" she asked.

"We'll go find Mica and ask him."

Sally looked at me, and by this time she was firmly convinced that I was insane. Maybe she had a right to be.

25

THE WESTERN TIMELINES

By the time the skudder came to take us back to Sally's world I had her sufficiently convinced of the truth of my beliefs so that she at least agreed to go along with me.

When the Krithian skudder materialized in the garden before the cabin, Sally was half way ready to accept once more the belief that Mica and his kind were the saviors of mankind. I wasn't, not quite, but least I was willing to accept them over the Kriths, whom I now *knew* to be liars on a scale I had never before imagined possible.

Well, as I said, the skudder materialized in the garden. The pilot stepped out, waved to us with a big grin.

"You people ready to go back?" he called as we walked down the path toward him.

"Try to smile," I whispered to Sally. Then louder, "No, not really, but I guess we have to. Everything in the cabin's on standby. I guess we can leave now."

"Good," the pilot said. "Kar-hinter said to get you back to him as quickly as possible. He has some news for you."

"What kind of news?" I asked, now within handshaking distance of the pilot.

"Didn't say. He just said that it was something that both of you would find very interesting."

"I guess we'll find out soon," I replied.

The pilot now opened the hatch, gestured for Sally to climb in, offered her his hand. "I've got clothes in here for you."

"Good," I said, keeping a false smile on my face.

"Must be nice here," he said as Sally placed one foot on the lip of the hatch, hoisted herself in with both hands.

For a moment the pilot's eyes strayed from Sally's bare buttocks to the cabin and the blissful, idyllic panorama that surrounded it. And that was exactly what I wanted.

I could see Sally in the hatchway out of the corner of my eye as she pulled herself erect, then slowly, carefully turned so that she was facing outward, then lashed out with her foot to the back of the unconcerned pilot's head.

I switched into combat augmentation and was satisfied that everything worked perfectly. The world slowed to my senses; sounds grew deeper and shifted toward the bass; light shifted toward the red.

"Aaaaaccchhh," the pilot groaned slowly, floating forward from the impact of Sally's foot. I grabbed him by the shoulder, spun him around to face me, threw my right fist into a face that had not yet registered the shock of the violent action. I put my left fist into his stomach, my right into his face again as he folded. Then he was unconscious on the soft green ground before he realized that he was being attacked. I cut out the augmentation.

"He's out," I said, bending over him, quickly running my hands over his body to see if he carried a weapon, which I doubted. "Nothing," I told Sally, then dragged him a few feet away from the craft and made him as comfortable as possible. They'd come after him soon, very soon, I feared.

When I got into the skudder Sally had already found the clothing that he had brought for us, standard civilian-type clothing from Sally's Line or one very near it. It didn't matter much to me how we were dressed since I had no idea what kind of costumes we'd find at our destination.

While I was dressing, Sally said, "Oh, Eric, I hope that we're doing the right thing."

"No more than I do."

"Are you sure you can find Mica's Paratime?"

"Sure?" I asked as I buttoned up the shirt brought for me. "No, I'm not sure, but I've got a fair idea; at least I do if Latham's book was true."

"What exactly do you mean?" she asked. "You never have really explained it to me."

"Okay, just a minute," I said, sitting down in the pilot's seat, feeling back under the control panel to where the energy pistol was supposed to be within reach of every skudder pilot. You never know what you might run into when you flicker across the Lines.

I found the cold metal butt, the stud that released the weapon. Click! The pistol snapped into my hand. I drew it out, looked at it for a moment. Standard-issue energy pistol. Full charge. You could do a hell of a lot of damage with that baby if you wanted to. I might want to. I slipped it into my belt, feeling more like a man than I had for a good long while and feeling a hell of a lot more confident of our ability to get away with our scheme. It's funny what a weapon can do to a man.

"Sit down there," I gestured toward the seat beside me, studying the familiar skudder controls. "Keep a watch on our friend out there. If he wakes up, we'll get out of here in a hurry."

"Okay, but tell me what you're going to do."

"Well, you've read Martin Latham's book, haven't you?"

"*The Greatest Lie*? Of course."

"You remember how he found the Albigensians?"

"Yes, he left his own Paratime and went West as far as he could."

"Okay, that's the key. I've read that part three or four times," I said, "and I remember it pretty well. Latham had a standard four-man skudder just like this one. He got it out of the skudder pool, so I'm pretty sure that when he did, the power cells were at full charge. They always are. He removed the governor and deactivated the telltale, but other than that, the skudder he used was exactly like this one."

"Uh-huh," Sally grunted.

I reached under the control panel again, fumbled, then found what I wanted and pulled at two wires. They broke free from their connections.

"Our telltale's off," I said. "They can't trace us by it now. It's just a safety device, so it's not hidden." I smiled to myself. "I'm not going to bother the governor. That's a job for a licensed mechanic—or an engineer like Latham. But we don't need to remove it anyway. We don't have nearly as far to go as Latham did, and we don't need top speed—I hope."

"Oh?" Sally said.

"Well, to get back to what I was saying: A skudder of given mass with a probability generator of a given maximum potential can only go so far on a set of full power cells, governor, or no."

"Oh, I see," Sally said, beginning to follow me. "You can tell how far Latham went from the amount of power he used. All you have to do is find his starting point, right?"

"Right," I said. "Now I don't know exactly where Latham started. He didn't give the Paratemporal coordinates, but I've got a pretty good idea, to within a few dozen Lines, anyway."

"What do we do then?" Sally asked.

In answer to Sally's question I flipped back the covering panel of the skudder's miniature computer and began tapping on the exposed keys.

A four-man skudder's computer is a simple-minded beast, not much more than an electronic slide rule, really, but given the right data, it can give you fairly quick and accurate answers. I just hoped that I was giving it the right data.

The Line where Latham had been working was a long way East, much farther East then the Eden Line where we were now—on the other side of my Homeline, I believed. The place where he had finally come to rest was a very long way West. We were now somewhere in between, though exactly where, I didn't know for sure yet. The computer would give me that too in a few moments, based on the skudder's power consumption, since leaving the only Line whose coordinates I was sure of, the Line from which Sally and I had originally come, RTGB-307.

A few minutes later I was satisfied with the approximate number of Lines that Latham had crossed before he ran out of power. Yes, it was a hell of a long way West.

Now, assuming that this skudder had come from Sally's Homeline, from our base at the Butt of Lewis in the Outer Hebrides which was still Kar-hinter's base of operations, and assuming that it had started out with full power cells—which I was sure it had, regulations required it—it had come exactly X number of Lines. X from Y, being Kar-hinter's base of operations, left *Z* number of Lines and our present location. Our location then, after a little more figuring using the computer, was *A* number of Lines to the Temporal West of the Line from which Latham had supposedly started his trip, plus or minus a dozen Lines to allow for my own errors. All this meant that we had about *B* number of Lines to cross to reach the place where Latham had run out of power—Mica's Homeline.

Okay, then, if my memory and assumptions were valid, and I hoped to all the gods that I knew that they were, we had enough power in the cells to make a round trip, plus. Very good, I thought, since we'd probably have to do a lot of maneuvering to find the exact Line we were looking for.

I sat back at last, dug a pack of cigarettes out of the skudder's supply compartment, and smiled a big smile at Sally.

"Are we ready?" she asked.

"We are now if we'll ever be." I glanced out through the skudder's dome. "Our friend's still out."

"You hit him pretty hard."

"Yeah. Okay, brace yourself. I'm not the world's best pilot but I can manage."

My hands slowly went to the controls. I cut on the probability generator, watched dials show the gradual rise of power, heard the hum that filled the air grow in intensity, become a whine, an almost physical sensation. While the probability potential grew I adjusted other controls. Initially I set the controls just a little short of where I expected Mica's Homeline to be, planning to stop and recon the Lines before plunging all the way in. I still wasn't sure enough of what we were getting ourselves into to jump all the way in at once. "Caution preventeth a fall . . ." or something like that.

"Ready?" I asked.

"I guess."

"Here goes."

I hit the activating switch.

"We're on our way," I said.

Flicker.

Fortunately we had both eaten before the skudder came, but even at that we began to feel hunger before the trip was into its

228

econd half. We'd just have to wait it out. There wasn't much in ne skudder to eat besides emergency rations, which I didn't vant to break open short of an emergency, and we didn't dare top anywhere. Not for a long while yet.

More than once I had a strong desire to bring the skudder out f probability into, well, "reality" to see what kinds of worlds ve were passing through now. By the middle of the trip we had one beyond the Lines known to the Kriths, and we were now in argely unexplored Lines, unexplored by the Kriths and 'imeliners, at least, though I assumed that Mica's people had een there, were probably there in force, though keeping them- elves hidden from most of the locals as they were on Sally's vorld. But, well, I didn't want to cause an incident by coming ut in some place where our kind was unknown, where we night be taken as alien invaders or something, maybe smeared 'ith thermonukes or shot with arrows or whatever kinds of veapons they might have.

So we waited and watched the dials indicate the passage of me and Paratime as the master destination dial said we were owly nearing the place where I had determined that we would ome out for the first time.

We didn't speak much, Sally and I. There wasn't too much ft to say now. We just waited and held hands and felt scared nd hoped that Mica or somebody would be waiting for us with pen arms.

The automatic destination settings terminated. The final ross-Line jump flickered. I held the energy pistol in my hand, fety off, held my breath and. . . .

We came out.

I don't know what we expected, but what we found wasn't it. was like nothing we had hoped or expected to see here, in a art of the Lines where we had expected to encounter a high and mplex civilization of cross-Line travelers.

Oh, there had been a high degree of technology here once, but ow. . . .

The transparent dome of the skudder gave us a 360 degree iew of the countryside surrounding us, if it could be called by generous a term as "countryside." The sky above us was blue-black, sprinkled with a smattering of the brighter stars, and in that sky hung an enormous, bloated sun whose corona beamed brightly around it. It was broad daylight, yet the sky was more than halfway dark, and I knew that this Earth had very little left of its atmosphere, more than the moon, but not enough to support human life or much of any other kind of life as we know it.

Before us a rocky, gray-brown plain stretched toward the horizon, then abruptly ended two or three miles away in a huge pile of rocks, a chunk of the Earth lifted up and tilted skyward, revealing a thousand centuries of geological evolution, though at the moment that didn't interest me very much.

In the other directions the view was essentially the same, gray-brown stone and earth, waterless, airless, lifeless rock, world that was totally dead, that might have always been dead, that might have never known life and men, though I doubted it. had seen worlds like this before, though I don't believe I have ever seen one so totally devastated.

A skudder's hull, the result of millions of man-hours of research and labor, is impervious to most forms of radiation except visible light which is allowed to pass through the dome. So I wasn't too worried when the counters on the outer hull were wild, measuring a nuclear radiation level a million times or more higher than it should have been.

"God, haven't they had a war here!" I said.

"What is this place, Eric?" Sally gasped, her voice filled with fear.

"The *where* is exactly the place where we started," I said slowly. "It's the Parawhen that matters." I paused. "There's been a war here, Sally. One hell of a war. This planet's good and dead. Let's get the hell out of here. We've still got a way to go."

The probability generator was standing by. All I had to do was spin the destination dial for a few Lines ahead, hit the actuating switch and flicker.

Flicker. Flicker. Flicker.

"I . . . I've never seen anything so horrible. How did happen, a war like that, I mean?"

"I don't know," I said. "I don't even want to know. Don't worry. We'll find Mica's Line."

Flicker. Flicker. Flicker.

We came out in a world that was different, but not very much. The sky was more like a sky, bluer but not as blue as it should have been. The Earth was desolate, the same dead gray-brown, and the radiation level was almost as high, and we were just a few hundred yards from the edge of an enormous crater that still glowed in its depths, down in the hot shadows.

"Not again," Sally gasped.

"Parallel war," I said. "Maybe not as bad as the other, but just as total as far as human life is concerned."

"What is this, Eric? Could we possibly be near Mica's Paratime? He never told me about anything like this."

"Maybe he was ashamed of what his relatives had done," I said, feeling a growing apprehension. "We'll go on."

But as I glanced at the controls and the dials and the computer read-out, I saw that we were very nearly smack on top of where I thought Mica's Homeline should be. Well, I thought, maybe his Line is an island in all this destruction. That's possible. It's happened before. But we'd better go a little slower.

Flicker.

The next Line was almost identical, except that the nearest crater was a mile away and the radiation level in the vicinity of the skudder was a few roentgens lower.

Flicker.

It was as if we were back in the first Line we had seen. The atmosphere was blasted away, and a naked sun blistered the naked rock of a dead, naked Earth. The radiation was high enough to scare me even inside the skudder.

Flicker.

The sky was almost blue. The earth was brown and barren, though here and there I saw the stark skeletons of what had once been trees, and a brown ash covered the earth that might have once been grass long ago. The radiation level was still far too high to allow any kind of life that I knew.

Flicker.

Blue sky, brown earth, radiation levels that perhaps men could survive if they were buried deep under the ground.

My heart was sinking, and there was a lump where my throat should have been. I was beginning to believe that my assumptions were pretty far wrong. Maybe Latham. . . .

"There just could be someone alive here," I said. "Mica's people could even have an outpost here."

I flicked on the skudder's radio, scanned the frequencies from the lowest up to the edges of microwave. Nothing. If there were anyone alive here, he wasn't using radio. I can't say that I was too surprised.

"We'll go on," I said.

Flicker.

Things were about the same on the next Line. The radiation level was a little lower, a few notches; men would have had a better chance of surviving here than on the last Line; Mica's people would be more likely to have an outpost, if we were anywhere near their Lines, which I had begun to seriously doubt now, though, according to my figures, we ought to be right about there.

The radio was dead. The air was silent. No one answered my transmissions.

We went on.

Flicker.

In the next Line the sky looked normal enough, though no clouds were visible. The earth, as far as we could see, was brown and gray, scorched grasses and burned trees and nothing much else. The radiation level was lower still, but high enough to kill an unprotected man almost instantly.

Out of a hope that I knew now to be foolish, I cut the radio's receiver on again, slowly scanned the frequencies—and nearly fainted when I picked up a carrier at 104 MHz.

"What is it?" Sally gasped when she saw the expression on my face, realized that the buzz from the receiver meant something.

"There's somebody here," I said.

"Paratimers?"

"I don't know. It could be locals who survived the war, or it could be Paratimers. No Krith or Timeliner has ever come this far to my knowledge."

"Talk to them."

"I'll try." Then I realized something and said, "I don't know the language. Albigensian, I mean. You talk."

"Okay, what do I say?"

"Just tell them who we are and why we're here."

"Okay. Show me what to do."

"Well, you just. . . ."

Ahead of us and to the right, maybe a hundred and fifty feet or a little more, the air shimmered and flickered for a moment, then a solid object materialized out of the nothingness, a squashed sphere that was unmistakable: a Krithian skudder.

I did not doubt for a moment who it was. I merely wondered how he had followed me so easily. What had I overlooked?

"Eric!" Sally cried.

"Easy."

"Who is it?"

"I can make a guess. The skudder pilot said that Kar-hinter had something to tell us. I guess he's come to tell us what it is."

"Oh, God, Eric, and we were so close."

"Don't worry."

"But they'll have guns."

"I've got one, too," I said. "There are no guns mounted on their hull. There's never been a reason for it before now."

"What are we going to do?"

"Well, as I see it, we've got three choices. We can try to call for help, but I don't know how much good that'll do or how soon. I'd hate to have to count on it. Two, we can run, but I don't know how much good that'll do either. If Kar-hinter could follow us this far, I suppose he could keep on following us until he caught us. Or, three, we can talk to Kar-hinter and see what he wants with us."

"What good will *that* do?"

"Damned if I know, but it can't hurt."

My hands fell to the radio controls and I switched to the Krithian/Timeliner emergency broadcast frequency, thinking that was probably what Kar-hinter would be using. It was.

". . . Eric. Please respond if you are receiving me."

"I hear you," I said into the microphone, satisfied that the voice on the other end was that of Kar-hinter.

"Eric," the Krith answered at once. "Please do not be a fool. You do not know what you are getting into."

"I have a fair idea," I said. "Listen, Kar-hinter, your false memories didn't take. I saw through them. We know now that there's no Cross-Line Civilization, and we can assume that all the rest of it is lies, too."

"You listen to me, Eric," Kar-hinter snapped back, anger in his voice, a very human-sounding anger. "We have already sent patrols into the worlds where the Paratimers claim to live, their world of origin and all."

"And where's that?" I demanded.

"Here, Eric. Here and there is no human life here, not a hundred Lines in either direction."

"Another lie," I said flatly. "There's someone on this Line using radio, Kar-hinter. I just picked up their carrier."

"I said *human*, Eric. The Paratimers aren't human either."

26

KAR-HINTER, KEARNS, TRACY,
AND DEATH

"Eric, this is Tracy," said another voice from the radio's loudspeaker, a voice which I recognized. "What Kar-hinter is saying is true, old boy. I've seen them the way they *really* are and they aren't human beings."

"You're crazy," I said because I couldn't think of anything else to say.

"No, it's true," Tracy's voice said. "We've been making recons into these Lines ever since we picked up you and Sally from Staunton, and we've found out the truth about the Paratimers. *They* have a base somewhere on this Line—and, for God's sake, Eric, they aren't people."

"Eric," Kar-hinter's voice said, "you know that there is someone using radio here. They will probably pick up our signals if we continue to talk by radio. We do not have sufficient force to defend ourselves from an attack on their own ground. I suggest, then, that we cease using radio and meet outside the skudders to discuss this further."

"How can I believe anything you say?" I asked.

"You can believe me, can't you, Eric?" Tracy's voice asked.

"I don't know what to believe anymore," I replied.

"We are going to turn off our radio equipment," Kar-hinter said. "We will dress in survival suits and leave our skudder. We will wait for you midway between our craft and yours. We will be unarmed. Please, Eric, give us—and yourself—a chance."

There was a click and the carrier of their transmitter died away.

For a long while I sat there silently before the transceiver, gazing blankly at its controls. *What the hell am I going to do now?* I kept asking myself, and I really didn't have any answers.

"It's a trap, isn't it, Eric?" Sally asked at last.

"Probably," I said, "but Tracy. . . ."

"Who's Tracy?"

"A friend of mine. I've known him for a long time. He was with us the night we kidnapped you."

"Oh, yes," she said, "the one who was wounded in the leg."

I nodded. "I don't think he'd lie to me," I said. "At least not intentionally."

"'do you think they're forcing him?"

"Maybe. No, I don't think so." Tracy wasn't the sort of man who was easily *forced* to do anything. "I don't know. Damn it, I just don't know!"

We were silent for a while longer.

The hatch of the other skudder opened, and three of its four occupants, clad in emergency survival suits, stepped out onto the barren, radioactive earth of this world. Two of the figures were probably human from their size and proportions. The third was tall, built like a Krith, built like Kar-hinter. The three slowly advanced across the scorched ground and finally stopped about halfway to our skudder. There they stood and waited. Assuming that one of the men was Tracy, who was the other? Pall? If so, who was still inside the skudder? Maybe my old buddy, Kearns. Or maybe it was the other way around. Did it matter? I'd learn soon.

"What are you going to do?" Sally asked.

"I'm going out there," I answered, finally making up my mind.

"But. . . ."

"I have to go," I said, cutting her off. "There's too much that we don't know. None of this makes any sense at all, and I've got to find out why."

I got up and walked back to the rear of the skudder, to where the locker containing the survival suits were kept.

"You stay in the skudder," I told Sally. "I'll leave the probability generator on, and I'll set the destination controls for your own Line. If anything happens, well, all you'll have to do is press one switch and the skudder'll take you home. I think we've still got the power to do that."

"Please don't go, Eric," Sally said as I opened the locker and pulled out one of the four survival suits.

"I've got to go," I said. "If what Mica and his people said is true, we ought to be in one of their Lines now. I really don't think that my figures were that far off."

"But you *could* be wrong."

"I could be, yes, but for some reason I'm convinced that I'm not. There's something going on here that they haven't told us about. Maybe what Tracy said is true. Maybe the Paratimers aren't human."

"That's not true, Eric," Sally said slowly. "Mica's as human as you are. I *know*."

I slowly turned to look at her. *That's right,* I told myself, visualizing Mica, naked and pale white, lying atop my Sally. Human or not, I hated him for a moment.

Still, if anyone knew, she would. She had been Mica's mistress; she had lived with him; if he weren't human, she would know it.

But what's human? I asked myself. And if Mica were, suppose, just suppose for a minute, some kind of alien being disguised as a man, well, what outside of moral scruples would prevent him from making love to a human woman if he wanted to and had the proper equipment. I mean, in situations where women—or other men—weren't available, men have been known to have sexual relations with creatures that certainly aren't human or even sentient. Everyone's heard stories of farmboys and their cows and chickens and sheep. I felt a little sick. Okay, maybe. . . .

"I have to go out there, Sally," I said slowly. "You can't talk me out of it. Please, just do as I say."

I pulled the survival suit over my clothing, jerking the straps tight. After tucking the helmet under my arm, I went back to the front of the skudder's cabin, adjusted the controls to return Sally to her own Timeline if anything happened to me.

"Just push that button," I told her, then led her back to the rear of the craft again.

"Be careful, Eric," she said as I helped her into a similar survival suit. When the skudder's hatch was opened, the interior would be liberally dosed with deadly radiation. In fact, the skudder would probably not be safe for an unprotected human being without some serious decontamination once the hatch had been opened in this world.

"I'll be careful," I said, slipping the energy pistol into one of the suit's capacious pockets. "I'm taking this pistol along just in case."

"Come back, Eric," Sally said. "I won't know what to do if you don't."

"If I don't, then get the hell out of here. Do what you can to . . . Well, just get home and hide."

I kissed her and then clamped the helmet down over my head, sealed it, and then turned toward the hatch.

"Good luck," Sally's voice said through the muffled speaker of her own helmet as she sealed it.

"Thanks, sweetheart."

The hatch opened before me, and I leaped down to the dry, burned, barren soil of this Earth. The hatch closed behind me. I walked toward the place where Kar-hinter, Tracy, and the other man waited for me.

I don't suppose that I thought about very much while I crossed those seventy-five feet of space between us. There wasn't much that my mind could do, except wonder. But the time for asking idle questions was over. I wanted some hard answers.

"I am glad you came to us, Eric," Kar-hinter said when I was within range of his voice as it came from the speakers of his survival helmet.

"I want the truth now," I said in reply. "I know that you've been lying to me."

"I will admit that there is no Cross-Line Civilization, as such, Eric," Kar-hinter said slowly. "It was a lie, but one that we told because we had to."

"And the Contratime communications business?" I asked.

238

"That also is untrue," Kar-hinter said just as slowly. "The truth is much more fantastic."

I ignored his last statement for the moment and looked at the two men with the Krith. One of them was Tracy. And the other was our old companion, Kearns, the same inexplicable expression on his warrior's face. Then was the fourth one, the one in the skudder, Pall?

"They both know," Kar-hinter was saying.

"I won't ask you why you lied," I said. "I don't want to hear it now."

"But you must hear it, Eric," Kar-hinter said. "It is. . . ."

"It's another lie!" I yelled. "And I don't want to hear any more lies from you! Tracy, who are the Paratimers?"

"I don't really know," Tracy replied. "They're from the West, a hell of a damned long way to the West. They do have a base here, but it looks like it's just one of many they have in these Lines. There are more of them farther West, but we don't know much about them yet."

"You said they aren't human," I said. "How do you know?"

"We raided one of their bases about a week ago. We captured some of them alive."

"Then what are they if they aren't human?" I asked.

Tracy spread his hands to show his ignorance.

"They are as different from you as we are, perhaps more so, considering," Kar-hinter said. "The ones you have seen have been surgically modified to look like men."

"Then what do they really look like?" I asked, still looking at Tracy.

"Well, they look something like us," he replied. "At least they're humanoid, except, well, they're almost hairless and their skin had a kind of almost bluish tint to it, and they have six fingers on each hand, and their eyes have pupils like a cat's. But, well, they're mammals. We caught one of their women, and there's no doubt about that. They're more—more like us in looks than the Kriths are, but, well, Eric, they don't think the same way. I can't explain it. They're *alien*, Eric, I mean real damned alien, and I think they hate us more than we could ever understand. I—I can't really explain it. You've got to be with

239

one of them, the way they really are and not pretending to be people, to know what kind of *things* they are.'' Then he seemed to run out of words to say the things he wanted to say.

"I find all this pretty hard to believe, Tracy," I said,

"I do too, Eric, but, well, it's true. I'm not lying to you."

"Do you think that one of them could make love to a human woman?" I asked.

"Yes, I suppose it's possible," Tracy said after a moment of thought. "I mean, they're physically capable of it. They're built a lot like us."

"That much?"

Tracy nodded.

"What do they want here?"

"I don't know. I wish I did."

"Listen, Eric," Kar-hinter said. "We are now in the Albigensian Lines. Much of what the one who called himself Mica told you is true. The Albigensians *were* a highly developed people. They may have developed skudder travel independently. But they encountered these *others*. What do you think caused all this destruction?" His hand gestured sweepingly around.

"War," I said bitterly.

"Damned right it was war," Kearns said. "War with the bluies. The Albigensians fought back, but they were wiped out. The war destroyed dozens of Lines before it was over and those blue bastards had won. Damn it, Mathers, you've got to make a choice. Now! Maybe you don't trust Kar-hinter. I don't know whether I do. But for God's sake, man, the Kriths never did anything like *this*."

"Eric," Kar-hinter said when I turned back to look at him, "given time, I could perhaps explain *our* motives to you, but now we do not have the time and you have stated an unwillingness to listen. But we, both mankind *and* Krith, are on the verge of war with these aliens. You must decide which side you are on. That of mankind or that of the blue-skinned aliens."

"He's right," Tracy said. "Eric, whatever else the Kriths are, and I think I know now, they aren't half as bad as—as these others."

"I don't know that."

240

"Damn it, man, look at this world!" Kearns said.

"I have only your word," I said, "and I'm sick and tired of taking other people's word for things. I'm going to find out for myself."

"You'll get yourself killed in the process," Kearns said.

"It's my life."

"Your life belongs to the Timeliners," Kar-hinter said, a sharp coldness to his voice that I had never heard before.

"The hell you say!" I yelled. Then, more calmly, "I'm sorry, but I can't take your word for anything any longer. I'm leaving." I started to turn away.

"Stay, Eric, we are not finished yet," Kar-hinter said in that same tone.

"Hold still Mathers," Kearns snapped and when I turned back I saw that he held an energy pistol in his hand.

"I thought you were supposed to be unarmed," I said.

"Don't be a fool," Kearns said in disgust.

The look on Tracy's face inside the helmet was blank astonishment. He had not known that Kearns was bringing a gun. "Wait," he finally managed to say. "We told him. . . ."

"To hell with what we told him," Kearns said. The pistol in his hand slowly came up, then leveled at my stomach. "You've talked yourself into this, Mathers, you damned, bloody, human fool."

Three things happened at once. I threw myself to the earth, rolling, grabbing toward the energy pistol in the pocket of my survival suit. Kearns' energy pistol rasped, sending a jet of hell through the radioactive air where I had been standing. Tracy threw himself against Kearns, knocking him off his feet. They both went down together.

As I rolled, I tugged the pistol out of my suit, but before I could aim and fire, the air was lighted by another energy blast, this one from a pistol in the hand of Kar-hinter. That was the first time in my life that I had ever seen a Krith hold a weapon—that I knew of.

Tracy's survival suit blackened, burst into flames, for it was he that Kar-hinter was aiming for. Tracy's screams were loud in the near silence of this dead world, but he died quickly.

Yet even before Hillary Tracy died, Kar-hinter joined him.

241

My pistol fired, poorly aimed, but aimed well enough, and the clothing covering Kar-hinter's chest flamed and disintegrated, as did the living flesh under it.

Even while all this was happening, I was able to see out of the corner of my eye the fourth figure emerging from the skudder. Whether it was man or Krith I couldn't tell. I was rolling to my knees, swinging the pistol around at Kearns, who was coming up, throwing Tracy's body aside. I fired. My beam seared off the top of Kearns' helmet, and the top of his head and bone and blackened brain burst out.

Kearns should have died instantly. Any *normal man* would have, but he didn't. His body kept moving, rising upward, coming awkwardly to its feet, the energy pistol still in its hand and firing wildly. I blasted again, and Kearns' half-headless corpse, now missing an arm, nothing left but a cauterized stump, staggered backward and fell to the earth, its legs still kicking.

I only know of one kind of higher creature that can live with its head blown away and that only because it has three brains and can go on living for a while without its head-brain. And I realized that there was a lot that I had never suspected about the Kriths—and I realized that the blue-skinned Paratimers weren't the only ones who could make use of plastic surgery. Kearns had no more been a human being than Kar-hinter. He had just looked more like one.

At the time I wasn't thinking about these things very much, though. I was thinking about the fourth figure who was running across the barren soil toward me, a seven-foot figure of a man with an energy pistol in his hand, aiming at me.

Perhaps I had the advantage of anger and adrenalin over Pall—for that is who it must have been. Perhaps he hadn't had the time to take it all in, time to prepare himself to kill. I had. And the weapon in my hand was surprisingly steady as it came up and fired, almost on its own, into the middle of the man's torso.

Pall stopped, then staggered backward, his chest and abdomen flaming, and finally fell forward on his face, still thirty feet from me. I didn't know whether he was dead or not, but if he weren't, he wouldn't last long in this environment.

I gasped for breath, felt myself shaking in reaction to the

violence that had just taken place, and looked at the three bodies close to me. Only Tracy's body was human, some part of my mind thought, and he had trusted the Kriths. It had cost him his life. I knew that I could never trust them again. Never. Nor ever believe anything that they said.

I shook my head sadly, bitterly, returned the energy pistol to the pocket of my survival suit and turned back toward the skudder where Sally waited—and had crossed no more than half that distance when I saw the other skudder, no, sautierboat, come sailing across the hills, its externally mounted machine guns firing—at me.

27

"THEY ARE ALMOST HUMAN"

There was very little protection out there. The nearest was thirty or forty feet away—the skudder—and I ran toward it. The aim of the machine gunner in the boat was fortunately lousy and I crossed the distance without getting myself killed.

Sally started to open the hatch for me, but I waved to her to keep it closed. I wanted to meet the men in that sautierboat, but I wanted to be alive when I did it.

I walked a few steps away from the skudder, waved my hands above my head, gesturing that I surrendered.

The gunner in the boat must have got my message, for the firing ceased and the craft came to earth a few yards from my skudder. I stood silently waiting, hoping that whoever came out looked like me and not like the things Tracy had described.

While the sautierboat settled and its hatch began to open, I let one of my hands slip back toward the pocket that held the energy pistol. I wasn't that confident yet. Maybe. . . .

The hatch was fully open now, and a figure clad in something that was probably a radiation protection suit climbed out, a long, ugly-looking weapon in his hands. Two more followed him, both as well armed.

The helmets that covered their heads and faces protected them from my view pretty well while they were in the shadow of the boat, but when they walked forward, speaking in some language that I had never heard before and knew wasn't Albigensian, and the late afternoon sunlight shone directly on and through their transparent helmets, I could see their faces—and I knew that at least Tracy hadn't been lying to me.

The faces well, they were almost human, but *almost* wasn't good enough. Their eyes were too big and their noses too flat and somehow their mouths weren't in the right place and their jaws were hinged wrongly and there was an unmistakable tinge of blue to their skins. And there was something menacing about them that was more than just their appearance.

Sally must have seen them, too, for she screamed, but she still had the presence of mind to open the hatch and yell, "Get in!"

All at once my energy pistol was out and firing, so close to my body that I felt the terrible backwash of its heat even through the insulation of the survival suit. And three sub-machine pistols were screaming and chattering in the space between the two craft, and the whole universe tried to come apart at the seams.

Something smashed through the fabric of my survival suit below my left thigh, and my leg suddenly became a column of mush that didn't want to hold me up and I felt the salty taste of blood in my mouth as I bit through my lower lip. But my energy pistol kept firing, and light and heat and flame filled the air, and the three alien figures before me, scant feet away, stopped coming forward, stopped firing at me, and fell apart screaming.

Then a woman's arms, impossibly strong, were pulling me backward, upward into the skudder's open hatch, and I tried to help, pulling with my arms and somehow together, Sally and I, we got my uncooperative body into the skudder as the machine gun on the sautierboat turned around and began to blast into the skudder's open hatch.

"Hit the switch!" I screamed, and Sally must have understood me. She stumbled across the skudder's deck under a hail of bullets and hit the activating switch on the skudder's control panel.

WHAM!

I aimed the energy pistol through the open hatch, held the firing stud depressed, searing at the metal hull of the sautierboat, until. . . .

Flicker!

"Get the hatch closed," I gasped.

Flicker.

"Are you hurt badly?" Sally cried.

Flicker.

"My left leg," I said, but all I remember after that is. . . .

Flicker. Flicker. Flicker.

28

OUT OF PROBABILITY

The machine-gun bullets from the sautierboat must have penetrated the skudder's hull, must have damaged the craft, for within a few minutes red warning lights began to flicker on in the craft's control panel. I don't remember it. Sally told me about it later.

She cut away enough of the survival suit to get to my leg, shattered by a bullet, and she was at least able to stop the bleeding, though she was afraid to try to do anything more with the radiation level within the craft still dangerously high.

When I finally came out of the grayness, hours later, I saw the danger lights, and I struggled to sit up.

"Eric," Sally asked, "what do those lights mean?"

"The probability generator," I said. "It's. . . ." Another light flickered on, and a dial swung into a red danger area.

"Open the hatch!" I cried.

"What?"

"Open the hatch. Now!"

Sally did, and I pulled myself across the deck, trying to ignore the pain that told me that I ought to lie down and die.

"What are we going to do?"

"This damned thing's going to blow up. Help me to the hatch. We're going to jump."

She didn't ask any more questions. She just helped me.

"Get me to my feet."

Painfully, more painfully than I like to remember, I came up, standing on one leg. Sally supported me on the other side. We stood in the hatch for a moment.

"I'm going to count," I said. "When I get to five, jump. Exactly on five and together, or we won't even end up in the same Line."

"Okay," Sally managed to say.

"One."

Flicker,

"Two."

Flicker.

"Three."

Flicker.

"Four."

Flicker.

"Five. Jump!"

We jumped.

Don't ask me to try to tell you what it was like—leaping out of a probability field into "reality." It didn't kill us. And that in itself is something of a minor miracle. We both were battered, and Sally's right arm was broken where she fell on it, and a couple of my ribs were cracked, but we lived through it, and that's about all that matters now. We lived.

29

"SOMETHING'S GOT TO BE DONE"

The rest isn't too important.

We found ourselves in a wood, but one that showed the works of man, tree stumps cut by power tools and footpaths, and off in the distance we could hear the sounds of surface vehicles on a paved road.

We took off our survival suits, and Sally, little more than half-conscious, made her way to the road and stopped one of the vehicles and asked for help in English and was more than surprised when the vehicle's driver answered in the same language. She told him, convincingly, I suppose, and with great presence of mind, that we were the survivors of the crash of an aircraft—she didn't say "airplane," though that is the word Here and Now—and that we had made our way through the woods this far.

The vehicle's driver, a kind, generous man, took us to a hospital where we spent the next few days, groggy and only halfway aware of our surroundings.

After a while, though, I learned that we had made it back to a Line that didn't seem to be too far from Sally's own world, but in this one the American rebels had won their war for independence nearly two hundred years ago.

The fact that our crashed aircraft has not been found has led to some questions from the American authorities, but we both claim to be British subjects—which is almost true—but that has created other problems that we haven't solved yet.

Now, well, now we are in a hospital in a world that doesn't suspect the existence of the parallel worlds and the almost unbelievable menace of two equally alien and non-human forces approaching each other across those Timelines, nearing the inevitable clash that might well mean the end of human life on all the Lines.

We're here, stranded, and there's no one to listen to us. But it can't end this way. By all that's holy, it can't! Something's got to be done. Someone's got to be told. Someone, somehow, must stop this hell before it destroys billions upon billions of human beings across the Lines and all the magnificent civilizations we've built.

And if nobody else will do it, I guess it'll be up to Sally and me.

But damned if I know how.